Praise for the novels of
New York Times bestselling author Lynn Kurland

"One of romance's finest writers." —*The Oakland Press*

"Both powerful and sensitive . . . A wonderfully rich and rewarding book." —Susan Wiggs, #1 *New York Times* bestselling author

"Kurland weaves another fabulous read with just the right amounts of laughter, romance, and fantasy." —Affaire de Coeur

"As always, Kurland does a spectacular job blending thrilling fantasy adventure with rich characterization—making sure readers are in for an exceptional ride!" —*RT Book Reviews* (4½ Stars)

"[A] triumphant romance." —Fresh Fiction

"Woven with magic, handsome heroes, lovely heroines, oodles of fun, and plenty of romance . . . Just plain wonderful." —Romance Reviews Today

"Spellbinding and lovely, this is one story readers won't want to miss." —Romance Reader at Heart

"Kurland infuses her polished writing with a deliciously dry wit . . . Sweetly romantic and thoroughly satisfying." —*Booklist*

"A pure delight." —Huntress Book Reviews

"[A] consummate storyteller." —ParaNormal Romance Reviews

Titles by Lynn Kurland

STARDUST OF YESTERDAY
A DANCE THROUGH TIME
THIS IS ALL I ASK
THE VERY THOUGHT OF YOU
ANOTHER CHANCE TO DREAM
THE MORE I SEE YOU
IF I HAD YOU
MY HEART STOOD STILL
FROM THIS MOMENT ON
A GARDEN IN THE RAIN
DREAMS OF STARDUST

MUCH ADO IN THE MOONLIGHT
WHEN I FALL IN LOVE
WITH EVERY BREATH
TILL THERE WAS YOU
ONE ENCHANTED EVENING
ONE MAGIC MOMENT
ALL FOR YOU
ROSES IN MOONLIGHT
DREAMS OF LILACS
STARS IN YOUR EYES
EVER MY LOVE

The Novels of the Nine Kingdoms

STAR OF THE MORNING
THE MAGE'S DAUGHTER
PRINCESS OF THE SWORD
A TAPESTRY OF SPELLS
SPELLWEAVER
GIFT OF MAGIC

DREAMSPINNER
RIVER OF DREAMS
DREAMER'S DAUGHTER
THE WHITE SPELL
THE DREAMER'S SONG

Anthologies

THE CHRISTMAS CAT
(with Julie Beard, Barbara Bretton, and Jo Beverley)

CHRISTMAS SPIRITS
(with Casey Claybourne, Elizabeth Bevarly, and Jenny Lykins)

VEILS OF TIME
(with Maggie Shayne, Angie Ray, and Ingrid Weaver)

OPPOSITES ATTRACT
(with Elizabeth Bevarly, Emily Carmichael, and Elda Minger)

LOVE CAME JUST IN TIME
A KNIGHT'S VOW
(with Patricia Potter, Deborah Simmons, and Glynnis Campbell)

TAPESTRY
(with Madeline Hunter, Sherrilyn Kenyon, and Karen Marie Moning)

TO WEAVE A WEB OF MAGIC
(with Patricia A. McKillip, Sharon Shinn, and Claire Delacroix)

THE QUEEN IN WINTER
(with Sharon Shinn, Claire Delacroix, and Sarah Monette)

A TIME FOR LOVE

Specials

"TO KISS IN THE SHADOWS" FROM TAPESTRY
THE TRAVELLER

Lynn Kurland

THE DREAMER'S SONG

BERKLEY SENSATION
New York

BERKLEY SENSATION

Published by Berkley

An imprint of Penguin Random House LLC

375 Hudson Street, New York, New York 10014

Library of Congress Cataloging-in-Publication Data

Names: Kurland, Lynn, author.
Title: The dreamer's song / Lynn Kurland.
Description: First edition. | New York, NY : Berkley Sensation, 2017. |
Series: A novel of the nine kingdoms ; 11
Identifiers: LCCN 2017027230 (print) | LCCN 2017030072 (ebook) |
ISBN 9780698198746 (eBook) | ISBN 9780425282199 (softcover)
Subjects: LCSH: Magic—Fiction. | BISAC: FICTION / Romance / Fantasy. |
GSAFD: Fantasy fiction. | Love stories.
Classification: LCC PS3561.U645 (ebook) | LCC PS3561.U645 D75 2017 (print) |
DDC 813/.54—dc23
LC record available at https://lccn.loc.gov/2017027230

First Edition: December 2017

Printed in the United States of America
1 3 5 7 9 10 8 6 4 2

Cover art by Mélanie Delon
Cover design by Katie Anderson
Interior map illustration copyright © 2012 by Tara Larsen Chang

To Kate and Nancy

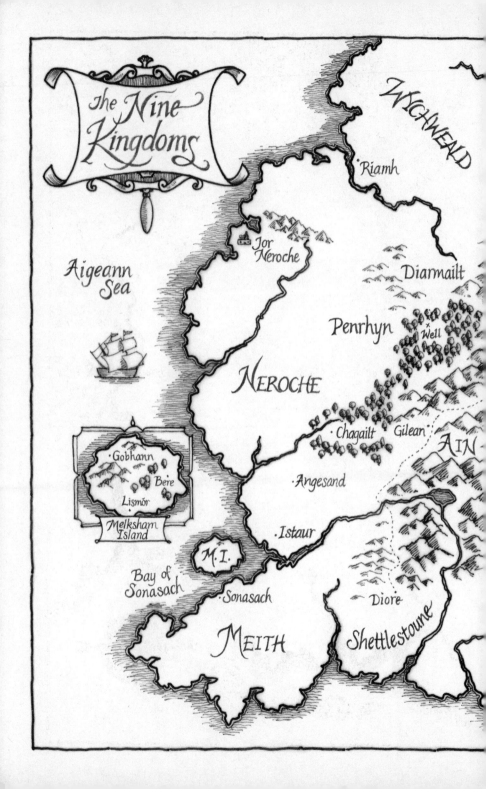

Prologue

A fair-haired man stood under the trees on the edge of a forest, watching the heavens as the world turned toward dawn, waiting for a miracle.

The stars were obscured by clouds that resembled nothing so much as a thin layer of wool that had been tugged and stretched to fit the glittering expanse, but they were still occasionally visible if one looked carefully enough. That was an apt metaphor, he supposed, for his part in the drama that lay before him, a drama he was doing his damndest to stay out of. He was, he had to admit, having far less success at that than he would have liked.

But what else was he to do? The fate of the world hung in the balance and for the second time in as many years, he found that he simply couldn't not at least reach out to steady the scales.

He thought he might not want to make a habit of it, actually.

He glanced at the woman who stood next to him, a woman he knew was a great deal less philosophical about their present business than he was. She was watching the sky with a frown.

"Is the spell of concealment they're using that good," she asked, "or have they fallen off their dragon somewhere between here and Tor Neroche and plunged to their deaths?"

The man paused, sought out the travelers with thought alone, then shook his head. "They're still alive."

"Your Highness, you could do more for the success of this venture than just make certain they're breathing every now and again."

"I don't like to interfere—"

His companion snorted rather indelicately. "You continue to tell yourself that, but how you manage not to choke on the words, I don't know."

He had to fight his smile. "Few dare speak to me with such frankness."

She looked singularly unimpressed. "I do not fear you. That, if you're curious, is nothing more than you deserve for rescuing me all those many years ago, then recently plucking me from my safe, comfortable obscurity only to drag me into events too large for my poor soul to bear."

"Yet here you are, in spite of everything," he noted.

"I have my reasons."

He had his reasons as well, though perhaps his weren't so personal. Being concerned about the fate of the world rather than the players involved tended to protect his heart, though he supposed he couldn't keep that up forever. He wasn't sure what he would do when the day came that he couldn't manage it, but perhaps it was something he could put off thinking about for a bit longer.

He continued to watch the sky for any hint of something more substantial than the stillness of the night air.

"Is he kind to her, do you think?" his companion asked suddenly.

He shrugged lightly. "Time will tell, I suppose."

"I absolutely despise it when you say that."

He looked at her in amusement. "Have you known me long enough to form such an opinion?"

She glared at him. "Almost a score of years, which is long enough to acquaint myself with phrases you use when you don't want to answer a question. And aye, I realize a score of years is likely younger than your favorite pair of slippers, but that's hardly my fault."

"Indeed it isn't," he agreed. He looked up, then nodded. "They have arrived."

She swore. "I can't see them—ah, damnation, I can see the edges of the spell." She let out an unsteady breath. "I'm not sure I'll ever accustom myself to that sort of rot."

He smiled a little at the thought of just how much of *that sort of rot* he had been privy to himself, then watched the spectacle in front of him with more jaded eyes. The spell of un-noticing covering the pair flying on that rather impressive dragon was a good one, which had likely served them well to that point. Unfortunately, he was who he was and he could see them perfectly well in spite of the magic covering them. His companion could also boast sight clearer than most thanks to her progenitors, but perhaps that was something he would be wise not to point out at present.

He supposed even a simple woodsman wouldn't have required any special powers to know what had arrived in that glade given how enthusiastically one of the riders was commenting on their descent. The dragon dropping out of the night with his claws stretched toward the ground was doing so without much mercy for the pair on his back. He tore through the spell of un-noticing and landed with a ground-shaking thump. If his fire-laced snort warmed the entire place up considerably without actually setting the glade on fire, well, who could complain?

Certainly not the man chortling as he hopped off the dragon's back and turned to hold up his hands for his companion.

If nothing else, that lad there had decent manners.

The dragon shook off his scales and resumed a very sensible horse shape whilst his two passengers indulged in a brief but salty discussion of their journey thus far. A third man unspun himself from a bit of swirling wind, then joined in the spirited but whispered conversation about spells, libraries, and the need for a decent breakfast sooner rather than later. Friendly curses were exchanged between the two men before the first man gathered up his horse's reins, offered his arm to his shivering companion, then walked off toward the gates of the city that squatted there in the distance. The third of their number was left to obviously follow or not, as he willed.

The blond man looked at his companion. "Satisfied?"

She closed her eyes briefly. "I'm not sure I have much of a choice. I know what you think already and I've made my peace with it, but I will say a final time that Acair of Ceangail has a horrible reputation."

"He's not exactly able to do anything to augment that reputation at the moment, as you well know."

"How is that better?" she asked sharply. "At least with his magic, he could keep his companions safe."

The man considered for a moment or two. His sight was, he

was the first to admit, sometimes a bit too clear to allow him to sleep easily at night, but, as he told himself more often than he liked, if there were no evil in the world, what would there be for good men to do?

He suppressed the impulse to shift at the memories of all the looks he'd had in return for stating that truth, looks ranging from incredulity to fury.

He let out his breath slowly. "He is a mage of terrible power," he conceded, "and questionable morals—"

"Wonderful!" she exclaimed, throwing up her hands in frustration. "Again, how is this better?"

"Because he's also damned clever," he offered. "He would also be the first to admit that keeping himself alive tops his list of things to do each day. I believe that enthusiasm for continuing to breathe extends to his traveling companions." He paused. "Well, perhaps not as far as to that prince of Neroche who travels with them, but to the woman he's obviously fond of? Aye, he'll keep her safe enough."

She looked at him seriously. "He would do better with his magic."

"Which he cannot use, for reasons you understand very well."

She cursed him as she pulled on gloves, then cursed a bit more as one of her fingers went through the wool. She looked at him sharply.

"Don't fix that."

"I hadn't intended to, actually—" He closed his mouth for the simple reason that he thought she might pull the dagger from her boot and stab him if he didn't.

"You have no bloody idea how tempting it is to seek out any of the women you're favoring with your attentions and warn them about you."

He smiled briefly. "My own reputation already does that, I fear."

"Then you have sympathy for that black mage wandering off toward Eòlas without anything but his wits to keep his company safe."

"More than I'll admit to."

She pulled her hood up over her head. "I've been away too long. I don't want to be missed." She took a step or two away, then paused and turned toward him a final time. "Anything to add?"

"I have said too much."

"You haven't said *anything*."

That wasn't true and she knew it, but, as he'd reminded himself earlier, he'd had no choice but to speak more than he'd wanted to and interfere more than he'd been comfortable with. In the previous month alone, he'd sent a black mage off on a noble quest, handed that mage a rune to use to summon him if aid was required, and put the finishing touches on a scheme he'd been reluctantly considering for two decades. The only way he comforted himself over any of it was reminding himself—he'd lost count of how often—that occasionally there were circumstances that required a bit of judicious meddling.

His companion had vanished into the night in a thoroughly unmagical fashion, following after that trio who had also decamped in the same manner, leaving him to either stand there and freeze or build himself a fire by thoroughly magical means. That was possible, of course, but unwise, and he was not unwise.

That he had to stand there for a moment or two and remind himself of that was more unsettling than it should have been, but it had been that sort of autumn so far. Winter was sweeping over the Nine Kingdoms with a fury, which he supposed wasn't going to help matters any, but there were things even he couldn't bring himself to change.

He cast a final glance in the direction of those who held the fate of the world in their unknowing hands, then turned and vanished into the bitter pre-dawn air.

One

Horses. Grain. Manure. Those were useful, reliable things a woman with any amount of good sense chose to fill her life with. Anything of a more untoward or unnerving nature was obviously something that same sort of woman should avoid like a pile of mouldy oats.

Léirsinn of Sàraichte stood in the shadows of a rather disreputable-looking pub, shivered, and made a valiant effort to focus on those things that had made up so much of her life so far. Horses were majestic creatures, grain kept them happy, and cleaning up after them was the price she'd paid for the joy of riding on their backs. It was a simple, predictable circle that had given purpose and meaning to her days. How she had strayed so far from such a pedestrian life, she couldn't say—

She sighed and stopped herself from even finishing that thought. She knew exactly how she'd come to be where she was

and how barn work had led her to such a terrible place. It wasn't
something she particularly wanted to think about, but she was
trapped where she was for the moment and she needed something to help her pass the time. It seemed like the least dangerous
of the things she could be doing, so she made herself more comfortable against the outside of the pub and allowed her thoughts
to wander.

They wandered without much effort to the moment when her
life had become something so thoroughly not what she'd been
accustomed to. There she'd been, innocently going about her
chores as usual, when a man had arrived at her uncle's barn
looking for work. What she should have done was take away the
pitchfork he quite obviously had never used and shown him the
quickest way out of the barn.

Instead, she'd stared just a bit too long at his truly spectacular
visage and apparently lost all her wits. Not only had she allowed
him to remain in her uncle's stables attempting work he was
singularly unqualified to do, she had listened to him long enough
to be convinced that her uncle wanted her dead and her only
hope was to flee. She had somehow lost her grip on good sense
and traded the three things she knew best for other, less comfortable things such as mages, magic, and mythical beasts.

A breathless race across the whole of the Nine Kingdoms in
the company of a madman and a shapechanging horse—two
horses actually, but who was counting?—had left her standing
where she was at present, trying not to gape at her surroundings
like the country mouse she most definitely was and wishing she
were safely tucked away in an obscure barn.

Where she was at present was Eòlas, the capital city of the
country of Diarmailt. She hadn't dared ask anyone to verify her
location, though she likely could have given that most of the in-

habitants of the Nine Kingdoms were on the same cobblestone byway with her. Never in her life had she seen so many people gathered together in one place.

To make matters worse, most of those souls seemed determined to either elbow her out of their way or grope various parts of her person as they passed by her, no doubt in search of valuables.

She frowned at a particularly irritating lad who seemed determined to pester her, but she wasn't sure what the rules were for ridding oneself of that sort of vexation. She thought a hearty shove or perhaps even a fist to the lad's nose might be the easiest way to make her wishes known, but she was unfortunately under an injunction to do whatever was necessary not to draw attention to herself.

"A bit of ale," the young man said, looking at her meaningfully, "then perhaps a quiet moment or two in a—"

"Ditch?" suggested a deep voice from directly behind him. "Or perhaps you would care to select a less comfortable final resting place."

The lad turned, squeaked, then fled.

Léirsinn understood. She looked at the tall, cloaked figure now standing where her would-be companion had recently stood and supposed that if she'd had any sense, she would have bolted as well. The man facing her, while terribly elegant, gave the impression that a good brawl was something he indulged in each morning just after sunrise and just before helping himself to a hearty breakfast.

Fortunately for her, he was her traveling companion and deliverer of the occasional bit of maudlin sentiment. If he also happened to be the youngest bastard son of the worst black mage in recent memory, well, she wasn't going to complain. He was sitting on her side of the table instead of sitting across from her and spewing spells at her. She didn't think she could ask for anything more than that, though she did snort silently at how freely thoughts of magic galloped across what was left of her mind.

Spells. What absolute rot.

She turned away from indulging in those thoroughly useless thoughts and focused on the man standing in front of her. Acair of Ceangail shoved aside another gangly youth, then joined her in leaning against the pub wall, as far out of the press of humanity as possible.

"Any trouble?" he asked.

"Nothing noteworthy," she said, "though I'm probably not the right one to judge that." She glanced at him. "I've never seen so many people in one place in my life and 'tis only dawn."

He pushed his hood back from his face. "It is an easy place in which to lose oneself, true. In your case, though, I can see why nothing would aid you in escaping the attentions of every lad in the area."

She ignored the flattery, mostly because the memory of their thoroughly unpleasant journey to their current locale was still very fresh in her mind and he was responsible for it. "Did hiding your face help you in the past quarter hour?"

"Barely," he said, straightening his cloak. "I vow I was accosted by no fewer than half a dozen maids with mischief on their minds."

"Good thing you're accustomed to it," she observed.

"Isn't it, though?"

She suppressed the urge to roll her eyes. She imagined he was very accustomed to the same and she further supposed he had rarely passed up an opportunity to indulge as many lassies in their desires as possible. Given that she had experienced his powers of persuasion firsthand, she knew those poor women weren't to blame for whatever straits they found themselves in.

She could scarce believe she had been just as overcome, but the man was hard to resist. He was also, as she had reminded herself just a moment or two ago, completely to blame for the terror-filled journey she'd made on the back of her favorite horse to places she'd never intended to go, where she had encountered people of various sorts she had never imagined existed—

"You're thinking pleasant thoughts about me," Acair murmured, leaning closer to her. "Planning on joining that list of my admirers?"

"I was actually wishing I had stabbed you with a pitchfork the first time I saw you," she managed.

He smiled, and she winced. She realized at that moment that it had been his smile to render her not only witless but unable to do him any serious bodily harm. The first time she'd clapped eyes on him, she should have clapped her hand over her own traitorous eyes and stumbled away to somewhere he wasn't.

"You aren't in earnest," he said with a small smile. "Do damage to this extremely fine form? I don't think you could."

"I'm not sure you want to test it after what you put me through last night," she said, trying to ignore the memories of that extremely bumpy ride on the back of a dragon who had seemed determined by his antics to wring shouts of laughter from the madman standing next to her. She dredged up the sternest look she could muster and attempted an abrupt return to the business at hand. "What now?" she asked. "Well, besides watching you step over the pile of lassies who have fallen at your feet, did you find anything unexpected?"

He propped his foot up underneath him and sighed. "Nothing out of the ordinary, which bodes well for success here. Unfortunately, that leaves us with nothing to do but continue to keep ourselves out of trouble whilst we wait for a certain finicky prince of Neroche to locate the sort of accommodations he might find to his liking, then we run away from them as quickly as possible and find something suitable."

"And then?" she asked. "I know you told me yesterday, but I spent so much time screaming last night that I believe the noise drove it from my mind."

He bumped her companionably with his shoulder. "You didn't scream the entire time."

"Nay, I fainted midway through the torment, which likely saved your ears."

He smiled. "I thought you were swooning for my benefit, so I'm not sure I'll accept anything else." He watched the shadowy press of humanity for a bit longer, then looked at her. "We'll find somewhere safe to leave our gear, then I need to nip in and out of the library and fetch that book I need."

She knew that, of course. She'd simply been hoping her ears had been failing her. Traveling to their current locale seemed like a great deal of fuss for not much at all. "You couldn't have found a copy of this book somewhere else?"

He opened his mouth, then shut it and shook his head. "Nay, though you've no idea how it pains me to say as much. The damned thing is of my own make, unfortunately, and whilst I usually make at least one copy of my notes to hide elsewhere, in this instance I was in a hurry and therefore less careful than I should have been." He shrugged. "I would prefer not to be here, but here we are."

She was tempted to ask him why he didn't just stash things under his bed, but for all she knew, he didn't have a bed, never mind a home to call his own. Perhaps he was forced to hide his priceless treasures in odd places just to keep them safe. Given that he seemed to endlessly travel the world, she wouldn't have been surprised.

The idea that she might travel the world in a similar fashion had honestly never occurred to her. In fact, if anyone had suggested the possibility of it to her even a pair of months before, she would have stabbed *them* with a pitchfork to give them relief from their stupidity. Getting herself even from her uncle's stables in Briàghde across the hill to Sàraichte, nothing more than a leisurely hour's walk, had seemed the very limit of what she could do. It had never crossed her mind that she might someday travel farther than that, never mind all the way across the Nine Kingdoms.

Yet there she was, hundreds of leagues from the only home she truly remembered, keeping company with a terrible black mage on holiday from his usual business of wreaking havoc, and looking forward to a nap in lodgings that had been sought for them by a prince of the royal house of Neroche. She had seen elves, mages, and horses worth a king's ransom. She had encountered kindness she hadn't deserved and refuge she hadn't dared hope for. It had been an adventure beyond her wildest imaginings and she knew it was far from over.

It couldn't be over yet because apart from the fairly pressing need to avoid having her uncle slay her, she had Acair's promise that once he'd done what he needed to, he would rescue her very ill grandfather from that same uncle's house. She was prepared to entertain all sorts of ridiculous notions of magic and mages in return for that aid.

That was, she admitted freely, why she found herself where she was with the task that was set before her, namely keeping an eye out for shadows lying on the ground. Not just any sorts of shadows, of course, such as might have been made by ordinary people standing just so against the sun, or the odd planter placed just outside a pub door to catch whatever light might be had. Nay, the shadows she was meant to be looking for were created by magic.

It was daft, of course, something she continued to tell herself because it allowed her to continue to breathe normally. She absolutely refused to admit that she might or might not have had her own unsettling experience with those spots of shadow where shadows shouldn't be found. With any luck, while about her looking she might manage to stumble over her missing wits.

She didn't hold out much hope for it.

"I think we'd best be off looking for that hapless prince of Neroche before he finds himself entangled in some madness or other," Acair said heavily. "He is definitely not the brightest flame that family has produced."

"He seems chivalrous enough," she offered.

"The man might know how to offer an arm at the right time," Acair conceded, "but that is the absolute limit of his gifts. I'd avoid him at all costs, were I you."

"What did he do to irritate you so?"

Acair reached for her hand and looked briefly both up and down the way before he pulled her into the crowd. "I would give you a list, but there is the lad himself. One can only hope he's found somewhere suitable for us to sleep tonight."

She supposed her standards for lodging were far below what either of her companions might consider acceptable because at the moment all she wanted was somewhere flat and unmoving to cast herself.

"Finally," Prince Mansourah said in disbelief, stopping in

front of them and causing several passersby to hurl curses at him. "Where have you been?"

"Waiting for you where we agreed to wait for you," Acair said with exaggerated politeness, "and all the while holding out a desperate hope that you would take a set of chambers somewhere discreet."

Mansourah glared at him. "I did, and I paid for them in local currency so as not to attract any notice."

"Then my skepticism is quite happily allayed," Acair said, "though I doubt that will last for long. Lead on and pray assure me there is a decent pub nearby as well."

"There is, though if I had any sense I would leave you scrambling to wash platters in return for your meal instead of putting myself out to pay for your breakfast myself."

Acair favored Mansourah with a look that Léirsinn imagined had sent more than one nobleman's butler scurrying for cover.

"I have coin enough," he said coolly. "Whilst I am not at my liberty to fill my own purse, my half-sister, your brother's thoughtful wife, was kind enough to do it for me, so please don't concern yourself about my poor tum. I have sufficient for myself and my lady without ruining my hands."

Mansourah pursed his lips. "Then your delicate fingers are safe for the moment, I suppose. Follow me and we'll see ourselves settled first."

Léirsinn was fairly certain Acair had made some sort of less-than-polite comment about Mansourah's tendency to find himself lost in the weeds while about any sort of meaningful quest, but she decided to let it pass. The sooner she could escape the press of city-dwellers getting on with their business for the day, the happier she would be. She glanced at Acair as they walked.

"How do you feed yourself?" she asked. "If that isn't too personal a question."

He shook his head. "My life is an open book, as they say. I mostly manage to find myself invited to supper at one superior table or another, which keeps me from starving. When I require funds, I go about acquiring them in the usual way."

She looked at him sternly. "If you use the word I can scarce bear to utter, I will do damage to you."

"Magic can be fairly useful," he said with a smile, "when you think about it."

She wasn't about to dignify that with any sort of response, not that there would have been a decent response for it. That happy time when she had lived her life blissfully unaware of anything but the rich smells of green grass, steaming oats, and freshly baled hay was gone. Being something just short of an indentured servant in her uncle's stables had been difficult, but there had been a certain peace that had come with living in such innocence. Things of a troubling and capricious nature had been easily relegated to her imagination while the tales her parents had told her in her childhood had been consigned to fanciful imaginings with equal ease.

Now, though, a being once relegated to her imagination was walking beside her, muttering under his breath about peasants, princes, and the condition of the boots he was wearing that were most definitely not his own.

A black mage who used magic as easily as she drew breath.

Well, not of late, but he certainly seemed to be familiar with the stuff. As for anything else, she wasn't entirely sure what to think. She kept count of the frisky lads that same black mage sent scampering off with either a warning look or a quick shove and reminded herself of all the reasons she had not to believe a damned thing anyone had said about him. His reputation was awful, true, but his manners were impeccable, he wasn't afraid to shovel a substantial bit of manure in return for having the privilege of riding a spectacular horse or two, and he had never once in all the time she'd known him worked even the simplest spell.

She refused to bring to mind what she had seen of him, *how* she'd seen him, when she'd been standing in a particular spot of shadow that shouldn't have existed outside her nightmares, all found within the king of Neroche's garden.

It occurred to her with a bit of a start that she hadn't seen a damned one of those shadows so far that morning.

That was odd.

She realized Mansourah had come to a halt only because she'd run into Acair's outstretched arm. She looked at the rather rustic door there in front of them and hoped she wasn't about to enter a place she wouldn't be able to get back out of easily.

"Here?" Acair asked in disbelief.

"Have you never stayed here before?" Mansourah asked.

"Well of course I've stayed here before," Acair answered shortly, "when I wanted everyone in the city to know I'd arrived!"

"The innkeeper is capable of discretion," Mansourah said smoothly, "though I generally find it difficult to hide my identity in spite of that." He looked down his nose at Acair. "The trials of noble blood and all that. And before you wring your hands overmuch, all they know is that I took rooms for myself, my affianced lady of quality, and you, my very silent and witless servant."

Léirsinn would have smiled, but she wasn't at all sure that Acair wouldn't strangle Mansourah right there in the street. He took a deep, careful breath, then gave their companion a look that Léirsinn was half surprised didn't have the prince blurting out an apology.

"When I am again sailing under my own power," he said seriously, "you had best find somewhere to hide."

Mansourah pursed his lips. "I would remember that, but I'm not sure 'tis worth the effort."

"I'll make a note of it for you," Acair promised, "at the bottom of my list of tedious but necessary engagements to be seen to the moment I am back fully to myself." He pulled his hood up over his face. "Let's stow our gear, then I want something marginally edible before we're about the true business of the day."

Mansourah elbowed Acair out of the way and held out his arm. "Lady Léirsinn?"

"I'm no lady—" she began.

"Your uncle is, I believe, lord of his own hall, which gives you station enough for me," Mansourah said gallantly. "Here, let me take your gear and give it to him whose task it is to carry it."

Léirsinn would have protested that as well, but Mansourah had already taken her pack and held it out toward Acair. Acair took it without hesitation, shot her a brief smile, then turned a look of fury on Mansourah. She wasn't sure the pair wouldn't kill each other before they managed to achieve their purpose in coming to Eòlas, but there was nothing she could do to change that. She simply followed Mansourah through rather worn and uninviting doors into the antechamber of an inn that revealed itself to be far more lavish than expected.

Her opinion of the inn only improved when they were shown to their accommodations. Mansourah managed to listen politely to the innkeeper falling over himself to make certain he was content while at the same time shooting Acair looks that promised him nothing more comfortable than the floor. She was torn between checking her companions for weapons or finding the first marginally suitable spot to use for a quick nap. All recent events aside, she was most definitely not accustomed to the methods of travel she'd recently been subjected to. If she never saw the Nine Kingdoms from farther off the ground than a decent horse put her, it would be too soon.

"She would be safe enough here," Mansourah said firmly. "She looks weary."

Léirsinn came back to herself to find herself standing in the middle of the chamber, staring at nothing and hearing not much more. She realized the innkeeper was gone and her companions were close to blows.

"I am absolutely not leaving her in some *slum* you've chosen," Acair growled.

"You said you'd taken lodgings here before," Mansourah protested.

"I have stayed here before because I have the means to protect myself, unlike my lady here," Acair said. "As for anything else, you know as well as I that the entire bloody city is dangerous."

"I have excellent taste in—"

"Pubs, no doubt," Léirsinn said loudly enough to be heard over their snarling. "Breakfast sounds wonderful, thank you." If the distraction of a warm bucket of grain was good enough for horses, it was surely suitable for those two there.

Mansourah looked as if he were having trouble choosing between finding breakfast and dealing out death, but good sense apparently prevailed. He left off with his glaring and walked over to the door. She followed him from the chamber with Acair on her heels, then found herself between the two of them as they made their way down the street to a pub that seemed to suit them both.

A meal was provided posthaste, which fortunately occupied her companions long enough for her to manage to gulp down what had been set in front of her. By the time she had fed and watered herself sufficiently, the sun had somehow managed to get itself above the horizon and make its presence known through the window she was facing. She was tempted to doze off right there, which made her wonder if she shouldn't have remained back in that chamber and taken a nap on what had looked to be a perfectly serviceable divan.

She fought an enormous yawn and turned her attention back to the conversation going on in front of her, if conversation it could be called. She reminded herself that stepping between two crotchety stallions was never a good idea, but at the moment she was very tempted. She needed those two fools to keep from killing each other long enough for Acair to see to his business so he could then help her see to hers. At the moment, she wasn't entirely sure she would manage it.

"I wonder if you understand whom you're dealing with here," Mansourah said, holding his fork as if he could hardly stop himself from plunging it into Acair's chest.

"Do *you*?" Acair returned.

Mansourah pursed his lips. "Aye, a black mageling with no power."

"That is a temporary condition, I assure you."

Léirsinn watched them in fascination, wondering if they actually believed they would draw blood with words alone. Mansourah was obviously quite used to having everyone jump to humor him, and Acair, well, she supposed if she had met him in a darkened alley, she would have done exactly what that lad earlier had done, namely turned tail and run.

"I wonder," she interrupted, "if it might be time to go."

Mansourah took a deep breath, then very deliberately set his fork down. "An excellent thought. I'll go see what the street contains."

"Oh, please do," Acair said, waving him off. "Can't wait to see what you scout out."

Mansourah swore at him, then rose and made his way to the entrance to the pub.

Léirsinn glanced at Acair to find him watching the doorway. Either he was considering the lay of the land himself or he was plotting their companion's demise. She honestly wouldn't have been surprised by either.

"You can't do what you're contemplating, you know," she said, because she thought she should.

He glanced at her. "What? Smother him in his sleep?"

"Aye."

He shook his head. "I'll forebear, but only because I might need his aid."

She toyed idly with her mug of ale. "Perilous deeds await, is that what you're saying?"

"Hopefully not. All we have to look forward to here is a pleasant stroll to the library, though I will admit I might need someone to serve as a distraction. I believe I know just the lad— and there he is by the door, obviously ready to be about the business of the morning." He rose and put his hand on the back of her chair. "Shall we?"

She couldn't think of a decent reason why not, so she pushed herself to her feet, then followed him across the room and out into the pale winter morning sunlight. It was chilly, true, but she was wearing a discreet but extremely well-made cloak given to her by the queen of Neroche so the cold didn't trouble her overmuch.

Unfortunately, it didn't seem to be helping the unease she felt. It was mad to think she was being watched, but she couldn't ignore the feeling. Perhaps it was nothing more than that lad from earlier, the one Acair had sent off with a stern look and a handful of harsh words—

"My lady?"

She blinked when she realized Mansourah was holding out his elbow toward her. Damnation, too late to run. She took a deep breath, took his arm, and nodded. Acair fell in on her other side, breathing out fiery threats under his breath.

"Do shut up, peasant," Mansourah drawled.

"I'll kill you the first chance I have," Acair promised.

"And find yourself swinging from the nearest tree before you managed it?" Mansourah asked with a yawn. "Wouldn't risk it, were I you."

Léirsinn heard Acair take a deep breath, then let it out gustily. Perhaps thoughts of murder were being shelved for the moment. She looked at him briefly, had a raised eyebrow in return, then took her own steadying breath. She would leave her companions to their business and concentrate on her own task of watching for shadows on the ground that she found herself particularly adept at seeing.

She could do no more. Their quest was begun with little more than their wits, a bad-tempered horse, and the company of a handsome, noble prince who she suspected would slip a knife between Acair's ribs if given half a chance.

She supposed others had trotted off into the fray with less.

She just wasn't sure she wanted to know where that lack had left them.

Two

❧

There was much to be said for the quiet, unassuming life of a black mage.

Acair of Ceangail walked along the cobblestone streets of a city he hadn't planned on visiting ever again without a very dire reason indeed and took the opportunity to indulge in a leisurely mental recounting of the pleasures of that normally quiet life.

He interrupted himself long enough to give a frisky lad a shove away from his companion and situate her more fully between himself and that empty-headed archer from Neroche, then he turned his mind back to his much-needed distraction.

He was never without an invitation to dinner. He nodded over that truth, then reviewed a small list of the elegant tables at which he'd enjoyed a prime seat, the stunning women for whom he'd poured wine, and the noble husbands and fathers with whom he'd engaged in battles fought with the tools associated with his class.

He had also enjoyed a wide variety of entertainments. Frolics on the stage, the occasional duel at dawn he thought worth getting up early for, and long, pleasant evenings spent listening to musicians who played in tune only began the lengthy list of pleasures he had enjoyed.

There were other things he relished, things that were perhaps a bit less gentlemanlike but absolutely to his taste. There were murders to boast of—and not a soul with the courage to ask him about the particulars—mischief to be about, and mayhem to inflict. His terrible reputation preceded him like a cleansing wind and trailed after him like so many neophytes wishing they had earned even a single word of the gossip that attended him. When he entered a gilded chamber, women swooned, men clutched the keys to their coffers, and mages scampered out the nearest exit.

And why not? He was the youngest natural son of the worst black mage in recent memory, and his mother was a witch. He had the wit, the courage, and the cheek to succeed at all sorts of ventures that might give a lesser man pause. Was there in truth any who possessed an existence such as his own?

"All right, bastard, where to now?"

He took a careful breath and reminded himself that killing anyone directly after breakfast might get the day off to a bad start. He clasped his hands behind his back where they wouldn't do something he might regret later, then revisited why he still had a use for that wee rustic from Neroche standing closer to Léirsinn of Sàraichte than he was happy about.

He was trapped in the middle of the city of Eòlas, a place he continued to wish he weren't visiting, preparing to mount an assault on the library attached to the city's university in order to retrieve something he'd hidden there previously. He couldn't use his magic, which left him relying on lesser souls to take care of any of that sort of business on his behalf. Not the most ideal of circumstances, but his life was not his own at the moment.

Mansourah of Neroche had been told all that already. If he had been left in the dark about a few things of note, that simply couldn't be helped. There were few whom Acair trusted with the complete particulars of any given plan, and that lad from Neroche, whilst surely a pleasant fellow, hadn't yet earned a place on that list.

Besides, what was there to tell? He needed a book that currently found itself in the university's library. If he wanted to see what sort of trouble his presence in the city might stir up as he went about liberating that tome from its spot, that was his business. If his business also included a visit to his tailor when time permitted, so much the better.

And last but certainly not least, if his companions slept deeply enough during the coming night that he could slip out the window and do a bit of snooping in the local ruler's private chambers, who could blame him? There was something in Eòlas that didn't smell quite right and that wasn't simply the trio of drunken, vomit-covered students sprawled on the sidewalk in front of him.

Exam time at the university, obviously.

He stepped over a moaning lad sporting ink-stained fingers and gave thought to the mystery that stank of something unpleasant.

Simeon of Diarmailt had been willing a pair of years earlier to trade his most treasured book of spells for a decent amount of the world's magic. The king had sworn on his signet ring that it was the only copy of said book in existence, a claim no doubt made to enhance its desirability. Acair had doubted that the oath carried its usual weight considering that Simeon had left his crown behind—unwillingly, or so rumor had it—at the gaming table of one of his northern neighbors, but quibbling over the details had seemed a bit gauche at the time. He had accepted the king's assurance about the exclusive nature of his book and hoped for the best.

He had wondered, of course, why the king wanted power badly enough to pay that sort of price, though the answer hadn't been long in coming. The simple fact was, Simeon had lost his throne and therefore a solid border between his own sweet self and Wychweald. Given that the man was one of the most unpleasant knaves spawned in the past century, charm alone was obviously not going to win him a return of crown and country. Power it would have to be.

"Acair?"

He pulled himself reluctantly away from thoughts of poking his nose into royal affairs that weren't his and brought his attention back to the matter at hand. The library was currently rising up before them in all its austere glory and getting inside without being discovered was going to be a challenge. He paused with his companions in the shadow of that imposing structure, then looked at the hapless middle—or thereabouts—prince of the house of Neroche.

"Where to?" he repeated slowly. "The library, which you already knew. I would like to pay said visit whilst shielded by as much anonymity as possible, which you also already knew."

"Why is that again?" Mansourah asked with something of a smirk. "I believe I've forgotten."

Acair imagined Mansourah hadn't forgotten a damned thing. The obvious reason for discretion was that he was being chased by black mages who were salivating over the prospect of doing him in, though that was nothing unusual. A more pressing problem would be finding himself also being chased by the crownless ruler of Diarmailt if the man knew he had come to town.

He supposed the king would have been justified in it. The unfortunate truth was that though he had indeed made Simeon a promise to deliver power in exchange for that book of spells, his plans to discreetly acquire a sizeable amount of the world's magic had gone completely south the year before. He'd sent along a note of regret to His Former Majesty, which, he understood via the grapevine generally used for that sort of thing, hadn't been received terribly well. Not that his welcome in Diarmailt had ever been particularly warm, but such an embarrassing failure had certainly not helped matters any—

"We're making for the library," Mansourah reminded him.

Acair noted the thoughtful frown gracing the prince's noble brow. No doubt the lad was struggling to imagine why one would ever want to spend any time in such a locale. What Mansourah of Neroche did with his days beyond inserting himself into places where the only results were social disasters was a mystery, but perhaps that was all the child could hope for. Acair thought it best to just let the matter lie.

"I'm here for a book," he said, hoping the use of small words would aid Mansourah in understanding what they were about. He was, as even those he'd brought to their knees pleading for mercy would admit, altruistic to the last.

Mansourah's brow puckered a bit more. "But Rùnach has your book."

Acair was fairly certain they'd covered that ground before, but he wasn't unwilling to cover it again. As he'd noted before, *altruism* was his middle name.

"Rùnach has the innards of *a* book," he said. "I might even go so far as to say that those innards might have belonged to one of *my* books. He has those, my young princeling, because I put them there for him to find. I knew he needed something with which to keep himself busy last year and I was happy to oblige him in the same. In return, I liberated the pages of *his* most cherished tome and deposited them in a safe place of my choosing."

He could have said more, of course, but there was no reason to go into details that would only keep Mansourah awake at night. Aye, he had pages from a book of Rùnach's and he knew very well what those pages contained. He could scarce wait to flex his fingers and dive into his half-brother's efforts to counter their father's dastardly spells.

Even more intriguing were the notes Rùnach had dropped all over the plains of Ailean that Acair had been, again, altruistic enough to scoop up for him, but those were equally well hidden and best forgotten about for the moment.

"What's in this book we've come for?" Mansourah asked. "Lists of pubs to avoid?"

Acair sighed lightly. He would have preferred to boast that the pages were full of his own lists of black mages of note, but the truth was, he was after something he'd liberated from under the blotter on his father's desk one evening when Gair had been suffering from intense tummy troubles that might or might not have been caused by Acair having spent the afternoon loitering in the kitchens near the stewpot. Those pages were hidden in a book of lists of other things that would *definitely* keep that wee prince there awake at night.

"The address of my tailor, rather," Acair said with a casual shrug. "You might find it useful."

Mansourah looked as if he were toying with the idea of taking one of the arrows in the quiver slung over his shoulder and plunging it into Acair's chest. Normally, Acair wouldn't have even yawned over such a possibility, but things were as they were and his only protections were threats and the rather unsatisfactory dagger stashed down the side of his boot. He reached out and clapped Mansourah companionably on the shoulder. If his hand got in the way of the man reaching for an arrow, perhaps it could be considered saving time and trouble for those who swept the streets.

"Just having a bit of sport at your expense, old bean," he said soothingly. "I'm here for my usual sort of thing: state secrets, terrible spells, and quite potentially the address of my father's bootmaker. You might want to order a pair whilst we're there. That ought to take up our afternoon quite nicely."

Mansourah glared at him, then turned a much more pleasant look on Léirsinn. "Please, get me away from him."

Léirsinn took his arm, then looked over her shoulder and raised her eyebrows. Acair smiled briefly at her, then settled for walking behind the pair. He was followed by his own constant shadow, a spell of death that was apparently charged with keeping him from turning vexatious princes into steaming piles of dung. He hadn't hit upon a way to rid himself of the damned thing yet, but that was definitely high up on his list of things to do. Obviously, the sooner he was able to be back to the business of proper black magery, the better.

He watched the crowd as he followed his companions toward the library's front doors. Those souls were students for the most part, lads and lassies fortunate enough to study at the university surrounding what was arguably the largest library in all the Nine Kingdoms. Perhaps not the most interesting collection of books, but definitely the largest. He wasn't troubled by the press, but he could tell by the way Léirsinn was occasionally flinching that she was. He leaned forward and tapped Mansourah smartly on the shoulder.

"Put her between yourself and the wall, dolt."

Mansourah apologized profusely, then did as he'd been bid. Acair turned back to watching for thugs and wondering just what sort of hornet's nest he might stir up with an innocent visit to the small collection of tomes he kept hidden in plain sight among other books of catastrophically boring subjects. His trio of books was covered in his own spells, spells which were designed to render them uninteresting to anyone with a merely rudimentary command of magic.

But he wasn't interested in lesser mages.

He was looking for a lad with power to match his own, perhaps. At any other time, such a thought would have had him perking up his ears and preparing a few dire things for use in a tight spot, but things were what they were at the moment. The best he could do was see whom he provoked, then be out of the vicinity when the storm arrived.

The truth was, he knew he was being watched. He knew that because the watcher had recently sent along a missive telling him as much. His catalog of enemies was substantial and, it had to be noted, very well deserved. But this felt different somehow. He was accustomed to outraged monarchs and papas coming after him for wives, daughters, and priceless treasures he might or might not have absconded with, but this . . . this was something else entirely. He wasn't sure whom he could have possibly angered recently in light of all the damned do-gooding he'd been engaged in, but there you had it. Life on the wrong side of black magery was unpredictable. If he could solve that with a little nipping in and out of the library, so much the better.

If he also used his time wisely enough to acquire a new pair
of boots and perhaps a decent shirt or two, who could blame him?

They continued on toward the library. Acair patted himself
figuratively on the back several times for resisting the urge to
pull the dagger from his boot and slide it between Mansourah's
ribs for spending more time chatting with that beautiful woman
on his arm than he did watching where he was going. At least
there wasn't much opportunity for getting lost between where
they were and the library's front doors. Mansourah came to a
halt a dozen paces away from the same, then stood there, frowning thoughtfully. Acair waited until it became painful to continue.

"What?" he asked shortly.

"I've been thinking," Mansourah said slowly.

"Ye gads, not that," Acair said before he could stop himself.

Mansourah gave him a look that Acair had to admit left him
almost impressed.

"You realize most everything precious resides in glass cases,"
Mansourah said pointedly. "Protected by impenetrable spells."

"The quality of those spells is debatable," Acair said with a
shrug, "but aye, I realize that."

"But if your book is hidden in such a place, how are you going to get past all that magic?"

Acair sighed. "Let me walk you through this gently. If you
were me—and you'll never manage that so don't try—and you
wanted to hide a perilous book, where, with your superior intel-
lect and cleverness, would you hide it?"

"Behind glass and impenetrable spells, of course."

Acair studied him. "The trouble with you, my young friend,
is that you fail to use any imagination when presented with these

conundrums. If you have a priceless treasure, you don't hide it behind something that screams *I'm hiding something priceless behind myself!* You hide the damned thing in plain sight."

Mansourah looked thoroughly baffled. "You're not afraid someone will simply pick it up and walk off with it?"

"Not when it's slathered with the kinds of spells I prefer to use for that sort of slathering."

Mansourah looked at Léirsinn. "I don't know how you haven't pushed him off the back of your horse before now."

"I have a strong stomach."

Acair would have preferred a compliment about his flawless face, but he had dragged her places she hadn't wanted to go. He had also called her hair *red*, which didn't begin to describe the glorious fire of that mane she was currently hiding under the hood of her cloak. He vowed to compliment her properly on not only her locks but her strong stomach later, then looked at Mansourah.

"We'll walk in as normal patrons, go to the appropriate spot without garnering any notice, then I'll retrieve my book. I suggest we not linger over any fashion papers, which I'm sure will be a great blow to you."

Mansourah bit back something, his agreement no doubt. He considered, then looked at Acair. "And your book is behind spells."

"As I said before, aye."

Silence descended.

It descended softly, as if it had been a delicate snowfall somewhere between the first sloppy business of autumn but not yet the brittle stuff of winter that sounded like glass shattering as it fell through the air.

It was a fairly substantial silence, actually.

Acair had known that moment would come, of course, because he never walked into any dodgy situation without first having studied it thoroughly. It had obviously occurred to him that what he needed was hidden behind his own spells that he couldn't very well undo in his present condition. He had also given thought to the master spell he'd laid there, a very pedestrian but useful thing that could be triggered by a single word.

Only he couldn't utter that single word without causing that damned spell currently resting its bony shadow of a chin on his shoulder to fall upon him and, as he would have told anyone willing to listen, slay him instantly. He flicked it off as if it had been an annoying fly, then waited for the abuse he knew was coming his way.

Mansourah arched his back and did everything but yawn hugely before he began to purr in satisfaction. "I suppose," he drawled, "that you might need my help."

Acair smiled instead of snarling because he knew which side his bread was buttered on, as the saying went. "Terribly kind of you, of course."

"It also seems as though you might need my aid in getting past the guards at the door given that they'll want a list of anyone in our party who has magic."

"Indeed they will and that would be absolutely sporting of you, Your Highness."

Mansourah was obviously enjoying the situation far more than it merited, but Acair wasn't about to spoil the man's pleasure. He was above all a pragmatist. If he had to use that empty-headed flirt to get what he wanted, he would and swallow his pride in the bargain.

Mansourah nodded toward the doors. "Léirsinn, stay close to me. If things go badly, we'll toss him to the wolves and escape whilst they're feasting."

Acair had heard worse ideas, so he kept his head down as they made their way to the front doors and waited with the rest of the rabble to be allowed inside. He didn't expect Mansourah to keep his own identity a secret and the lad didn't disappoint. Léirsinn was introduced as his fiancée, a practice Acair fully intended to put a stop to sooner rather than later. He was himself presented as a lowly servant with enough magic to his name to find his master's slippers but not quite enough to prepare morning chocolate in any but the most pedestrian of ways. He didn't argue, but he made a mental note of the insult for future repayment.

He followed along behind Mansourah and Léirsinn as deferentially as possible. He spared a look over his shoulder and wasn't at all comfortable with the notice they were still attracting from those at the front door. Mansourah might have been a prince from that rustic hovel of Tor Neroche, but he wasn't at all shy about using any of his nobility credentials. The head librarian was still in a bit of a swoon, leaving a handful of under librarians saddled with the task of holding him up.

It could have been worse, Acair supposed. The lad with the nose for magic they generally used for sniffing out interlopers could have been standing there as well. He was perhaps off having his morning ale, which was definitely a boon for them.

Acair gave Mansourah directions to an unassuming spot in an even more unassuming stack of extremely dry and rather poorly written—he'd checked previously, of course—tomes on the production of various varieties of cheese to be found only in the country of Meith. He'd been to Meith several times and whilst he could definitely say they were masters at their craft, they were also quite possibly the worst writers in the whole of the Nine Kingdoms. He paused with his companions, endured an opinion or two about his taste in literature that Mansourah couldn't seem to keep from sharing, then turned his mind back to the business at hand.

He shared the single word necessary, then stood back and waited to see what would happen.

He honestly wouldn't have been surprised if the entire library had come crashing down on their heads, which was one reason he'd pulled Léirsinn over to him where he could keep her safe in the case of such an event. Fortunately for the patrons within, however, not even a vigorous vocalization of the appropriate magical key had any effect. He considered Mansourah's failure to obtain that slim, worn volume he could plainly see hiding there and came to the only conclusion possible.

He was a damned good mage.

Obviously his spells were every bit as formidable as he'd always considered them to be. He examined that particularly marvelous piece of work there to make certain it hadn't been tampered with, but saw only what he'd left behind several months ago.

"What now?" Mansourah asked shortly. "Given that this is a dead end."

Acair was disappointed, of course, but not ready to consign the whole of the journey to the rubbish heap. He hadn't made a copy of his book, true, but it was possible perhaps to find the pertinent information in other places. Whether or not he wanted to go to those places was another matter, but it looked as if he might not have a choice.

He smiled gamely. "We'll continue the search for what I need, of course. The journey has certainly not been wasted. The city does offer other delights worthy of our visit."

"If you tell me we're here to sit by and watch as you have another pair of boots fashioned," Mansourah managed, "I will take them and shove them down your throat."

"I'd rather see my tailor, actually," Acair said without hesitation. "He always keeps a few things on hand for my sartorial emergencies. I might or might not have an extra pair of boots tucked into his workroom as well, so not to worry."

Mansourah's mouth fell open. It was possible he made one or two inarticulate sounds of amazement, but Acair thought it wise not to comment.

"You," Mansourah said, apparently finding his tongue, "dragged us here to see your *tailor*?"

"My barber as well, if we've the time—"

He had to admit that the present moment wasn't the first time he'd used Léirsinn of Sàraichte as a shield, and it was true that she'd stepped in front of him of her own accord, but there would come a day when he wouldn't allow that sort of thing any longer. Convincing her of that might prove to be another thing entirely.

He peeked at Mansourah over her head. "Don't bother with your puny spells."

"I won't need a spell to help me shove my dagger into your chest!"

Acair tsk-tsked him. "Lower your voice, lad. This is a place of study."

Mansourah looked as if he might benefit from either some fresh air or a strong glass of port—perhaps both—so Acair didn't waste any time urging Léirsinn around that choking piece of royalty and forging on ahead out of the stacks. He imagined Mansourah wouldn't resort to murder in such a place, but he wasn't at all sure that would last once they reached the outside.

Slipping out a back door he had used more than once in the past was accomplished easily enough and without any unwanted additions to their number. He continued on with his companions through the press of souls about their morning business, stopping only when he felt they'd gained enough distance from the library to be safe.

Mansourah shoved him aside. "Léirsinn, let us be away," he said crisply. "We'll retreat to our lodgings and share a bottle of wine in front of the fire whilst I decide how best to inflict a well-deserved and long-overdue death upon my servant."

Acair didn't waste breath arguing. He would absolutely prefer that Léirsinn be safely behind heavy doors whilst he spent the afternoon roaming the streets, keeping his eye peeled for any trouble he might have stirred up.

He walked behind the prince and a woman who would surely never lower herself to wed that same prince back to the most exclusive and, admittedly, expensive lodgings in town. If there were a pair of rough-looking lads leaning negligently near the very unassuming door that led to a much less unassuming courtyard, so much the better. Léirsinn would be safe, Mansourah would likely fall asleep in his ale, and he himself might manage to do a bit of nosing about.

He wasn't above playing the part of a servant as they were again shown upstairs to that fabulously appointed sitting room. He found himself complimenting the prince of Neroche on his good taste before he could stop himself.

Mansourah glared at him. "Don't plan on staying in here. I believe they have a spot by the coal bin downstairs that will be more fitting for your station."

Acair hadn't planned on anything, actually, though he couldn't stop himself from eyeing a rather comfortable looking settee. He watched Léirsinn stumble over to it, sit, then lean over. She was asleep before she managed to even remove her boots. He did the honors for her, had a barely audible *thank you* as a reward, then covered her with a luxurious blanket that had been tossed over one of the armrests for just such a need. He straightened and turned to assess the lay of the land, as it were.

Mansourah was watching him. Acair didn't suppose he wanted to know what was intended by that look, so he put on a polite smile and rubbed his hands together purposefully.

"I think I'll go for a walk."

Mansourah tossed his cloak over the back of one of the chairs in front of the fire. "I suggest a visit to the garden instead. No time like the present for a bit of swordplay."

Acair snorted. "If you think I'll lower myself to brawl with you—"

He stopped speaking abruptly for the simple reason that he became distracted by the rather fine rapier Mansourah had simply drawn out of thin air, then tossed at him. It arrived hilt-first, which he supposed was something of a concession. He examined the blade and found that it was very sharp indeed. He considered, then lifted an eyebrow.

"I thought you confined yourself to shooting little arrows into things."

Mansourah looked at him coolly. "I believe you'll find that I can do far more than that." He nodded sharply toward the door. "Outside."

"Is that an invitation?"

"Would you prefer that I prod you along with a spell of death?" Mansourah growled.

"Don't you lads from Neroche have a prohibition about that sort of thing?" Acair asked politely.

"Aye, 'tis called honor, which is why I'll take great pleasure in killing you in the usual way, with a sword through your chest, not your back."

Acair supposed that was fair enough, though he had no intention of dying that day. Humoring his half-sister's husband's brother—he didn't like to think about how that left him related to the grumbling prince currently exiting the chamber—seemed the very least he could do, however. Perhaps the lad could be prevailed upon to produce funds for a decent supper if he'd been taken out and exercised properly for a bit.

Acair made certain Léirsinn was still sleeping comfortably before he left the chamber and pulled the door shut behind him. He thanked Mansourah politely for the discreet spell of protection he dropped over the door, then followed him down the stairs to the inn's great room. He made good use of the time by reminding himself of a few things he hadn't particularly wanted to think about before.

He was on, he thought he could say without too much of a twitch, a Noble Quest.

He wasn't one for those sorts of things, as it happened, being much more inclined to sit by the fire with a hearty mug of tasty ale and indulge in ribald mocking of those who embarked on the same. It was truly an indication of how far his life had gotten away from him that he had become the one trotting off into the Deepening Gloom.

His father would have had an attack of the vapors if he'd known.

But damnation, what else had there been to do? Someone was cluttering up the world with disturbing spots of shadow that left anyone who walked through them adversely affected. There seemed to be no one else with the stomach to take up the trail, which had left him forgoing the impulse to bolt to more elegant surroundings to instead hoist the proverbial sword in the world's defense. If Léirsinn's grandfather needed a rescue from the clutches of her dastardly uncle, and Léirsinn herself needed protection from that same unsavory relative, well, all the more reason to lay hold of whatever nobler instincts he could dredge up and be about his business.

That was made substantially more difficult by an injunction that he not use even a smidgen of his formidable magic, a vexing charge of which Acair found himself endlessly reminded thanks to that damned spell of death that threatened to fall on him at the first sign of even a casually muttered spell.

Finding the rogue who had sent that spell to dog his heels was, he had to admit, very high on his list of things to do whilst questing.

He shook his head wearily. His task was daunting, his resources scarce, and his survival depended on nothing much past his formidable wits. Those lads from heroic tales could scarce lay claim to anything much more noteworthy than that.

"Acair? Hallo?"

He pulled himself back to the business at hand and looked at Mansourah. "A bit of a stroll first, to warm the blood."

Mansourah considered. "Interested in seeing what you stirred up this morning?"

Acair bestowed a smile upon the poor lad. "There is hope for you yet."

"You won't escape crossing blades with me later."

"My dearest boy, I would count it a great disappointment to miss such an opportunity. Now, can you possibly be discreet?"

Mansourah shot him a dark look, but Acair expected nothing else. He was happy to list the lad's flaws at length, but he had to admit that there had been the odd tale or two circulating about that one there having accomplished the occasional Heroic Deed. Even those lads from Neroche didn't manage that without some small bit of skill.

He followed his companion out of the inn and prepared to spend at least a pair of hours mingling with the workaday types.

It would be interesting to see what the afternoon might bring his way.

Three

Léirsinn woke to the sound of metal ringing.

She sat up and looked around herself quickly. She was alone, which was a bit alarming, but at least her chamber wasn't full of ruffians, which was less alarming. She rubbed her hands over her face and tried to make sense of what she was hearing. If she'd been in her uncle's barn, she would have assumed that noise was just tack jingling. In her present locale, though, she thought it sounded quite a bit like swords.

She pushed off the blanket someone had obviously draped over her, pausing briefly to appreciate the fact that it wasn't covered in horse hair, then rose and made her way unsteadily over to a window. The curtain was made of fabric finer than she had ever put her hand to, but perhaps that was nothing more than she should have expected given the luxurious nature of their accommodations.

She pulled back the curtain, surprised to find that it was well into the afternoon but somewhat less surprised to see that a pre-supper duel was in the offing. The mystery of the noises she'd been hearing was solved, as was the location of her companions. The only question that remained was whether or not the two fools going at each other with rapiers down there in the garden would manage to kill each other before she could stop them.

She looked quickly for her cloak, and then left the chamber at a dead run for the ground floor. The innkeeper, a sturdy, sober man of a decent age, only watched her as she skidded to a halt in front of him. She made a manful attempt to gather her dignity back around herself, then looked at him with as much hauteur as she could manage.

"The garden, good sir," she said. "If you please."

"Of course, lady," he said. He nodded to one of his lads, then instructed him to show her the way to the garden.

Léirsinn followed the boy outside, then frowned when he stopped and looked at her pointedly. She would have asked him what he wanted, but he had already glared at her and gone back the way they'd come before she could. It occurred to her then that she likely should have given him a coin for his trouble, but it was too late. It was also too late to ask him if she could escape back inside with him, so she turned to face the madness she had come to stop.

She stood on the edge of a finely laid stone path and won-dered how best to make her presence known. It only took a mo-ment or two to decide that even if those swordsmen there might notice her, they wouldn't dare take the time to acknowledge her. She considered shouting at them, then decided that there was no point. She knew better than to step between two feisty stallions, so she looked for somewhere to sit until they'd gotten out of their system whatever was bothering them.

The nearest bench was already heavily in shadow, but it looked far enough away from the field of battle that perhaps she wouldn't be caught by a stray sword. She walked over to it and perched on the edge, shivering in spite of herself. She wrapped her cloak more closely around her, looked at the two men in front of her, then wished rather abruptly that she'd just remained upstairs.

Who would have thought that watching two extremely handsome, thoroughly angry men fight with elegant swords would be so overwhelming?

She rolled her eyes and grasped for her last vestiges of good sense. She was a woman of action, not a wide-eyed lord's daughter who'd never been out of the nursery. If she occasionally found herself a bit weak-kneed over the thought of taking a peerless horse for a sprint across a large pasture with decent footing, who could blame her? That was the absolute limit of any propensity she might or might not have had to swoon.

Hadn't she easily ignored the lads she had ordered about in her uncle's barn? Even more quickly dismissed had been the men who had come to buy horses they couldn't possibly appreciate from her uncle, one of the worst specimens of manhood she had ever encountered. Unpleasant, unchivalrous louts, all of them.

Nothing at all like the lads out there, trampling the last bits of fall's brittle vegetation.

She considered, chalked most of her breathlessness up to the stress of her journey to Eòlas, then decided it couldn't hurt to have a look at prince and prince's bastard son about their noble business. For the sake of scholarly study, of course, which seemed particularly appropriate given her location.

She shifted to look at the man to her left. Mansourah of Neroche could have easily stridden across the pages of a Hero's tale and captured the heart of any maid with a book in her hands. He was handsome, chivalrous, and he had a very nice nose. If he'd been a horse, she would have immediately paid a premium price for him and considered it an excellent investment. He was obviously skilled in the sort of dangerous swordplay he was currently engaged in and his ability to hurl slurs and curses with equal ease likely came from years of consorting with his brothers as they saw to their royal doings.

All in all, it was understandable that a gel of lesser self-control might feel the need to give him a second look.

She wasn't at all sure what to say about the man facing him. Whatever Acair of Ceangail's abilities with a foul spell might have been, if she'd been watching him come at her with that sword in his hand, she would have tossed hers at him, turned, and hoped she could outrun him. She half wondered why he bothered with steel when his terrible reputation alone was likely enough to send his enemies bolting off in the opposite direction.

Then again, perhaps most saw what she saw: a terribly handsome, thoroughly elegant, perfectly fashioned man any woman with any sense at all would want sitting next to her at supper, twirling her about in the patterns of an intricate dance, or hoisting a sword in her defense. He was absolutely worthy of the fluttering of a feminine heart or a very casual fanning of the face.

She shifted on the slab, not because she was uncomfortable with her thoughts, but because it was damned cold. Her thoughts were just the usual ones a body had while looking at a black mage and a prince who could spew out spells as easily as curses.

She looked about for something else to dwell on and found

herself mentally trotting around in a circle and winding back up in about the same spot, only she realized her current unease didn't come from the fact that she was consorting with those types of men out there, it came from the experiences she'd had in their company.

As she continued to feel compelled to remind herself, magic and all its accompanying ridiculousness was nothing more than what made up her parents' most cherished nighttime tales.

It was a damned shame she couldn't bring herself to believe that any longer.

Unfortunately, that had everything to do with what had befallen her while watching Acair fight off a different prince of Neroche but a pair of days earlier. She had seen things, and not just the sorts of things one might normally find loitering in a garden. She had been faced with a perfect view of what she had spent a lifetime believing couldn't possibly exist.

She had seen magic.

Even the thought of that sort of thing possibly happening again was enough to leave her wanting to hop up and bolt back to her uncle's barn where, though she might face her own demise, she absolutely wouldn't encounter anything of a more otherworldly nature. She had to force herself to take several deep, steadying breaths to calm her racing heart, but it didn't help all that much. It might have been easier, perhaps, to recapture her hold on a very normal, unmagical life if she hadn't been watching the younger brother of a mage king and the bastard son of a different sort of mage prince go at each other with swords because they either didn't care to or couldn't use spells.

She was no coward, though, so she closed her eyes and thought back to that particular moment in Tor Neroche's garden when she'd first encountered that otherworldly ability to see.

There should have been nothing untoward in that garden save an untended vegetable patch or two, yet there seemingly had been. Stepping on a particular sort of spot on the ground had somehow sharpened her vision—or rendered her daft. At the moment, she wasn't sure which it was. The simple truth was, she had stepped backward, apparently put her foot in a magic pool of shadow, and seen things—

She opened her eyes and squeaked.

Acair's minder spell, the spell that was apparently tasked with slaying him should he use any magic, was sitting next to her on the bench. She shouldn't have been able to see it, but there it was just the same. The damned thing had somehow taken the shadowy shape of a youth, slouching negligently on the stone next to her and watching its charge with a sullen tilt to its head. If spells could fashion themselves into something resembling a man, of course, which Léirsinn wanted to doubt.

Well, either it was a new shape for the beast or she was viewing it with clearer eyes than usual. She just knew she wasn't about to ask it to lie on the ground in front of her so she could step on its belly as she'd stepped on that shadow in Tor Neroche and hopefully see things she shouldn't have been able to—

Or perhaps she didn't need a spell any longer.

She looked at Acair and Mansourah, fighting with the enthusiasm of men who wanted to do each other a goodly amount of damage, then closed her eyes. She willed herself not to see, but to *see*, then opened her eyes again.

Mansourah and Acair were still in front of her, but she could see both of them. *See* them, rather, as if she'd been privy to an endless collection of pieces from their souls and what they were made from—

A squeaking distracted her. It occurred to her that she was

the one making that sound, but she wasn't sure how to stop it. She blinked and the vision vanished, but Acair's minder spell was sitting as far away from her as possible, curled up into itself. She looked out into the garden to find Acair and Mansourah gaping at her.

She would have pointed out that she'd done nothing except use a formidable imagination she hadn't known she'd possessed, but apparently no explanation was necessary. They looked at each other in consternation, then seemed to remember what they'd been about but a moment before. The renewed ringing of their swords was a happy distraction from what she couldn't possibly have seen.

She looked about herself for anything else to concentrate on and jumped at the sight of the innkeeper standing a few feet from her. Damnation, would the urge to run never end? She had no idea how long he'd been there, but perhaps not long enough to watch her acting like a fool. She stood up and looked at him coolly, trying to imitate Acair at his most snobbish.

"Aye?" she asked, hoping her tone would take his mind off what he might or might not have just seen.

"A messenger arrived from the king." He held out a gilt-edged missive. "For His Highness, the prince of Neroche."

She took the folded sheaf of paper and tried not to look as much like a stable hand as she currently felt. "The prince seems to be quite occupied with his work over there, so I'll let him know when he finishes."

The innkeeper didn't move. "I host many powerful men here, my lady." He looked terribly torn. "I must say, Prince Mansourah's servant bears an amazing resemblance to someone else I know."

"He has that sort of face," she said without hesitation, though she held out absolutely no hope of putting the man off the scent. While Acair didn't have a clue what to do with a pitchfork, he didn't suffer the same problem with a sword. It was obvious he was no servant.

"He looks very much like Prince Gair, cousin to King Ehrne of Ainneamh," the innkeeper continued relentlessly. He shot her a look. "Gair of Ceangail, as others might call him. A very elegant, powerful man, that one."

"I've heard tales," she said, though that perhaps wasn't as true as she would have liked. She'd heard rumors about Gair's evil, but she hadn't wanted to delve more deeply into his tale lest she find something there she didn't want to know. "I'm sure 'tis nothing more than a coincidence."

The man looked at her carefully. "Lord Acair has been my guest here before, you know."

She opened her mouth to attempt some other sort of diversion but found herself without a single thing to say to counteract that. She just looked at the innkeeper helplessly.

He smiled faintly. "Not to worry, my lady. I have a very exclusive list of lodgers and an ability to keep my mouth shut."

"I'm sure those two out there appreciate both," she managed.

The man glanced at the men hurling insults at each other, then smiled briefly at her. "They have both paid me handsomely for that discretion in the past. Not, I imagine, that either of them needs my aid."

"You never know," she said faintly.

The man lifted his eyebrows briefly, then inclined his head before he retreated slowly back inside.

Léirsinn waited until the doors had closed before she looked at the missive in her hand. She had never in her life seen any-

thing so fine, but what did she know? She waved at the two exclusive lodgers still trying to kill each other, but they ignored her.

"I have a message from the king!" she finally shouted.

Acair caught the guard of Mansourah's rapier with the tip of
his blade and flung it up into the air. Léirsinn watched as it
flipped hilt over blade several times, glinting in the last of the
afternoon sunlight, before it clattered to the ground at her feet.
She jumped to avoid having her toes sliced off through her boots,
then watched Mansourah shove Acair out of his way before he
crossed the garden to her.

Léirsinn jumped as the rapier in front of her simply disappeared. Acair seemingly lost his sword at the same time—and in
the same manner—but he was obviously accustomed to that sort
of thing. He only cursed at Mansourah and followed him across
the garden to her. She held out the invitation to Mansourah.

"From the king," she repeated. "Or so the innkeeper claimed."

"Lovely," Mansourah said, accepting it and popping the wax
seal on one side.

"I'm not sure we have the time for supper at the palace," Acair
protested.

"Given that I doubt you were invited," Mansourah said, "I'm
not sure this is anything you need to worry about." He glanced
at the missive, then smiled. "Ah, a late, light tea in His Majesty's
private solar." He looked at Acair. "No servants necessary."

Acair snorted. "He is no longer the king, which you well
know, so I'm not at all certain why you would want to humor him."

"*He* believes he is still the king, which is enough for any courtesy I, as a member of the royal house of Neroche, might feel
disposed to show him." Mansourah shrugged. "For all we know,

he might take a stab at another game of cards and have his crown back, so what's the harm in it?"

Acair levelled a look at him. "The harm is what might happen to Léirsinn whilst you are burrowing into a plate of sweet cakes."

"I'll eat beforehand," Mansourah assured him. "As for anything else, she will be perfectly safe whilst being escorted there by a man with magic."

Léirsinn stepped between the two of them before she realized she'd moved and she supposed she was fortunate that she was facing Mansourah and not Acair. She didn't imagine, based on the way Mansourah took a step backward, that she would have wanted to see the look on Acair's face.

"Here I am with an invitation and not a thing to wear," she said, blurting out the first thing that came to mind. She was fairly sure she'd heard more than one high-born lady exclaim that in similar tones of despair while shopping in Sàraichte, though she'd never understood it herself. She'd spent a lifetime wearing things worn by others before her. The only things she ever splashed out on were riding boots, but given that she'd only ever owned one pair at a time, there hadn't been much call for worrying about making fashion choices.

As she'd said before, life was so much simpler in a barn.

"I'm sure a gown will be waiting for you in our chambers," Mansourah said. "Master Acair, I'm assuming you can amuse yourself back here at the inn for a few hours?"

Acair let out a gusty sigh. "I'll attempt the same."

"I have boots that need polishing," Mansourah said, examining his fingernails. "Seems a fitting task for someone of your birth."

Léirsinn eased herself from between them carefully, not sure if she were more grateful for lack of spells or lack of steel. She looked at Acair who was obviously nurturing a very warm anger and marveled at his self-control. Then again, the spell that endlessly trailed after him was standing there at his elbow like a gentleman's second, hissing insults at Mansourah that seemed more like echoes of something she might have heard in a dream.

She wondered if perhaps another nap was in order before she lost her wits completely.

Unfortunately, she suspected not even a peaceful sleep would alter what she was seeing. It was odd, that spell there. It was still nothing more than a shadow of something that resembled a tall, gangly youth, but even she could see that it shared Acair's fury. If she had been Mansourah of Neroche, she might have been nervous.

"I do believe I feel a bit of heat in my right hock," she said, wondering if she might distract the men with a clever lie. "Or pains in my head. I'm not sure which it is."

Acair took a deep breath, let it out very slowly, then took a step backward. He looked at her and smiled, every inch the grandson of a prince.

"Prince Mansourah will keep you safe," he said politely. "You should see the palace, I daresay, before our illustrious monarch loses that as well. Not to be missed." He made her a bow, then inclined his head to Mansourah. "After you, Your Highness."

Mansourah didn't move. "Are you going to plunge a knife into my back?"

"And miss the future pleasure of watching terror cross your features as you realize my spell of death is falling upon you and there isn't a damned thing you can do to stop it?" Acair asked mildly. "I think not."

"An honorable black mage."

"Hardly that," Acair said seriously. "I'll spare my lady the depths of my depravity. You, however, will see the full measure, I promise you." He gestured elegantly toward the door to the inn. "After you, Your Highness."

Léirsinn wouldn't have blamed Mansourah for hanging back but the man was obviously not a coward. He was also apparently no fool, for he only gestured for her to go ahead of them without bothering to offer her his arm.

She was grateful to reach their chamber safely, relieved to sit and have something very ordinary to eat, and too tired to fight the appearance of a maid who was soon called to help her dress. She endured what was required to make her look presentable, then happily showed the girl out of their chambers and shut the door behind her. She went to stand close enough to the hearth to try to warm her hands without setting herself on fire. Acair was sitting in a high-backed chair nearby, staring so thoughtfully at the flames that she couldn't bring herself to disturb him.

She shifted, trying not to be distracted by the very lovely sound her skirts made. She had no idea what the fabric was, but she knew the color looked a great deal like the pines near Tor Neroche and she didn't dare touch the damned thing.

"Lovely gown," Acair remarked.

She glanced at him then and realized he didn't look as peaceful as she'd first supposed. "Are you plotting something?"

"Perish the thought."

She tried a different tack. "You have a remarkable amount of self-control."

He looked up at her with eyes that she supposed might be likened to the sea, though surely not the dark business that she was familiar with. Perhaps a bay of greenish-blue water in some secluded spot. She wondered rather abruptly how it was that any woman still breathing managed to look away from him.

"I need him alive," he said mildly.

"Mansourah?" she managed. "For a sparring partner?"

"He's hardly worth the effort of drawing my sword," he said seriously. "The only reason he's still breathing is because I need him to keep you safe."

"Me," she said, wishing she sounded a bit more like she was scoffing instead of choking. "Surely not."

"I am willing to travel in rather unsavoury circles to keep myself safe," he said with a half shrug. "You? I wouldn't take you within a hundred leagues of them, which leaves me relying on that fluttering faery to do what I cannot."

She shook her head. "Who *are* you?"

He smiled briefly. "At the moment, I honestly don't know but don't think that uncomfortable self-examination will last long." He looked at her, then shook his head. "Mansourah will be protection enough for the evening, but I'm already thinking on other means of assuring that you and I both see the spring."

She would have expressed an opinion on that, but she was interrupted by Mansourah coming back inside the chamber from points unknown.

"Ready?" he asked pleasantly.

What she was ready to do was hike up her skirts and go hide behind the nearest curtain, but she supposed it was too late for that. Acair bundled her up in a cloak and herded her and her escort to the door. He held on to the wood at the level of Mansourah's throat, his forearm preventing the prince from leaving.

"Kiss her," he said distinctly, "and I will slay you with my bare hands."

"I think she can decide that for herself," Mansourah said coolly. "Let's be away, Léirsinn, before he works himself into a state over things that are none of his affair." He ushered her out into the passageway and pulled the door shut behind them. "Tea awaits."

"May you choke on its bitterness!" was hurled at the other side of the door.

Mansourah smiled. "I don't think that was directed at you."

"I don't think he means anything by it," she offered. "We're not—" She had to take a deep breath. "Well, we're not . . . you know."

"I think our friend inside has a different opinion on that," Mansourah said, "but let's ignore him for as long as possible. Simeon has never set a very fine table, but one can hope his cook won't ruin tea and biscuits."

She had her own thoughts on how easily food could be ruined, but she supposed there was no point in saying as much. She nodded, then followed Mansourah toward an evening she was fairly sure she wasn't going to enjoy.

An hour later, she was walking down a poorly lit passageway and wishing she had traded places with Acair and remained behind as the servant.

It wasn't that Mansourah wasn't delightful company, because he was. The man she cared quite a bit less for was Simeon of Diarmailt, a rather smallish man with beady eyes and restless hands. She didn't suppose it was polite to wonder if he picked guests' pockets while they were otherwise distracted, but she was a cynic when it came to men with titles—and he didn't even still have his title, if what she'd heard was true. All she knew was that the palace was very shabby, which she thought spoke rather loudly either of a family fallen on hard times or a master of that family who couldn't manage his funds properly. *A lesser relation of a once powerful, magical house* was how Acair had described him back at the inn, which she supposed had been a rather kind thing to say.

In the end, she didn't care who was pretending to sit on the Diarmailtian throne, presently past wishing she could make a curtsey to him and go.

"Here we are," the king said, opening the door to what was apparently his private solar. "After you, Lady Léirsinn."

She entered in front of Mansourah and their host, looked as usual for all possible exits, then realized the solar wasn't as empty as it could have been. She came to a teetering halt, causing the men behind her to stop abruptly. She supposed that was a boon given that it drew the attention of her two companions who made every effort to assure themselves that she wasn't unwell.

She wasn't unwell; she was terrified.

Damn that Acair of Ceangail. She would have wagered her only pair of riding boots that he was the man who had just flung himself over the settee placed at the back of the room. How he'd gotten himself inside the king's solar was a mystery, but she suspected he had quite a list of unsavoury skills to boast about. At least he was fortunate that the sofa found itself far enough away from the fire to be comfortable if one were about some sort of strenuous mischief.

She sat where invited to and tried to pay attention to the king and Mansourah. There were no noises coming from that particular corner of the chamber where she thought a particular intruder might be having a wee rest, but perhaps anyone who had made it to the king's inner chamber wasn't fool enough to wheeze while about his nefarious activities. At least that lad didn't have to feign any interest in polite conversation. Once she finally managed to listen to what Mansourah was discussing with the king—the latest batch of wine from some country she'd never heard of—she was left wishing she'd taken a tumble over the back of that splendidly upholstered sofa herself.

"I would enjoy that very much," Mansourah said politely. "Léirsinn, darling, King Simeon has invited us to go take a turn in his gardens with him."

Léirsinn dragged herself back to the conversation at hand. "Ah, well, wouldn't that be lovely," she managed, scrambling for an excuse not to go. "If only it weren't so cold."

"Of course," Mansourah said gently. "You are of a delicate constitution, so perhaps the chill should be avoided." He turned to the king. "It was a rather difficult journey here, Your Majesty, and my lady is rather fragile. I wonder if we might leave her here in comfort and perhaps visit your wine cellar instead?"

Simeon smiled, but his smile didn't reach his eyes. "I'm not parting with any of my private supply, lad."

Mansourah laughed politely. "I wouldn't presume to ask, of course. I might, however, be able to identify the remainder of what you sent my late brother the king for his coronation all those many years ago, if that would amuse you."

"Adhémar did love his drink," Simeon agreed. He rose and paused. "If you're certain your lady won't feel neglected."

Léirsinn shook her head quickly. "It would be a great kindness, actually, to be able to simply sit and enjoy your lovely fire," she said, doing her damndest to sound as noble as possible. Telling him to take his sorry arse out of his solar so she could shove the man she needed alive to rescue her grandfather out the window was likely not the right thing to say.

"As you will. Come, Prince Mansourah, and we'll take a torch downstairs. I'll leave guards outside the door for your lady's safety."

Léirsinn watched them go, looking as fragile as possible until the door closed. She waited a bit longer just to be safe, then hopped up and bolted across the room. She knelt on the sofa and looked over its back, utterly unsurprised at the identity of the man lying there with his hands folded over his chest.

"What are you doing here?" she whispered fiercely.

"Collecting payment for something I failed to provide," Acair said, sitting up and brushing dust off his shoulders. "Though why I'm bothering, I don't know."

She could scarce believe her ears. "You're *stealing* something?"

"I'm not sure I would use that word," he said, heaving himself to his feet, "but you can if you like."

She gaped at him, but either he didn't notice or he was accustomed to those sorts of looks. She honestly wouldn't have been surprised by either.

He walked over to a glass case sitting on a large, ornate table near the window. He didn't hesitate before picking the lock on it as easily as if he'd done the like hundreds of times before, which she suspected he had. He slipped his tools back into some sort of pocket, then opened the lid of the case. He paused and looked at her.

"You might not want to watch," he said seriously.

"Who will rescue you if you run afoul of trouble?"

"Ah—damnation. Don't save me."

She watched him leap across the chamber and dive over the

back of the sofa. There was no point in telling him that she had
no intention of even trying to rescue him, mostly because she
assumed he already knew that. She almost managed to get herself to her own seat before the door opened, but not quite. She
clutched the back of her chair and found a theretofore untapped
ability to feign illness as she looked at the king.

"Your Highness," she rasped, wondering if putting the back of
her hand to her forehead would be too much. She considered, then
decided it was best to continue to hold onto her chair. At least that
way, she could heave it at the man if he did anything untoward.

The king rushed to her side and took hold of her elbow.
"You're unwell."

"I think I am," she said, grasping for the first thing that came
to mind. "I thought standing for a bit might aid me, but I think
perhaps a turn in your garden might be best. Fresh air and all
that." She hesitated to ask him where Mansourah had gotten
himself to on the off chance she was going to soon be joining the
prince of Neroche in the dungeon, but she was no coward. She
took a deep breath. "Where is His Highness?"

"On his way," the king said smoothly. He leaned his hip
against the chair facing the one she was clutching and looked at
her. "So, my dear," he said without preamble, "who are you?"

"Just a country miss," she said as politely as possible, "trying
to navigate the shoals of a very large world."

"Then why is the prince of Neroche pursuing you?"

"It is," she said honestly, "an utter mystery to me."

She wasn't entirely sure she hadn't heard a snort from the
corner, but couldn't fault Acair for it.

"From whence do you hail precisely?"

"Ah, the East," she said, latching on to the first thing that
came to mind.

"The East is a very large place."

She actually had no idea about any of that save a rather unpleasant trip up the river from Sàraichte to Beinn òrain, then an even more unpleasant trip from there to an elven land where she *had* been tossed in a dungeon, but that had been west of everything she'd ever seen. In truth, she had no idea what the East contained, but it sounded uncharted enough for her purposes—

"Ah, Léirsinn, my love," a voice said suddenly from the doorway. "I feared you might have become lost."

She suppressed an enormous sigh of relief, mostly because she didn't think she should be indulging in that sort of thing while they were still inside the palace walls. She was beginning to suspect that was a dangerous place to be.

"The king was kind enough to rescue me," she said, pushing herself away from her chair. "Thank you, Your Majesty."

Mansourah rushed into the solar, looking terribly concerned. He looked her over, then turned to the king. "I believe she is very unwell. Forgive us, Your Majesty, if we cut our visit short."

Simeon pursed his lips. "Another time, then," he said dismissively.

"Assuredly so," Mansourah said, inclining his head slightly.

Léirsinn thought she might go back to her uncle's barn before she paid another visit to Simeon of Diarmailt, but she supposed no one cared about her thoughts. She listened to Mansourah and the king make polite, royal chitchat and forced herself not to look behind her to see if Acair might be visible from where she stood. She wasn't unhappy when Mansourah managed to get them out of the solar and heading off toward the front doors. The king coming along was simply a happy bit of good fortune, to her mind.

"If you tire of Tor Neroche," the king said, "do consider making another visit."

She realized he was talking to her, then wished she'd remained oblivious. She forced herself to smile when what she wanted to do was clout him on the nose.

"What a tremendous offer, Your Majesty," she managed. "I'm sure His Royal Highness and I would count that as a great honor on our honeymoon tour. Wouldn't we, Mansourah, my love?"

Mansourah lifted an eyebrow. "A delightful idea, of course. Thank you, Your Majesty, for the courtesy. I'll make certain my brother the king hears about your graciousness."

If the erstwhile king of Diarmailt said anything else, Léirsinn didn't hear it. Mansourah was very proficient at making a hasty yet polite exit and before she knew it, she had been bundled into a carriage and they were heading out of the gates at a decent clip. Mansourah didn't look concerned, so either he didn't know Acair was in the palace or he didn't care.

The third possibility was that he refrained from commenting on the location of their companion because they were still surrounded by the king's guards and those guards didn't seem particularly friendly.

She could only hope Acair wouldn't find himself similarly surrounded because there wasn't a damned thing she could do to rescue him if so.

Four

It was one thing to pinch the odd, priceless treasure whilst masquerading as a peasant, yet still having one's magic to fall back on if things went a bit sour. Making an escape without the ability to turn oneself into a brisk winter wind in order to whip past any potentially offended owners of priceless treasures was quite another.

Acair was, he was willing to concede, nothing if not versatile when it came to saving his own sweet neck whilst still holding onto the goods, so he carried on with bolting through back alleyways and across gardens, Simeon of Diarmailt's cherished book of spells tucked securely under his arm. Truly, there were few in the world with his ability to borrow and bolt, as his mother was wont to term it. He had to admit that watching a few less-than-savvy lads attempt the same at her expense during his

youth had been extremely instructive when it came to what not
to do.

He let himself into the inn's garden through a gate in the
hedge that he'd used more than once in the past for just such a
thing, then tiptoed across the garden, keeping to the shadows.
Why he bothered in the dark, he couldn't have said, but there it
was. Old habits died hard.

A quick hop or two up very useful bits of building and a careful scoot along a ledge left him sliding open the window he'd left
unlocked on his way out and rolling back inside the chamber just
in time to hear voices at the door. He flung his cloak onto the sofa
and leapt over to one of the chairs in front of the fire.

If he sat down rather quickly without remembering that he
had a damned book wedged into his belt and it subsequently tore
what felt like a gaping hole into the flesh of his lower back, well,
that was the price for the spoils. He shifted a bit to alleviate the
worst of the pain, then assumed a casual pose before the door
opened and Léirsinn rushed inside.

She came to a skidding halt halfway across the chamber.
"Oh," she said. "You're here."

He was desperate to gasp in a few restorative breaths, but
that damned busybody from Neroche was hard on her heels. It
wouldn't do to provide anything interesting for that one to poke
his nose into.

"Of course," he said, trying not to wheeze. "How was tea?"

"Terrible," Mansourah said, tossing his cloak onto the sofa
without apparently noticing what was already there. He accepted Léirsinn's wrap, then saw Léirsinn seated in the unoc-
cupied chair there in front of the hearth. He looked at Acair.
"Move."

At any other time, Acair would have simply responded to the

offer with a cool look, but the present moment demanded a bit more discretion than usual. He heaved himself up out of the chair and was happy to use that exertion as an excuse to catch his breath. He looked at Léirsinn to find her watching him more closely than he was comfortable with—

That thought was enough to leave him wanting to clap his hand to his forehead. Never in all his years had he ever complained about a woman favoring him with a lingering look, no matter her reason.

Truly, his life was no longer his own.

Mansourah sat down and stretched his legs out. "I hope you kept yourself sufficiently busy tonight."

"Polishing your boots, of course," Acair said, attempting a casual lean against the mantel. "Pedestrian labor, of course, but I'm nothing if not accommodating. How was the pretender tonight?"

"As unpleasant as he usually is," Mansourah said with a gusty sigh. "I'm surprised someone hasn't poisoned him yet, but perhaps no one finds him worth the effort. His magic could certainly use a bit of propping up."

Acair agreed, of course, but that was probably best left unsaid. As for anything else, the things he knew about Simeon of Diarmailt's desires for a substantial bit of additional magic would have given the rest of the world nightmares, he was sure.

"Léirsinn, what did you think?" Mansourah asked.

"I didn't like him at all," she said carefully. "His solar was not a place I would have cared to linger." She paused. "I'm not sure why anyone would want to pay a visit there."

"I couldn't agree more," Acair said. "'Tis a bit overdone of late, if you ask me, particularly that new settee—"

The chamber went rather silent. Acair supposed that was

what happened when men with lesser wits were having things occur to them that required all their powers of concentration. He preferred a few gasps echoing in any given chamber before silence fell, but he was that sort of lad. Theatrics were his lifeblood.

Now, if he could learn to curb his instinct to slander poorly appointed solars when the opportunity presented itself and keep his own bloody mouth shut instead, he might have something.

Mansourah shifted in his chair and gaped at him. "You were in his solar tonight!"

Acair decided there was no point in denying it. "Someone had to make certain you didn't have too much wine."

"I am *not* Adhémar," Mansourah growled.

"I never said you were, old thing," Acair said soothingly. He removed the book from where it resided halfway dug into his lower back and placed it carefully on the mantel. "I had business there of my own, so I thought I might as well pop round and see that you two were safe."

Mansourah pointed at the book. "What—and please don't think I'm actually curious—is *that*?"

"It is," Acair said slowly and distinctly, "a book."

"I can see that!"

"It never hurts to clarify these sorts of things for those with lesser minds." He shrugged. "Trust me, Simeon will never notice what's missing until we're very far away from here—"

A pounding on the door had him quickly revising his opinion of the king's ability to sense when he'd been robbed. He tucked the book back into his belt, then rubbed his hands together.

"Time to go."

"Time to go," Mansourah repeated incredulously. "What do you mean—and what *is* that book?"

"Best you not know," Acair said promptly. "Now, if you would be so good as to do something about my lady's clothes?"

Léirsinn looked at Mansourah, startled. "My clothes?"

Mansourah was, as Acair found himself forced to acknowledge with regularity, a gentleman. The prince shouted a demand for a moment to prepare himself to receive guests, then looked at Léirsinn.

"My apologies in advance," he said with a wince.

She would no doubt have protested, but before she could apparently blurt anything out, the change was made. Her gown was gone, to be replaced by very fine traveling clothes, a sturdy but obviously warm cloak, and an exceptionally handsome pair of boots. Acair didn't bother to ask if he might have a similar outfit. He suspected Mansourah would prefer to leave him standing there in his altogether just for the sport of it. He would simply make do with less.

"I don't suppose you're going to bolt out the window," Mansourah said grimly.

"It seems preferable to attempting the same through the door," Acair said. He looked at Léirsinn. "Are you afraid of heights?"

"I love them," she said through gritted teeth.

A fine lie, he had to admit, from a truly sporting gel. He reached for her hand.

"I've already been up and down a perfectly safe route tonight, so not to worry." He looked at Mansourah. "I don't suppose you'd be good enough to keep the rabble at bay for a few more minutes."

Mansourah glared at him. "For Léirsinn's sake."

"Of course," Acair agreed. "Let's rendezvous at the barn. I believe I'll make a little detour to my tailor, but that won't take long."

At the rate the pounding was intensifying, he suspected that door wasn't going to last long either, so he clapped Mansourah on the shoulder, avoided a fist headed toward his own very fine nose, then hastened with Léirsinn to the window. He climbed out, helped her out onto the ledge, then spared a brief moment to reflect on the fruits of his evening's activities. He had the feeling he was about to pay a heavy price for having tampered with Simeon of Diarmailt's most treasured book of spells, but it wasn't as if he'd bothered to steal the whole thing—

He paused, cursed his damnable propensity to always tell the absolute truth, then had to admit that while he should have only liberated a page or two, he had succumbed to temptation to take the whole bloody thing. He'd deposited another of the king's books in its place, turned in a way that shouldn't have left the man noticing the theft right off. Suspicious whoreson. If he'd been a bit more at his leisure, he would have sat down and penned a sharply worded complaint to the local monarch. Extremely bad form, that.

He stood on the ledge just to the right of the chamber's window and made himself a mental note to compliment Mansourah of Neroche on his ability to shout in the manner of an outraged nobleman missing out on his rest whilst holding the chamber door closed long enough to give his companions time to bolt out the window. It begged the question of whether or not the lad had done that sort of thing before, but perhaps that was something that could be investigated later.

At the moment, he was busy congratulating himself on having come in that same window earlier in the evening. If he hadn't, he wouldn't have realized the best he would manage would be a ledge hardly wide enough to hold up a plump bird, never mind a man with escape on his mind.

He looked to his right to find Léirsinn standing there—clinging to the side of the inn, actually—with her eyes closed, looking as if she might faint. He covered her closest hand with his.

"Léirsinn," he whispered, "there's a roof a trio of paces to your right—"

"Are you daft?" she asked tightly. "If I move, I'll fall!"

He decided against pointing out to her that the worst a fall might result in would be a broken bone or two. The woman didn't care for heights, something she had let him know very clearly several times in the past.

He didn't share her fear. He couldn't begin to count the number of times he had gleefully thrown himself off whatever castle wall, abbey spire, or rickety bridge he'd found himself atop, waiting until the very last moment possible before changing his shape into whatever came to mind at the time. The higher the perch, the longer the drop, the more time that passed before he gave himself the power of flight, the better.

Being forced to move about as a mere mortal was extremely inconvenient.

"If you can shift your feet just a bit at a time," he said, trying to sound as encouraging as possible, "we'll reach that little overhang in no time at all. After that, I'll go first, then help you down."

"All the way to the ground?"

"It won't be much farther than getting off the back of any number of horses you've mastered," he lied. "I'm sure."

"You're not sure of a damned thing."

"I am sure of several things, one of which is I can guarantee our pampered companion will be exiting the inn by way of the front door. Think on how you'll then be able to taunt him with your exploits when he next vexes you."

"He doesn't vex me," she managed.

"Then you can defend my abused honor," he said. "Or you can instruct him in the proper way to attempt a duel. Were you not witness to that childish display in the garden earlier this afternoon? I was embarrassed to be a part of it. Now, if we could just ease to our right a bit, I imagine we'll be able to hop right down to the ground. Perhaps we'll take a moment or two and examine this afternoon's battlefield, just to see how consistently our companion was forced to retreat."

He continued to babble in something just above a whisper, mostly in an effort to distract her. He stopped speaking when she glared at him, but perhaps that had been just the thing she needed. She took a deep breath, then inched her way over to that bit of something protruding from the side of the building that might have charitably been called an awning. It wasn't that the overhang was poorly made, it simply wasn't terribly large.

"I am here alone I tell you!"

Acair froze, grateful that he and Léirsinn were far enough away from where Mansourah was hanging out the window that they hopefully wouldn't be seen. He breathed lightly, listening to that hapless prince of Neroche trying to talk his way out of getting himself thrown into the king's dungeon.

Acair rolled his eyes in despair. That one there was altogether too accustomed to waving his title about to get himself out of trouble. Obviously lessons were needed in the fine art of prevarication necessary to save one's sorry arse when faced with guards carrying swords.

Time crawled by. He didn't dare move, particularly after he heard the innkeeper directly beneath him arguing with the lad who was seemingly the captain of the detail sent out to search for the thief who had broken into the king's private solar and taken one of his treasures.

Acair shook his head. Only one? Simeon was terrible at sums. He'd pinched at least three things earlier that night that he could bring to mind without effort, mostly in repayment for the way he'd caught the king looking at Léirsinn. Having perfected the art of peering over the backs of sofas whilst remaining unobserved himself had obviously been time well spent.

More time passed more slowly than he would have liked, but the voices below finally faded as the innkeeper and his late-night visitor went back inside. He eased past Léirsinn, then tested the awning for sturdiness. He had definitely seen worse, so he left Léirsinn sitting on the edge before he swung down to the ground. The threat of death always tended to leave him feeling rather spry, so after congratulating himself on not landing on an upturned rake left lying where a pile of snow had covered it, he turned his mind to coaxing Léirsinn down from the roof.

He couldn't fault her for being cautious. He tended to rush forward into things because he enjoyed the looks of astonished dismay he generally received thanks to that sort of thing, but he'd always had magic to fall back on if things went awry.

He was starting to understand why the average bloke spent such an inordinate amount of time down at the pub.

"Just jump," he said finally, trying not to sound as exasperated as he felt. Exasperated was better than alarmed, he supposed, and he was alarmed enough without any help.

She jumped. He caught her—barely. If he held her in his arms perhaps a moment or two longer than necessary, well, who could fault him for it? The only thing he appreciated more than a finely wrought spell was a beautifully fashioned woman.

"Let go of me, you lecher."

He patted her back, then released her from his embrace. "Just trying to keep you warm."

Her teeth were chattering. That might have come from fear, which he doubted, or the bitter cold, which seemed more likely. He rubbed her arms briskly, wishing he'd had the luxury of conjuring up a hot fire by which they could take their ease. Unfortunately, things were as they were and he had made do with much less in the past. He imagined Léirsinn had as well.

"Where to now?" she whispered. "I'm assuming we're not going back to our chamber."

"I'm actually planning a quick visit to my tailor, if you don't mind."

She looked at him as if she couldn't decide between complimenting him or stabbing him. He wasn't unaccustomed to that sort of look, though, so he carried on with getting them out of the garden by way of a gate disguising itself as part of a shrubbery. He pulled it shut behind them, then looked at her.

"Stay right with me," he advised.

"And miss out on more of this glorious adventure if I don't?" she said, looking as if she might rather be doing exactly that. "You must be mad."

He smiled briefly, because she was spectacular and full of good cheer even under adverse conditions. She was also shivering so badly, he was half tempted to strip off his cloak and put it on her. Because he knew that would leave any stray females walking the streets so late swooning at the sight, he decided they would simply have to resort to a hasty trot along back alleyways. He took Léirsinn's icy hand in his and concentrated on not getting them captured.

Running was, he supposed after a half-hours' worth of the same through places he might have hesitated to go alone but necessity left him with no choice but to pass through with an innocent horse miss in tow, at least a decent way to warm up. He found an empty doorway and pulled Léirsinn into it. He wrapped his arms around her—an altruistic and definitely not self-serving gesture—and waited until a burly night watchman had passed them by before he allowed himself to breathe easily.

"Was that a palace guard?" she whispered.

He shook his head. "Just a regular lad making the rounds of his neighborhood, doubtless keeping his eyes peeled for black mages and their fire-breathing companions."

She might have huffed a bit of a laugh or she might have simply been wheezing from the cold. The weather was typical for that time of year and location but not terribly pleasant when one was enjoying it not from a choice spot in front of a roaring fire.

"Why did they send guards after us—after you, rather—or do I need to ask?"

He shifted so he could keep his eyes peeled for miscreants while still keeping Léirsinn shielded from as much of the icy breath of wind as possible.

"'Tis possible that my activities earlier this evening included liberating a collection of kingly scribblings and stuffing them into the waistband of my trousers," he whispered. "I refuse to admit to anything else which may or may not have happened as an intended insult to someone I might or might not have, as my mother is wont to say, done dirty in the past."

She sighed deeply. "You're incorrigible."

"Your confidence in my ability to stir up trouble is gratifying," he said. "There is more to the tale, of course, but I'm not sure now is the proper place to relate the particulars. Let's just say that Simeon and I made a bargain last year and there were a few loose ends remaining."

"And those loose ends were to be found in his solar?"

"One of them, aye." He patted her back. "I'm as surprised as you are to find he doesn't hide his treasures in a more secure location, but not my worry."

She snorted. "I would think he would be coming after you then, not Mansourah."

Acair shrugged lightly. "'Tis possible I left Simeon a note telling him that his spells needed more protection than a lock that even Mansourah of Neroche could pick."

"You didn't," she breathed.

"I hadn't intended that he find it right off, which is why I placed it inside the book that I substituted for the one I now have."

"Did you lock the case back up?"

He patted her. "Of course, and your appreciation for my altruism does you credit. I will admit that Simeon is no fool," he continued. "He likely put the proverbial two and two together and realized that perhaps Mansourah might be keeping company with those far above his station in a magical sense. I had hoped it would take him longer to come to that conclusion, but there you have it. Mansourah has the chance to act indignant and you and I have the glorious opportunity to make a run for it." He smiled. "I promised you danger and peril, didn't I?"

"I should have taken you more at your word." She looked at him seriously. "Someday you're going to poke at the wrong hornet's nest."

He didn't want to mention that he suspected he already had, mostly because she knew he already had. He hadn't been entirely forthcoming about his desire to see what a visit to Diarmailt stirred up, but he supposed she knew that already as well.

There were strange things afoot in his life.

He stood with her until the street was as free of guards as it was going to be, then nodded up the way. "Let's slither through the shadows as best we can."

"We aren't really going to visit your tailor, are we?"

"He has things I need."

"If you tell me we are here for cravats, I will bloody your nose."

He smiled. "Nothing so pedestrian, actually."

"Will he be awake?"

"He keeps rather unusual hours," Acair conceded, "but better still is his uncanny ability to keep an ear to the ground for all sorts of unusual arrivals. I also might have sent a lad with a message to him earlier."

She looked at him in surprise. "Do you think *he* told the king you were here?"

"Never," Acair said confidently. "I likely don't need to mention that we have a particular understanding."

"He keeps his mouth shut and you let him live?"

He stopped and looked at her in surprise. "I'm not sure if I should be flattered or alarmed."

She only smiled briefly. "It was a guess."

"A good one," he said frankly, "but in this case, my reputation for dishing out the odd bit of retribution doesn't serve me. The simple truth is, I aided him many years ago in what for me was a profoundly uncharacteristic display of good will and he's repaid me with the finest couture in all the Nine Kingdoms ever since. That and he keeps a thing or two for me under very tidy piles of superior neckwear."

That was ignoring the heart the matter, but the whole truth was something he didn't want to discuss. Unfortunately, he couldn't avoid examining it in his own head.

The absolute heart of the matter was that he needed something from Odhran of Eòlas's back workroom that he had put there for an exigency he had never intended to face. That there was a need driving him to seek out that failsafe was profoundly unnerving. He considered a handful of words as they walked until he hit upon the one that best described the sensation that was continually nipping at his heels, threatening to overcome him if he allowed it to.

Fear.

He could hardly believe he was even acknowledging the same, but things in his life were not as they should have been. He who had never once since reaching his majority faced off with another being and felt even so much as a twinge of unease? He who had walked places that his father would never have dared go? He who had fought duels with spells and sword that would have had any of his brothers—or any number of other pompous, boasting mages—scampering off with tails tucked?

He didn't like the feeling.

He ducked into another alley with Léirsinn until yet another city guard had passed, then squeezed her hand and continued on. Easier that than standing still and allowing things to rattle about in his empty head. There was a full tally of vapid thoughts endlessly coming from Mansourah of Neroche; he didn't need to be adding his own to the collective thoughts being considered in the wide, uncivilized world.

Who will keep Léirsinn safe?

The man with magic ...

The salient parts of that very brief conversation were what he couldn't seem to stop hearing, try as he might to pay them no heed. It had galled him almost past reason that such was his lot in life at the moment, partly because his pride had been stung and partly because he had feared that if something dire happened, in truth, he wouldn't be able to keep Léirsinn safe.

Hence a trip to retrieve something he'd never thought he would ever be in a position to need. He might not have been able to use the power he possessed, but that didn't mean he couldn't use something that required nothing from him—

"Here?"

He looked at Léirsinn and realized he'd come to a stop in the middle of the sidewalk. Fortunately for them both, the streets were completely empty. Unsurprising given the time of night, but still a little unsettling. He frowned, nodded, then drew her over to the appropriate shop door.

He knocked softly. There was no answer, but that didn't trouble him. Ofttimes the man was slow to answer simply because he occasionally worked far into the night, toiling over silks and woolens that were truly enough to make a gentleman of substantial means shed a tear in the privacy of his own dressing closet. Perhaps he had paused in his labors, put his head down atop a pile of fine silks, and descended into a comfortable slumber.

The puzzling thing was, though, that Master Odhran knew to expect him.

He put his ear to the wood, but he heard nothing.

"I can see someone just sitting there." Léirsinn looked at him. "Just inside, there by the hearth. But there's no fire."

Acair found himself very rarely startled—he was too calculating for that, he would admit—but her words sent a chill down his spine that was not at all pleasant. To be sure, Odhran was very careful about the delicate balance between keeping his shop warm in the winter and burning the place to the ground thanks to a stray spark, but he couldn't imagine the man simply sitting in front of a stone cold hearth.

It reminded him sharply of another soul he'd heard tell of, the youngest son of a particular horse breeder who had been reduced to simply sitting and staring. That lad had been rendered thus because of repeated encounters with a certain sort of shadow lying on the ground where shadows shouldn't have found themselves.

But surely that couldn't have anything to do with what was going on behind the door he was currently opening . . .

"Is there a lock you cannot best?"

He shook his head, not bothering to make any protestations of false modesty. He let them inside, had the presence of mind to make sure Léirsinn followed him in, then heard her shut and lock the door behind them. He pocketed the tools of his very unmagical trade, then scanned the shop before he walked carefully over and looked at the man sitting there, staring at nothing.

Léirsinn didn't move. "Is he asleep?" she whispered.

Acair put his fingers to the man's neck, paused, then looked at her.

"He's dead."

Five

Léirsinn stood in the front chamber of a dead man's shop and had to put her hand over her mouth to keep her gasps inside her where they belonged. She wasn't unaccustomed to death; it was a part of working in a barn. She had never seen a man, though, simply sitting, motionless, in front of his cold hearth as if he'd let the fire go out and been unable to bring it back to life.

She looked at Acair leaning over his tailor, his expression scarce visible. There were street lamps outside, but so far away from where they were that they were of little use. She had to wonder if that might have been deliberate, given the tailor's unusual clientele. It certainly hadn't served him very well that evening.

"What now?" she croaked. She cleared her throat and tried again. "Can you aid him?"

Acair straightened. "Your faith in me is gratifying, but this is far beyond my poor art. Death is that final journey from whence no man or woman returns."

She wrapped her arms around herself. "Poetic."

He started to speak, then shook his head. "And perhaps not as true as I'd like it to be for some mages who dabble in things they shouldn't. I'm surprised to find it isn't anything I wish to think about at the moment."

She wasn't surprised to realize that it was something she would want to think about never. "What will we do now?"

"Slip out of here before anyone thinks we're responsible," he said without hesitation. "But I must have a look in the back first."

She looked at him in surprise. "For shirts?"

He sent her a look she couldn't begin to decipher, so she didn't bother to try. She was torn between wanting to fling herself out the front door and run until she couldn't any longer and wanting to stand right where she was and see if Acair did anything to redeem himself. At the moment, he seemed a right proper bastard with absolutely no heart at all.

He reached out and closed his tailor's eyes.

"Sleep well, Odhran of Eòlas," he said quietly. "You will be missed."

If he added, *and avenged*, she suspected he didn't want to be heard. She closed her mouth when she realized it had been hanging open and decided abruptly that trying to judge Acair of Ceangail was an impossible task. Hadn't she seen that already when she'd been faced with that terrible vision of him in the king's garden at Neroche? A perfect balance of light and darkness, something she suspected he wouldn't have acknowledged if he'd seen it himself. He was vowing to avenge his tailor one moment, then off on the hunt for other clothing the next.

He walked around the deceased, put his hand under her elbow, and leaned close enough to whisper against her ear.

"I fear we aren't alone," he murmured. "I need something specific from his workroom, but feel free to be as outraged as you like to distract those potential watchers whilst I search." He pulled back and smoothed his hand over his hair. "Of course, shirts," he said huffily. "Why else would I come to a tailor's shop in the middle of the night?"

Her mouth was very dry, but she found that she could spit out a bit of fury just the same.

"A man is dead," she said, ignoring the crack in her voice, "and all you can think about is what you're wearing?"

"Or not wearing, which is precisely the point," he said. "A black mage's best accessory is his garb."

She babbled something that she tried to tinge with as much disgust as possible. It distracted her from the almost overwhelming urge to look around her to see who might be there, lying in wait to kill them both.

Acair took her hand. "Let's go into the back. You can tell me if you approve of the cut of my fresh garments. Master Odhran was truly without peer in his craft."

His fingers were cold, which led her to believe he was perhaps feeling as unsettled as she was.

"What I'm most interested in," she managed, "is a pair of shears to stow in your black heart."

"You look for those whilst I am about the heavier labor of seeing if there might be a decent pair of boots set aside for me. I am simply shattered by the figure I'm cutting in what I'm wearing at present."

He stopped at the doorway to what was apparently the workroom and released her hand. She would have protested that, but saw soon enough that he had simply gone back out in front for a candle and a match. He paused next to her, bent, and struck the match against the stone floor. She would have asked him why he didn't just use a spell, but the sudden sight of his minder spell standing behind him almost left her shrieking. She stood, shaking, in the tailor's back room and decided that while there were many things she didn't care for, that list was topped by shadows, things that made loud thumps in the dark, and lingering in a shop where the owner was no longer present in the current world. The sooner they were gone, the better.

"Did Master Odhran hide a record of your foul deeds here?" she wheezed. She wished she could have sounded a bit more irritated and quite a bit less terrified, but things were what they were. She supposed Acair was fortunate she was still on her feet.

"Oh, his workroom is hardly large enough for that," he said, setting his candle down on a tall worktable. "A brief list of the more notable pieces of mischief, perhaps, but nothing more."

Léirsinn would have advised him to look instead for a hook on which to hang that light, but a pair of things stopped her. First, she had absolutely no desire to look around Master Odhran's workroom for anything on the off chance she saw many somethings she wasn't going to care for. The other thing was, there was apparently no need for worry. Whatever else the tailor had done with his time—several unsavoury and dangerous things came more easily to her mind than she would have liked—Master Odhran had been extremely tidy. His worktable was spotless.

The rest of the room was less so. The wall to her left was lined with shelves on which were stacked an endless number of boxes and many piles that listed in various directions. The wall to her right boasted row after row of various threads and tools, some of which had definitely not been put back properly. She was fairly certain if she'd wanted to plunge a pair of shears into Acair's chest, though, she would have managed to find whatever she required over there without too much trouble.

Another long workbench was pushed up against the wall facing her, and the window above it ran almost the entire length of that bench. One of the panes of glass there reflected the light of the candle, something she found thoroughly unsettling. Who knew who might be standing outside that window in the shadows, watching them?

She looked at Acair to see if he might be just as bothered by it only to find him standing in front of a shelf, still as stone.

She ignored the window and moved to stand next to him. "What is it?" she asked. "Nothing here to suit your finicky tastes?"

"It occurs to me," he managed, "that one of my brothers has no doubt decided to have a good laugh at my expense by filching some of my spare cravats."

She realized at that moment that she had seen several expressions on his ridiculously handsome face, but genuine surprise had never been one of them. It wasn't a pleasant surprise, though, which was more alarming than she would have thought it might be. Worse still was the icy nature of his fingers when he casually laced them with hers.

She looked at the empty box he had laid down on a workbench and couldn't begin to imagine how he had decided one unmarked box amongst dozens of unmarked boxes was his, but perhaps the idea wasn't so farfetched. She knew when tack went missing, so why not neckwear?

"I'm sure you'll shed tears over their loss," she said.

"Buckets," he agreed. "One never knows when the right bit of silk at the throat will turn the tide of a seduction."

She would have smiled, but found that she simply couldn't. "You are an honorless bastard."

"I'm offended," he said, squeezing her fingers gently, then releasing her hand. "I have a great deal of honor when it comes to exploits in and out of the bedchamber and taking my place in the center of any dance floor. You are at liberty, of course, to inquire about any of them."

"I'm not sure I want to," she said seriously. She looked at him as casually as possible. "Are you certain you have the right box?"

"There's one way to tell, isn't there?"

"I imagine your tailor is too dead to care whose goods you rifle through," she muttered, "so search away."

He lifted his eyebrows briefly, then nodded. She had no idea what to look for, so she settled for putting boxes back in their places after he'd searched them. She couldn't help herself. Riding was so much more pleasant when one could easily find one's boots and gloves.

He came to a stop near the window and looked at her. She thought he looked a bit as if what he truly wanted was to find somewhere to sit down.

"Gone?" she asked.

"Every last bloody piece of anything I left here," he said with a heavy sigh. "A travesty, truly."

She didn't bother to ask if he were certain or not, because she'd just watched him go through an entire wall of goods. He sighed heavily as he walked over to the other side of the chamber where his tailor's tools were stored. He pulled a stool over to a cabinet in the corner, then stepped up onto it and opened the uppermost door.

Léirsinn watched him take a deep breath, then reach inside.

She half expected something to leap out at him, but apparently the only thing to be flying at the moment were curses. Those curses were soon joined by the things that Acair started flinging onto the table. She made a grab for the candle and held it out of the way scarcely a moment before a pattern—or so she supposed it was—landed atop the flame. She was rather surprised by his sudden change of mien, but perhaps he saw no reason to be subtle any longer. Whoever had chosen his gear from all the things in that work chamber obviously hadn't done so by accident.

If she had expected him to stop flinging once the cabinet was empty, she would have been mistaken. She tidied the piles of patterns on the worktable as she watched him continue to feel around inside the cabinet as if he actually expected to find something still there.

"Is this not everything?" she asked finally.

He swore enthusiastically, then stepped down off the stool and came back around the corner of the worktable. He started shuffling through the patterns there, but with an unusual lack of care. She put her hand on his arm to stop him.

"What are you looking for?" she asked.

"Something besides an invitation to your wedding to Mansourah of Neroche," he said grimly.

She smiled in spite of herself. "I don't think you're in any danger there."

"I hardly dare hold out any hope." He shook his head. "Well, there's obviously no reason to hide my true reason for being here given that I've obviously been robbed." He put his hands on the table and took a deep breath. "I'm looking for a spell."

"Of course," she said, knowing she shouldn't have expected

anything else. "Is this spell written down on one of these patterns?"

"Nay," he said slowly. "You're right to assume what you have, but the truth is, this spell is of a different sort. It might or might not look like a very thin wafer made from a cobweb spun by a very particular, artistic sort of spider. I think 'tis golden in appearance, but I vow it's been so long since I laid eyes on it, I've forgotten."

She smiled, prepared to chide him for having her on, then realized he was perfectly serious. She looked at him in surprise. "You're mad."

He smiled very briefly. "Believe that, my gel, if it lets you sleep more easily at night."

"I haven't been sleeping at *all* at night, which is absolutely your fault and not for any less gentlemanlike reasons," she said pointedly. "As for the other, I don't believe you."

She waited for him to agree that she had every reason to think he was utterly daft, but he only stood there, watching her gravely.

"But spells don't just lie about like abandoned pieces of tack," she protested. "Do they?"

"If you are truly interested—"

"I'm not."

"Which is why you've asked," he finished. He took a pile of patterns, then very carefully started to sort through them. "In general, you have it aright. Most spells are simply words until a mage puts his power behind them. If a local wizard is exceptionally clever, he might write one of his spells in a book and add a bit of magic to it should he ever not feel quite up to making a full effort to sling that same spell at a bothersome youth or crotchety old sorceress."

She supposed that since she was already knee-deep in the madness, there was no sense in not continuing to wade farther from the shore. "Is that what you did with your book in the library?"

He shook his head. "That was simply a spell of un-noticing layered over a very businesslike spell of protection. What I'm talking about is writing down a spell and depositing a bit of power along with the ink." He glanced at her. "So the spell has a life of its own."

"Rubbish," she said faintly.

"Or not, but we can argue that later. It is also possible if a mage is either exceptionally gifted or perhaps even more cynical, to take a decent amount of his own power and bind it into some small object along with a spell of his choice. Elves do it constantly with their damned runes they draw on each other for their own fathomless purposes."

"Why?" she asked, though she honestly wasn't sure she wanted to know.

He shrugged lightly. "Such a thing might come in handy if a mage didn't particularly care to make a display of his own mighty power."

"Or if he couldn't use any of that mighty power?"

He looked at her seriously. "Precisely."

She found she had absolutely nothing to say to that. All she could do was stare at him and wonder how she had ever become caught up in events so far beyond her ken. She was fairly sure it had all begun in a barn, which she knew she should have found appalling somehow.

"The spell I'm seeking," Acair continued, "has the delightful ability to explode into scores of shadows that then distract and disorient an enemy. Better still, as we've already discussed, it requires nothing more to set events in motion other than to find itself flung in the proper direction."

She set aside her first instinct, which was to roll her eyes, and forced herself to think in a different way. She considered, then looked at him. "Could anyone use something like that, or must you be a . . . well, you know."

"Ah," he said, nodding knowingly, "now it begins. Thinking to take it out for a trot around the meadow if you find it first?"

"Perish the thought," she said without hesitation. "I'm just wondering about the danger of someone else finding it before we do."

"More an annoyance than a danger," he said, "but I would rather have it in my pocket than someone else's. Hence my interest in Master Odhran's work chamber."

She wasn't about to argue with him, and she absolutely didn't want to know anything else. Unfortunately, she felt something run down her spine, her own fear or perhaps even the icy breath of someone she hadn't seen come into the chamber. She glanced over her shoulder to make certain they were still alone, then watched Acair continue to sift through his tailor's scribblings.

She didn't see anything that looked out of the ordinary, but what did she know? She was a stable hand with a love for horses and a healthy skepticism for anything she couldn't, as Acair had so correctly put it, take out for a trot through a meadow. She was accustomed to scanning the earth for unstable footing, not—

She put her hand on Acair's arm more suddenly than she meant to, but he didn't seem to mind. She pointed to the corner of something that was peeking out from beneath a pile he had yet to go through.

Acair took the piece of paper with a hand that was far steadier than hers holding the candle. He glanced at her, then took the candle from her and held it over the missive.

I'm watching you, but you knew that . . .

"Rubbish," he said crisply.

That wouldn't have been her word for it, but she didn't think she needed to say as much. "It looks familiar," she offered.

He pursed his lips. "Are you telling me that when I examined a similar piece of refuse in Mochriademiach of Neroche's private solar, you were merely pretending to doze in front of his fire?"

"I'm a light sleeper," she said, "and you were swearing rather loudly at the time."

"I was expressing a polite bit of dismay."

"You almost put out the king's fire with your shouting—"

The sudden banging on the front door sent her stumbling into his side. He shoved the missive into a pocket, smothered the candle flame, then reached for her hand.

"Side door," he said quickly. "Trust me."

Surprisingly enough, she did. She took a brief moment to appreciate the concessions Master Odhran had apparently made for those who might want to make a less-than-visible exit from his shop, then followed Acair quickly out into the night.

She was lost within moments, but that didn't surprise her. She hadn't been able to keep track of all the twists and turns they'd taken simply to get to the tailor's shop. Running through alleyways and as many unlit streets as possible left her utterly disoriented. The only thing that eased her mind any was realizing that the doorway Acair soon found for them to rest in was empty and the pounding she was hearing was only the blood thundering in her ears, not booted feet chasing them.

She propped herself up against the very worn doorway and looked at him, leaning over as he was, gasping for air with almost as much enthusiasm as she was herself.

"Were those palace guards?" she whispered.

"More than likely." He heaved himself upright, then collapsed back against the door with her. "Not lads I would care to encounter at the moment."

"Have they come after the book you have?"

He hesitated. "Possibly."

She shot him a look. "Are you going to explain, or should I guess?"

He chewed on his words for a moment or two, then sighed deeply. "'Tis possible that the king made a bargain with an extremely powerful and canny mage to exchange this unimpressive book of spells for a rather generous amount of the world's power."

She wondered if the time would come where she was no longer surprised by what came out of his mouth. "Is *that* what you did?"

He opened his mouth—no doubt to give her the entire tale—then swore softly instead at the sound of a shout or two in the distance. He pulled her over more fully into the shadows of the alcove. *Shadow* was, of course, not a word she was particularly fond of for reasons she didn't need to explain to herself.

It was also fairly inaccurate given that the whole damned place was dark. They had definitely left behind anywhere that boasted streetlamps, something she suspected Acair had planned. She could scarce make out his face in the darkness, but she supposed she didn't need to look for signs of lying. His greatest fault, according to the man himself, was his lamentable propensity to always tell the truth.

It also wasn't as if she needed him to give her the particulars. She had recently listened to an elven king and his lads go on at length about Acair's having attempted to steal quite a few things, including all the world's magic. At the time, she had thought the entire lot of them absolutely barking. Now, though, she had to admit she could see it was exactly something Acair would have done.

That she was taking any of it seriously . . . well, she was past the point where she could do anything but shake her head over her ability to accept things she wouldn't have wasted the effort to disbelieve but a fortnight earlier. She closed her eyes and leaned her head back against the wood of the door behind her until the voices had faded and they were left with nothing but silence. She opened her eyes and looked at her companion.

"And?" she prodded.

He pulled her closer and wrapped his cloak around her. "If you must know the particulars, I did indeed promise Simeon power in trade for the book that is currently leaving bruises on my poor back."

She was shivering because it was very cold out, not because the thought was so ridiculous she could hardly stop herself from snorting in derision.

Surely.

"So, this isn't just a nasty rumor started by the king of those elves?" she asked.

"I'm afraid not."

She took a deep breath. "Did you manage it?"

"Sadly, nay," he said, "and that wasn't for a lack of trying, believe me. I beg you not to force me to reveal any of the more

humiliating particulars. There are many and each equally unflattering."

"I'm surprised you failed."

"Ah, your faith in my ability to make mischief is heartening,
to say the very least." He sighed deeply. "I will admit that Simeon's spellbook was something I wanted rather badly, as you
might gather from the lengths I was willing to go to in order to
have it."

"I'm not surprised by *that*."

"I am a simple man," he agreed, "with simple needs."

She was too tired to even smile. "I suppose he wouldn't have
merely let you have a look out of the goodness of his heart."

Acair snorted. "The man is notoriously stingy. It was all or
nothing, as they say. He was willing to part with the entire thing
in return for power enough to restore his kingdom back to
rights, but that was the only bargain he was willing to make." He
paused. "It begs the question of where all that power went to
begin with. Was it lost at the gaming table with his crown or had
it been already lost and the wager was an attempt to regain it?
Whatever the case, Diarmailt has certainly suffered for it."

"His home was a bit worn around the edges," she said, "for
something meant to be a palace."

"The whole bloody country could use a bit of sprucing up,"
he agreed. "As for any bargain we might or might not have made,
in the end I was forced to offer my regrets when I wasn't able to
obtain what I needed for the trade."

She pulled away far enough to frown at him. "So you went
ahead and stole the book just the same?"

"I hadn't intended to *steal* it," he said, sounding offended. "I
was just planning on having a look, memorizing the useful bits
as I went along." He looked at her archly. "If you must know, I

wasn't entirely certain that rustic gadfly you went off with tonight was capable of keeping you safe. I thought being to hand
might be useful. If I happened to linger in the king's solar whilst
on that errand, well, so much the better."

"You are incorrigible," she said in disbelief.

"Opportunistic," he said, "which seems to go along quite
nicely with all that altruism that afflicts me like a constant rash.
Unfortunately, tonight I was forced by circumstances I hadn't
planned on to simply filch and flee, as my mother might term it."

"You could have left the book undisturbed, you know."

"I could have, but I didn't want to because Simeon is a colos-
sal ass—and a rather dangerous one." He frowned fiercely.
"There it is again, that damnable impulse to do good that I am
finding myself less and less able to control. I should leave the
whole bloody world to its own sorry fate, but there I seem to go,
endlessly into the breach." He looked at her seriously. "You must
admit that he is a vile little man."

She let out her breath slowly. "I didn't trust him."

"Neither do I, which is why I wonder what it was in his book
that could possibly be worth such a price."

"You haven't looked yet?"

"Haven't had time for anything but a glance. So far, it is absolute rubbish. Hardly the sort of stuff that one might use in
ruling a large kingdom, unless one fancies childish spells of revenge and nastiness." He shrugged. "Honestly, I had intended to
have a look at it overnight, then leave it with my tailor on our
way out of the city. He would certainly have found a way to see
it returned to the proper royal hands."

She shivered. "Impossible now."

"Thoroughly. Now, 'tis left to me to find another way to return it to Simeon with a polite note of regret over the tome hav-

ing inadvertently fallen into my clutching hands." He shrugged.
"One attends to social niceties as best one can." He leaned past
her a bit to look up and down the street, then nodded. "We should
go whilst we can."

She took his proffered hand and was probably more relieved
than she should have been that his fingers weren't chilly. It was
ridiculous perhaps, but she was more comfortable when Acair of
Ceangail was striding off to do foul deeds than when he was
hesitating to do the same.

"Is the king vengeful?" she asked quietly as they walked. "Or
was that just my impression of him at the palace?"

"He's a right proper bastard, but without any of the charm
and elegance possessed by the rest of us," Acair said easily. "Vin-
dictive enough to murder those who cross him, surely."

"Did Master Odhran vex him?"

He paused in mid-step, then continued on, frowning thoughtfully. "I wondered the same thing, but there was something about
that scene in the front of his shop that struck me as odd. I'll have
to give it thought when we're free of the city and relaxing in front
of a hot fire."

"Any ideas on where that fire might be found?" she asked,
fully expecting to hear that such a thing lingered in some mythical elven king's hall she would never manage to reach.

"I believe we might wish to make a visit to my mother."

Léirsinn swallowed with no small amount of difficulty. "Isn't
she a witch?"

"A superior specimen of the same," he said cheerfully, "but I
am her favorite son and you breathe fire. We'll at least have a
decent meal out of her before she comes to a decision about how
long she'll allow us to live. All in all, not our most pressing
worry."

He said it with ease, but she suspected he didn't mean it as easily. She understood. The journey to Eòlas had been dangerous, their time spent there too short, and what they were taking away was apparently not very useful.

Never mind the message she supposed Acair had tucked into his purse with the other one he'd been given in Tor Neroche.

"Let's go fetch our pony and be away," Acair said. "Lovely night for flying, what's left of it."

She had several things to say about any sort of night that might require them to fly and *lovely* didn't find itself on that list. But she was traveling with a black mage who was being pursued by a nameless enemy and he'd just added an angry monarch to his own list of unlovely things.

She sincerely hoped that might be the last of the unpleasant things they would need to put there.

Six

❧

A cair kept to the shadows, though he had to admit he wondered why he bothered.

I'm watching you, but you knew that . . .

He did, though he'd be damned if he had any idea who that watcher might be—and that in spite of now having had two of the same sort of messages delivered to him. It was obviously a poor jest. His brothers were too stupid to have concocted such a dull piece of sport, so perhaps when he had an opening in his diary he would take the time to speculate on which of his enemies might have had the wit to combine the same. It would be an extremely short list, to be sure.

That he might not have *any* name to put on that list was what was leaving him looking over his shoulder far more often than he usually did. It was that looking over his shoulder that was surely the only reason he almost walked himself and Léirsinn directly into a clutch of mages.

He pulled her off the street and into a darkened corner so quickly, he feared he had caused her to squeak. That she didn't bloody his nose for the way he wrapped his arms around her and voiced a few endearments of the sort a man with a paid companion might offer was something of a mercy.

"To the eastern gates, then," said a voice behind him. "We'll lie in wait for him there."

"Won't he be expecting the like?"

There was a lengthy discussion about where the most advantageous spot for snaring an unsuspecting mage might lie. Acair suppressed a sigh. It was honestly a wonder he hadn't simply perished from boredom long before the present moment. So few decent mages possessed the ability to execute a decent bit of mayhem. Obviously, based on what he was hearing, Simeon wasn't able to pay what a more exclusive worker of magic would require.

A tap on his shoulder almost sent him pitching forward into Léirsinn, but he maintained his composure and limited himself to a grunt of annoyance.

"Seen any suspicious lads in the area," asked the mage behind him, "or were you too occupied with your very pedestrian business there?"

"Oy, master," Acair said in his best workaday accent, "I've only a bit longer 'afore me witch at home wakes, so I've no time for lookin' about."

The cluster of fools laughed, entertaining themselves with comments about the superior nature of their magely endeavors and the substandard entertainments of the local rabble before they walked off. Acair shook his head in disgust. He despaired for the future of his profession, truly he did.

He waited until the hunters had disappeared around a corner before he pulled back and looked at Léirsinn.

"My apologies," he whispered.

She looked unsettled. He wasn't sure if it was because of him or those feeble lads he'd just avoided, but decided abruptly that it might be best just not to know.

"The king's mages?" she managed.

"If they could be termed thus," he said, "aye."

"What are we going to do now if they're hunting you?"

"We'll do our best to keep our unflattering comments on their skill to ourselves and settle in for a bit of a wait. It might be useful to have somewhere to hide."

"But we're not going to look for Mansourah," she said, shaking her head as she said it.

Acair took that as a sign that she didn't particularly want to go look for their companion and he was happy to agree. He suspected that not even that notorious busybody Soilléir of Cothromaiche could determine the whereabouts of that bumbling prince of Neroche, who had admittedly done a fine job of allowing them time to get out the window but was currently making up for that by not being anywhere he could be easily found. Acair could only hope they weren't trapped thanks to the delay.

He considered the things he could do to keep himself awake for the foreseeable future and settled for the idea of having a quick peek at Simeon's spellbook. It might be the only thing that kept him out of trouble where that red-haired horse miss was concerned.

"Let's find a bit of light," he said. "I'll have a look at my prize whilst we're waiting."

She pursed her lips, which he supposed said everything he needed to know about her opinions of his activities, but what else could she have expected? For all they knew, he was doing the world a very great service by removing a dangerous book of spells from the grasp of a king with just enough magic to get himself tangled in the proverbial weeds.

Altruistic to the last. He would have that inscribed on a headstone and tuck the damned thing in his mother's garden for future use. He could do nothing less.

Finding a suitable spot was as difficult as he'd expected it would be, but surely no more than a quarter hour had passed before he was loitering negligently near a lit streetlamp, turning the pages of what he soon discovered were the scribblings of a madman.

Little wonder the kingdom was in shambles.

He tried to make sense of what he was reading, but it was impossible. It was nothing but page after page of notes about everything from what the man had eaten for supper to how visiting dignitaries had been dressed. Acair would have made sport of it if he'd been sitting in a comfortable solar with people who might leap into that sort of gossipy fray with him, but as it was, he was standing in a barely lit alcove, shivering and wishing he were not being chased by the local monarch and his minions. The time for mockery was not the present one.

The one decent spell he found was something that only someone up to their necks in the copying of manuscripts might value. Who else would possibly care about the qualities of inks and how to affect the drying times of the same?

He shook his head in disgust. The lengths he had gone to— and the power he had promised the king—in return for the damned thing . . . well, it was obviously a blessing in disguise that he'd failed.

Léirsinn suddenly put her hand on his arm, then nodded up

the street. He pulled himself farther into the shadows, then waited whilst a wheezing piece of royalty staggered along the cobblestones toward them. He reached out and hauled Mansourah of Neroche out of the faint lamplight only to have the man almost collapse at his feet. He dropped the book of spells perforce, but he didn't drop the prince of Neroche, which he supposed might count as a fair trade. Léirsinn retrieved the book, then reached out toward Mansourah.

"Don't," he gasped.

Drunk was Acair's immediate assessment, then he realized that there was something very odd about the way Mansourah was holding his right arm.

"Battle?" Acair asked sympathetically.

"I fell off the ledge back at the inn," Mansourah said, through gritted teeth.

"And you couldn't have changed your shape on the way down?" Acair asked in astonishment.

It was truly a testament to his own ability to see so well in the dark that he was able to make out with perfect clarity the murderous look their feeble companion was giving him.

"I was taken by surprise." Mansourah took a deep, unsteady breath. "If you tell anyone the same, I will kill you."

"Well, I doubt you'll manage that, but let's set that aside for examination later. What did you do to yourself, land on your arm?"

Mansourah only growled, which Acair supposed was answer enough. He drew the prince out into a bit more light and was forced to acknowledge that the man looked thoroughly wrung out.

"I don't suppose you would be so good as to fix this," Mansourah said, sounding as faint as he looked.

Acair would have—a gentleman never bypassed another in need, even if the aid rendered was limited to nothing more than a boost toward that peaceful rest in the East—but his minder spell cleared its throat in a way it absolutely shouldn't have been able to. Acair ignored the fact that he'd become so accustomed to the damn thing that he hardly noticed it unless it poked its shadowy nose into his affairs, then looked at Mansourah and shrugged.

"Sorry, old bean. Can't help you."

Mansourah looked at Léirsinn in desperation. "No magic?"

Acair watched something cross her face, regret perhaps. Leftover tummy upset from whatever Simeon of Diarmailt had served for tea, more than likely.

"I'm sorry," she said helplessly. "I could set it, if that would help."

"I need to sit first," Mansourah said, looking as if he might fall down before he managed it. "Anywhere, even the ground. But perhaps not here, aye?"

Acair couldn't have agreed more about the somewhat exposed nature of their current locale. He encouraged the prince with soothing words and friendly taunts to take a stroll up the street. He hauled the lad into the first likely alleyway he came to and helped him sit atop the first wooden crate they found. It creaked dreadfully, but there was nothing to be done about that.

He considered the conundrum before him and wondered if it might just be easier to clunk the fool over the head and leave him behind. It was somewhat reassuring to find that that solution left him without a single twinge of conscience. Perhaps he hadn't lost himself entirely in the endless months of do-gooding he'd endured.

Léirsinn moved to stand shoulder-to-shoulder with him, which left him waving a fond farewell to the idea of a rap on the child's head and a hasty scamper in a useful direction.

"I can't believe I'm asking this," she said, looking as if she wished she could scamper away herself, "but why can't he just use magic on himself?"

"That is a question for someone far wiser than I," Acair said, "though I could speculate, if you like."

"Oh," Mansourah said through somewhat gritted teeth, "please do."

Acair shot him a look he was certain could have been better appreciated by daylight, but with the right circumstances he was certain he would be able to reproduce it. He looked at Léirsinn and settled for a hasty bit of theological conjecture.

"Men are selfish bastards," he said, "and I don't hesitate to include myself in that lot. I suspect that whatever humorless being created the rules of magic-making all those many eons ago simply decided that it would be amusing to watch a mage stagger from one locale to the next with a sore tum, looking for someone to help him."

"Do you think so?" she asked.

Acair shrugged. "I have no idea, in truth. All I know is that magic comes with limits, no matter how much we wish it didn't. Perhaps 'tis for the best. A mage who could heal himself could heal himself endlessly. If he were a very bad mage—"

"Know any of those?" Mansourah interrupted tightly.

Acair spared the lad the cool look he deserved only because he was already suffering enough. "If he were an evil mage," he repeated, "then his evil would always triumph. No chance of a plate of bad eggs giving the rest of the world a chance to balance the scales, as it were."

Léirsinn frowned. "But that doesn't make sense. If Mansourah can change his shape—and I'll deny this conversation if you repeat it—then why can't he just change his arm back to what it was before he landed on it?"

"An excellent question," Acair said, "and I believe we may have touched on this fascinating subject before."

"I'm sure I ignored you."

He didn't doubt it for a minute. "A shapechanging spell is only a temporary change, no matter how long it lasts. 'Tis a bit like donning a suit of clothes. You put the shape on, you take the shape off, but underneath, you're still the same strapping, terribly handsome lad you were before you used the spell. Healing isn't a temporary change."

"Is it like essence changing?"

"What have you been telling her?" Mansourah gurgled.

Acair ignored him. "It is exactly like essence changing," he said. "*That*, I'm certain, was a gift from someone back in the mists of time lest the whole of mankind perish because we're too stupid to take care of ourselves."

He watched Léirsinn send Mansourah a rather pointed look and thought it might be less-than-sporting if he didn't join her. He supposed the only reason Mansourah didn't spew out a complaint or two was because he obviously was in a great deal of pain.

"So, anyone can use a spell of healing?" Léirsinn asked. "As long as you use it on someone else?"

"Aye," he said, though for the first time in his life, he wondered if that was as true as he'd always thought it to be.

It was a staggering thought, actually. If a mage could endlessly heal himself, *by* himself, then what was to keep a worker of magic from living forever? That damned Soilléir of Cothromaiche seemed ageless. Then again, so did his own grandmother, Eulasaid, but she was surely a soul worthy of a lengthy life.

"What about what you were looking for in Master Odhran's shop?"

Silence, as seemed to be its habit of late, fell. Acair wondered if that would be his lot in life as long as that life included the woman next to him. She said the damndest things, things that he was thoroughly embarrassed not to have been thinking right along with her. He looked at her.

"I see."

She shrugged helplessly. "Would it work?"

"For the sake of the world? I certainly hope not."

She smiled. He was half tempted to join that mewling babe there on that crate and weep right along with him. Ah, damn that Soilléir of Cothromaiche and his cohort Rùnach of Tòrr Dòrainn. The two of them had likely foreseen the exact moment Acair would find himself standing in currently and had had a right proper guffaw over the sound his heart was making as it shattered into more pieces than a black heart ever should.

"I am," he said in all seriousness, "not worthy of you."

Mansourah blurted out a string of curses that should have alerted any and all night watchmen in the area to their where-abouts, but fortunately for them all, he descended rather quickly into a fit of wheezing. A broken arm perhaps did that to a man.

Acair decided action was more useful than speech, so he took his knife and cut off a strip from the bottom of his tunic. He laid it on the frost-covered cobblestones at Mansourah's feet, then slid his knife back down the side of his boot.

"What madness is that?" Mansourah croaked.

Acair squatted down in front of him because he thought it might terrify the lad less if he did so. "Enspell that with what-ever rot you use for healing, wrap it around yourself, and let's be off."

Mansourah looked utterly confused. "What in the hell are you talking about?"

"Take a spell," Acair said slowly, "infuse it into this piece of rather fine weave my sister gifted me, then add a bit of your own power so it stands on its own. Put it over your arm and there you have your cure. Unless you haven't any idea how to do the same, which is what I suspect."

Mansourah glared at him. "I'm no neophyte."

"You're worse," Acair said briskly, "because you've no idea just how much you don't understand."

"*I* don't understand it," Léirsinn said. She looked down at Acair and shrugged. "I don't believe it either, but you already knew that."

Acair did and at the moment, he had no time to attempt to convince her otherwise. He rose and looked down at Mansourah.

"I cannot heal you, nor can Léirsinn, so you'll have to do it yourself. This is all I can think of on short notice."

"You want me to take some of my power and put it on that strip of linen?" Mansourah asked blankly.

"Have you never done this before?" Acair asked, finding himself genuinely astonished.

"Why would I need to?"

Acair opened his mouth to make a list of several reasons why a man might want to keep a goodly amount of his treasure far from where he slept, then he reminded himself with whom he was dealing. Mansourah of Neroche had likely never had a subversive thought in his life, so why would he need to prepare for that sort of contingency?

"Because, my young friend," Acair said, "there might come a day when you are skulking about where you shouldn't be, keeping your magic under wraps to avoid detection, and the ability to fling a bit of distraction or mayhem in the direction of your enemies might save your life. Or heal your arrow-grasping arm, which I'm assuming is the one you shattered."

Mansourah shut his mouth around whatever it was he had obviously planned to say—Acair couldn't imagine it had been polite—then took a deep breath.

"Very well," he said. "I'll attempt it."

He wove a very sturdy, businesslike spell of healing over the cloth, then stopped short. He stared at the cloth at his feet for several moments, then looked up.

"I haven't got a bloody clue what to do now. How do you do it? *Why* can you do it?"

Acair looked at him evenly. "'Tis all that black magery, my boy," he said. "I'm accustomed to leaving bits of my soul behind, or isn't that common knowledge?"

Mansourah looked a bit unwell. "I didn't think."

"Most people don't." He blew out his breath, then realized he didn't have a bloody clue how to explain to that man-child there how one went about trading parts of one's essence for power. Soilléir likely could have waxed rhapsodic about the whole business for hours on end, but the thought of that was enough to leave Acair wanting to flee. In truth, he wasn't entirely sure how he did it either, something he might need to remedy if he were to leave behind important notes for the betterment of the world.

"I could set it," Léirsinn offered quietly, "though I think it would be best if we could escape the city first." She paused. "Just in case."

Acair understood what she was getting at and thoroughly agreed. Mansourah looked as though he might soon become senseless, and they were, as it happened, still within a city full of mages who weren't setting the table for a friendly evening of supper and cards.

He looked at the wounded prince of Neroche. "We'll have to escape first. Your Highness, if you can stand?"

Mansourah might have been a fool, but he wasn't stupid. He accepted a hand to his feet, then didn't spurn the offer of a shoulder to use as a crutch. Acair looked at Léirsinn from around Mansourah's chalky visage and nodded.

"We'll make for the barn and collect my horse. After that, we'll make do."

"Where are we headed?" Mansourah wheezed.

"Somewhere safe."

Mansourah grunted. "You're off on the hunt for another book you can't fetch, aren't you?"

"Aye and this one is cunningly hidden in my mother's library behind *The Noble History of Heroes from Neroche*, which I imagine is covered with at least an inch of dust. My offering will have remained undisturbed, I assure you."

"Your mother's library," Mansourah gasped. "I should slay you for suggesting the same. Save us all a great deal of trouble."

"Your code forbids your slaying a defenseless man."

"You aren't a defenseless man, you're a damned black mage with a reputation almost as vile as your sire's—"

"Almost?" Acair huffed. "I'm insulted."

"And still breathing, something I would like to remedy."

"What surprises me is that you're still talking," Acair said, though he was rather relieved by that fact. Whatever else their failings might have been, those lads from Neroche were cut from sturdy cloth. Acair could bring to mind several very dangerous mages who would sit on the edge of the closest flowerpot and weep over a hangnail.

He pulled up short at the sight of the gates squatting there in front of him, sooner than he'd expected. He propped Mansourah up against a wall, then peered around the corner at the stables. Léirsinn looked over his shoulder and caught her breath.

"Mages," she said.

He smiled in spite of himself. "You've become suspicious."

"At any other time," she murmured, "I would have thought them only ordinary travelers. Tonight, I find myself looking at any man hiding behind the shadows of a hood with a jaundiced eye and an immediate suspicion of their potential for magic-making."

"Very wise," Acair agreed, then hardly managed to catch himself before Mansourah's hand on his shoulder almost sent him sprawling.

"Your sort of lads?" Mansourah said hoarsely.

"They could only dream of it," Acair said without hesitation. "It does present something of a problem for me at the moment, however, given that I'm not at liberty to engage them."

"I could try to attract their notice, then lead them astray."

"Subversion," Acair said approvingly. "Look at you, lad, walking in less than fastidious paths."

"Crawling along them, you mean," Mansourah said faintly. "I'm not sure what would be left of me if I shapechanged at the moment." He leaned heavily on Acair's shoulder. "You certainly disturbed a few unpleasant sorts here."

"I'm beginning to think so," Acair agreed. More interesting still would be finding out who those men were, but he supposed that pleasure would need to wait for a bit.

"How fast can your pony go?" Mansourah asked.

Acair glanced at his wounded companion. "Faster than a princess of Meith running from tidings of your arrival to court her."

Mansourah looked at him with a bit more warmth than perhaps the moment merited. Warmth, fury, who could tell the difference in the gloom?

He looked back at the lay of the land and wondered how best

to proceed. It was, as he'd noted several times recently, extremely inconvenient to move about as a mere mortal. If he'd been at liberty to do what he did best, he would have stridden out into the courtyard of the stables, fought a delightful little duel with those lads there—singly or in a group, as it suited them—then swept off as a bitter, screeching wind toward the promise of more mischief in another place.

As it was, he could only be appallingly grateful, if not a little surprised, when his horse landed on his free shoulder and nipped at his ear.

He sighed. Some things never changed.

Sianach, that sterling fellow, hopped down to the ground, then changed his shape into a rather slim but eminently terrifying black dragon. Acair caught his eye before he spewed out a bit of fire in the wrong direction, then made a hasty decision.

"You and Léirsinn go," he said to Mansourah without hesitation. "I'll follow."

Léirsinn looked gratifyingly horrified. "On foot?"

"I've done it before," he said cheerfully. "You go on and keep our injured princeling from falling to his death. I'm guessing he can find my mother's house and keep you covered in a useful spell of concealment, even with his wounded wing."

"Your mother's house," Mansourah said, almost soundlessly. "I thought you were making a poor jest."

"She's a very competent healer," Acair said, "as well as one who sets a delightful table for supper. As long as you check her spells before she uses them on you or slips them into your tea, you'll be fine. Off you go, lad. Léirsinn, don't let him fall."

If he expected an argument, he didn't get one. What he did have for his trouble, however, was a brief peck on the cheek from Léirsinn and the same attempt made by Mansourah. And damn that bloody middle child of the fierce and irreverent maker of inappropriate jests Desdhemar of Neroche if he didn't simply laugh and hop up on Sianach's back with only a minor groan. Acair watched Léirsinn clamber up onto Sianach's scaly self, then send him a look full of meaning. He supposed since the gloom was so complete, he could read into that look anything he liked.

He scarce managed to duck before Sianach heaved himself up into the sky with a shriek that should have woken half the city. That horse-turned-dragon spewed out a fierce blast of fire in the direction of that vexatious clutch of mages, causing a handful of them to frantically strip off their cloaks and beat the flames into the dirt. Acair watched his companions disappear under a spell of un-noticing and felt a rather unwholesome wave of relief wash over him. They were away and safe. He could hardly ask for anything more.

He was momentarily distracted by a bag of something dropped at his feet—*on* his foot, rather. He picked it up and hefted it experimentally. He had a look inside as well, because he was a suspicious bastard and it wouldn't have surprised him at all to have found that the traveling funds Mansourah had obviously left for him were nothing but useless blanks. They were actually Nerochian gold sovereigns that certainly bit as though they were the genuine item, so he tied the purse to his belt and strode out into the courtyard.

Someone had thoughtfully lit a lamp or two, which he supposed would aid him in what he intended to do. He realized with a bit of a start that one of the men carrying a lantern was glaring at that equally irritated group of mages with a fair bit of enthusiasm and that the man was accompanied by a serving maid who was also holding up a light.

He thought it might be a reflection of the state of his life at present that he hadn't noticed either of them before.

Well, their arrival hadn't left him as much leisure as he might have liked, so he took matters into his own hands right away.

"The king's book of spells," he shouted, holding the thing up. He waited until all of them were looking at him—and recognizing him apparently—before he hurled the book over their heads with as much force as possible.

Mages scrambled to catch it, but they failed. Acair wasn't prepared to credit his endless amounts of do-gooding for anything, well, good, but he had to admit that perhaps there was something to it. He watched in astonishment as the serving girl plucked the king's book of spells out of the air as if she'd been using a spell to do the like. She fumbled with it, tossing it up in the air repeatedly as mages fell over themselves in an effort to grasp it.

There was magic afoot. Acair could smell it at twenty paces.

The serving girl seemingly lost control of her juggling and the book went flying into the hands of her master.

"Oh, my lord, don't *steal* that," she pled.

Mages converged on the man as one, flapping their metaphorical wings like a pack of damned vultures. Acair stood there long enough to see the servant look at him, then point rather pointedly at the gates.

Well, he would be damned.

He would have thanked her, but she looked as if she were capable of unleashing a bit of temper on him, so he made her a quick bow and dashed for the gates, keeping as much to the shadows as he could. He wasn't one to let something as insignificant as a city wall keep him from the sweet freedom of bucolic countryside, so he scaled the wall, rendered unconscious a pair of burly lads with mischief on their minds, then dropped to the other side without breaking any bones.

And with that, the night could quite properly be considered a success.

He had a final look at the city behind him, caught sight of the serving wench slipping past gate guards as if she'd been practiced at the same, and considered going back to ask her if she needed aid. He dithered, something he never did, but there it was again. Too much cozying up to his softer side had definitely done a foul work upon his good sense.

He was still trying to latch onto the cold, calculating, nobler part of himself when he found himself facing a wench who certainly was rather cheeky for her station.

"Are you daft or stupid?" she demanded, shoving her hood back off her hair. "I've helped you escape, now go!"

Acair very rarely found himself without a single thing to say, but at the moment all he could do was gape at the woman standing in front of him and wonder how it was that a complete stranger could look so much like Léirsinn of Sàraichte.

"Are you—"

She threw up her hands. "I'm no one! You will be no one as well if you don't flee."

She made a very reasonable argument, one he was perfectly happy to concede. He would have thanked her for her aid, but before he could even begin, she had melted into the shadows. Whether or not she simply vanished into the morning mist or climbed a tree to watch whatever mayhem might ensue, he couldn't have said. What he did know was that she had indeed saved his life and left him with the unhappy burden of needing to do yet another good turn for someone else.

He sighed deeply, then considered the journey that lay in

front of him. He could run for a great while—and had numerous times in the past when skirting the odd clutch of enemies—but his mother's house was on the far side of Ceangail and the country between his current locale and her rather unwelcoming abode was not insignificant. It would take him likely a se'nnight of travel on foot to arrive at her hearth and that was time he didn't have. The only thing he could hope was that Sianach would decide that returning for his beloved master was more important than making a pig of himself in some stack of hay.

He cursed, then strode off into what remained of the night.

Seven

Being in charge of a shapechanging horse wasn't for the faint of heart.

Léirsinn considered the truth of that as she struggled to keep her seat on a dragon that was flying quite a bit faster than the average dr—er, well, what she *thought* the average dragon should be . . . ah . . . flying—

She took a figurative step back from the thought, because it was ridiculous. She would have taken a deep breath, but the wind in her face was just short of a gale, even hiding behind Mansourah of Neroche as she was, so she settled for giving herself a hard mental shake and forcing herself to concentrate on what made sense to her.

She spent less than a trio of heartbeats on that path before she gave up there as well. The truth was, she was traveling quite swiftly to a destination she wasn't sure of, trying to keep her seat

on the back of her, ah, conveyance, and all the while holding on
to a prince of a royal house so he didn't pitch off the side into thin
air. The fact that it was late afternoon and she could see very
well things that should have remained in her nightmares—things
such as the ground farther beneath her than should have been
possible—was not helping matters any.

The only bit of truth that felt as ordinary as it should have
was the realization that she was actually missing Acair of Ceangail and not just for his endless amounts of courage and saucy
remarks.

The world was obviously on the verge of ending.

He had told her he would follow on foot, something she
hadn't been in a position to argue with. The man was hardly a
child and surely knew the dangers of his situation. All she could
do was carry on and try not to think about her future, a future
that would likely include first gaining entrance to his mother's
house, then attempting not to wind up in whatever cauldron the
woman might be endlessly stirring.

The journey felt interminable, but perhaps that had to do less
with the distance than the discomfort her thoughts were causing
her. She wished she could have consigned the whole experience
to that place where her dreams lived, but it was more difficult
than she'd expected. She continued to find herself in places so
far out of her realm of experience, she hardly recognized her life
any longer.

Perhaps she shouldn't have agreed so quickly to flee her uncle's barn so she could save her own sweet neck. She likely
shouldn't have gone with Acair to Beinn òrain where she had
then watched her favorite horse sprout wings. She absolutely
should have refused to go any farther after she had watched an
elven king heal her dying horse in some mysterious way she

didn't want to think about, then listened to that same monarch and his aides make a list of bad deeds committed by one Acair of Ceangail.

She would have been perfectly happy to chalk everything up to weariness, worry, and more adventure than she had ever thought she might be subjected to. That she had lost count of the days she'd spent being a gawking witness to the utter chaos that was Acair's normal way of living likely said all that needed to be said about the condition of her wits.

She shifted on Sianach's back and made certain Mansourah was awake before she allowed herself to continue to let her thoughts wander. Unfortunately, they seemed to continually lead her to the same place: a spot of shadow where shadow shouldn't have been. Once she started thinking about that particular spot, she couldn't not think about how whatever blindness she had experienced when it came to magical things had been completely stripped from her eyes.

She was no longer an observer; she was a full participant in the madness.

She fretted over that thought until she realized the sun was setting behind them. The only thing that accomplished was to leave her absolutely desperate to find somewhere relatively flat to lie down and sleep. She forced herself not to think about the man who was running to catch up with them. The last thing she suspected Acair would want was sympathy. Flattery, perhaps, or a decent glass of wine to enjoy while describing his latest piece of mischief—

"Down there," Mansourah shouted suddenly.

She almost fell off Sianach's back in her surprise. She took a deep breath and looked down to her right, past dragon wings that were only slightly more substantial than a fond wish.

"In the clearing," Mansourah croaked.

She wondered if Mansourah might be delirious or if he knew where they were. She had told Sianach where they were meant to go, Mansourah had made certain the pony—er, dragon—had some idea of where that spot might be located, and she had trusted that Acair had given the naughty thing decent directions in the bargain.

"Have you ever been here?" she asked.

"Never."

She wasn't sure how that was meant to be useful, but she supposed the sooner they were on the ground, the better.

The truth was, something—or some*one*—had caught up to them a pair of hours earlier. It couldn't have been Acair because whoever—or *what*ever—it was obviously possessed enough magic to fly so hard on their heels. That she was simply noting that without shrieking was perhaps the most unsettling realization she'd had in at least a fortnight.

Sianach at least seemed to find that hint of a clearing in the forest to be a suitable place to land. Léirsinn didn't argue with him. Instead, she closed her eyes and hoped that the damned pony wouldn't run them into the ground.

To her surprise, he landed with a surprising amount of care, folded his wings, then dipped his head. Léirsinn didn't bother to comment. She simply sighed, then tumbled off her mount and landed on Mansourah who had wound up sprawled atop a decent amount of snow.

She got to her knees, which seemed to be as far as her shaking limbs would take her. Sianach stretched out his neck and rested his head next to her which gave her the excuse of scratching him behind his scaly ears until she had caught her breath.

Feeling that things were likely as peaceful as they were going to get, she ventured a look around. There was a house to her right; that much she could tell by the light streaming out the open front door. A woman who looked remarkably like a slightly younger incarnation of Cailleach of Cael stood there, apparently waiting for company to arrive.

Léirsinn left Sianach to his own devices, then helped Mansourah up into a sitting position. He cradled his arm against his gut and shivered.

"We've arrived," he said.

Léirsinn didn't dare ask any details, so she kept her hand on his back and wondered if it might leave her looking cowardly if she used him as something to hide behind.

"I understand the witchwoman of Fàs has spells at all her doorways," he murmured, sounding as if he very much wished to avoid encountering any of them. "I suppose if I offer to share secrets of state with her, she won't slay us."

Léirsinn found that her mouth was suddenly quite dry and it had nothing to do with hours of, er, flying. "Do you think so?" she managed.

"I have no idea, actually," he said. "The rumors of her magic are many and terrifying."

"Worse than her son's?"

He glanced at her. "I'm not sure I'm equal to comparing the two, actually, but I would say they are definitely cut from the same cloth."

That's what she was afraid of. "Then how do we proceed?"

"I'll make introductions and we'll hope for the best."

Léirsinn wasn't sure there was anything else to be done, so she nodded and helped Mansourah get to his feet. She hardly flinched at all as their dragon jumped up in the shape of his own surly equine self, but it had been that sort of day so far. She pulled Mansourah's good arm over her shoulders, then walked with him across the front yard toward a woman who was watching them with only mild interest.

Acair's mother had no witchly wand to hand, but perhaps she didn't need sticks to do her business with.

The resemblance to Mistress Cailleach, the fishwife she knew in Sàraichte, was uncanny. To learn that Cailleach was not the ordinary old woman selling her wares Léirsinn had believed her to be but instead a witch had been ridiculous.

That Acair's mother was Cailleach's niece and therefore possessed a full complement of otherworldly skills was absolutely believable.

Mansourah made the woman a low bow and almost went pitching forward onto his face for his trouble. Léirsinn hauled him back upright and steadied him. Mansourah coughed a time or two, then carefully inclined his head.

"Mistress Fionne of Fàs," he said faintly, "if I might introduce myself—"

"No need for that, young prince of Neroche," the woman said. "I know who you are."

"Then my companion—"

"I know who she is as well."

Léirsinn had no idea what one was supposed to do when making the acquaintance of a reputed witch, but she decided a brief curtsey couldn't go wrong. Acair's mother lifted her eyebrows briefly, then looked her over from head to toe.

"Hmmm," was apparently the result of that looking.

"That's your son's horse," Léirsinn said quickly, hoping that might help them curry a bit of favor. "Your son, Acair."

The witchwoman of Fàs made a noise of disgust. "The little

rotter. He never writes, never comes to visit. I'm left to gather tales of his mischief-making from other, less reliable sources."

"That must be a terrible disappointment," Mansourah managed. "I can assure you, Mistress Fionne, that he has done you proud out in the great wide world. He has left a trail of vile deeds and terrible spells from one end of the Nine Kingdoms to the other."

The witchwoman of Fàs considered that for a moment or two, then nodded. "I'm interested in the more notable escapades as always, even given secondhand." She turned toward her house. "Bring in the young prince of Neroche, my wee horse miss. We'll see to his arm by the fire."

Léirsinn didn't bother to ask the woman how she had any idea where she'd passed the greater part of her life, mostly because she didn't want to know. Acair's mother was welcome to her speculations and their uncanny accuracy.

She squeezed Mansourah's arm. "Don't faint."

"I'm very near to it," he said, looking as if that might be the case. "Keep your fingers crossed that she doesn't slay us the moment we cross her threshold."

"At the moment, I'm not sure it wouldn't be a relief," Léirsinn said half under her breath. She smiled briefly at Mansourah. "I don't mean it, of course. I'm happy to clip you under the chin, if you'd rather face the rest of the evening senseless."

"It would be the kindest thing you could do—and I have to assume you didn't learn that from me."

"Life in a barn has its perils."

She didn't care to describe them and he didn't ask her what they were. That might have been because he was trying to stay on his feet. She followed Acair's mother into her house, trying not to look around as desperately as she wanted to, and stopped at the entrance to a modest but comfortably appointed kitchen. There was a round table precisely in the center of the room, with a large hearth to one side of it and cupboards and other things to the right. The witchwoman of Fàs pulled out a chair at the table and nodded.

"Over here, lad, and let's have a look at what ails you. Léirsinn, there's drink on the sideboard. Let's have something very strong."

Léirsinn wasn't sure when Acair's mother had learned her name, but she set that aside as something she likely wouldn't ask about later. She helped Mansourah sit, then went to look through the bottles huddling a healthy distance away from bowls, platters, and a collection of shiny knives.

Ye gads, as Acair would have said, what had she gotten herself into?

"Nay, gel, don't linger at the task," the witchwoman of Fàs said briskly. "Bring me that amber bottle. 'Twas a gift from the current ruler of An-uallach. Not the best-tasting whisky in the world, but very efficient for our current business."

Léirsinn found the correct bottle, fetched a glass, then poured a substantial amount. She set it in front of Mansourah and supposed he would drink it when he thought best.

"You should sit as well, dearie," the witchwoman of Fàs said absently. "Don't want you falling into the fire."

Léirsinn sat, because it seemed like a very sensible thing to do. She didn't argue when Mansourah pushed his glass toward her. She had a healthy sip, then wished she hadn't. The whisky burned all the way down her throat to then set up a robust bonfire in her gut. She had to admit, though, that she felt slightly less anxious than she had but a moment before, so perhaps that was all she could ask for. She handed the glass back to Mansourah with a shrug. He closed his eyes briefly, drank, then gasped for a bit until he could apparently breathe again.

"You're handsome," the witchwoman of Fàs observed, "but a bit of a gel when it comes to strong drink."

"Have you tasted that bilge?" Mansourah wheezed.

"I take only discreet, ladylike sips," she said archly. "I've appearances to keep up. Now, let's see what you've done to yourself, ye wee babe."

Léirsinn wasn't weak-stomached, but the sight of Mansourah's forearm bent at a spot where it shouldn't have been was unsettling, to say the least. The witchwoman of Fàs clucked her tongue at him.

"The follies of youth, obviously."

"Of course, Mistress Fionne," Mansourah managed. "If I might call you that."

"You might call me several things, my wee princeling," Acair's mother said, "and that would be the least of them." She considered, then looked at Léirsinn. "No magic, eh?"

Léirsinn shook her head. "Not a drop."

"Life is simpler without it, but a far sight less exciting." She looked at Mansourah. "Acair couldn't see his way clear to do anything about this?"

"He is enjoined from using any magic for the time being," Mansourah said, wincing as he shifted. "I'm certain he'll tell you all about it when he arrives, though that may take some time. He's walking here from Eòlas."

"Do him good," the witchwoman of Fàs said without hesitation. "Let's have a closer peek at your arm, young Mansourah."

Léirsinn exchanged an alarmed look with Mansourah, but she had absolutely no idea how to stop what they'd set in motion.

His sleeve was carefully cut away and tossed into the kitchen fire. Acair's mother shook her head, tutted, and uttered the occasional salty curse. It was nothing Léirsinn hadn't heard before from Mistress Cailleach, so she didn't think anything of it.

She was genuinely appalled, however, to watch Acair's mother drop words like feathers onto Mansourah's arm and see how they sank into his flesh. She could have sworn she heard his bones snick back together—

Mansourah poured himself another generous glass of whisky, then tossed it back with abandon. He gasped, his eyes watered madly, then he looked at Acair's mother.

"My most sincere gratitude, my lady," he rasped.

The witchwoman of Fàs put her hand to her throat and colored a bit. "Don't you have pretty manners, child. My lady, indeed."

He set his glass down with an unsteady hand. "I must repay your kindness," he said. "I am your servant."

Léirsinn watched Acair's mother consider him calculatingly for a moment or two and wondered how high that price might be.

"I have nieces," the witchwoman of Fàs said slowly. "They would appreciate a delicious piece of goodness such as yourself. That, and I owe their mother a great whacking favor."

"Ah," Mansourah began, looking absolutely panicked.

"Come along, Léirsinn," Acair's mother said without hesitation. "We'll leave our young prince here to contemplate future delights whilst we give your pony instructions on where to go look for that blasted Acair. He'll come limping in at an unseemly hour and cause a great ruckus if we don't find him first."

Léirsinn looked at Mansourah, shrugged, then followed Acair's mother through her house and back out the front door. Words were beyond her. That magic back in the kitchen . . . all she could do was shake her head. It had been as real and tangible as any piece of tack she'd ever put her hand to.

She decided abruptly that she had had enough magic for the day. She knew what she'd seen but she didn't want to believe it, never mind all that rubbish about essence changing and shapechanging when all she wanted to do was change the topic of conversation—

Unfortunately, she was starting to see why the stuff might come in handy, which was probably the most appalling thought she'd had in a solid fortnight of absolutely shattering thoughts.

She came to a teetering halt next to that worker of dangerous magic and gaped at Acair's dragon, who was currently in mid-chew of something with feathers. He looked at Acair's mother, then tossed whatever he'd been eating up in the air, caught it again, then swallowed it in one bite.

Léirsinn thought it might be time to have a little lie-down.

The witchwoman of Fàs only laughed. "A fitting match for my youngest. How do they get on?"

"Sianach tries to bite him every chance he has," Léirsinn said weakly.

"Perfect," the witchwoman of Fàs said. She walked over to the dragon and looked at him sternly. "You may not want to do this, but he's your master, ye wee fiend. You'd best go find him, hadn't you?"

Sianach snorted out a very discreet, almost chagrined bit of smoke from his nostrils. He heaved himself up, waddled backward a step or two, then leapt up into the sky.

"Wind is faster," the witchwoman of Fàs shouted at him.

He threw back his head, roared, then disappeared. Léirsinn wasn't sure she wanted to know what he had become, mostly because she'd already been on his back when he'd chosen a different shape than horse, Pegasus, or dragon.

Chosen a different shape. She laughed at the thought, truly she did. If she laughed silently and it sounded thoroughly unhinged in her head, who was to know?

Acair's mother returned, shaking her head. She stopped and looked at Léirsinn.

"I'll see you settled, gel, then you can decide to wait up or not. Acair'll manage to get here or he won't. Worrying won't change that."

Léirsinn scrambled for something to say. "I wasn't worried."

The witchwoman of Fàs grunted at her, then nodded toward the door. "You should be," she said bluntly. "That boy takes terrible chances, but he's old enough to make his own choices. Children leave the nest and all you can do is bar the door so they don't come back in and eat through your larder. I'll do him the favor of reworking the spell here so it doesn't fall on him and slay him instantly, should he manage to outrun whoever is chasing him at the moment. 'Tis the least—and the most, I'll admit—that I can do for him."

Léirsinn shut her mouth when she realized it was hanging open. She was beginning to see why Acair had such a tolerance for shocking things.

She put her head down and followed the woman inside, hoping she wouldn't see anything more than she already had. That had been more than enough for the night.

It was a pair of hours before dawn when she heard the front door open. It wasn't that she'd been listening for that, of course. She'd had plenty of her own concerns to see to.

She'd watched Mansourah be placed in the best guest bed-chamber with the same sort of care a baker might use while popping a delicate batch of cakes into an oven. She'd been quite happy to be offered a spot on the divan in front of a roaring fire in the Lesser Parlor, then spent the better part of the night pacing. If she'd fallen asleep for an hour or two, sitting on that divan with her cheek propped up on her fist as she leaned against the rolled arm of the sofa, who could blame her?

That she knew without thinking how to make a quick dash for the front door said nothing but that she was thoroughly committed to being able to find the nearest exit, should such a necessity arise. If she made a complete ass of herself by throwing her arms around Acair of Ceangail's neck and shaking right along with him for far longer than was perhaps circumspect, well, who was to know?

She pulled away from him, took his cloak and hung it on a hook by the door, then put her arm around his waist.

"You're soaked," she said. "Your mother has whisky, though I suppose you already know that."

He only nodded, looking thoroughly exhausted. She realized he wasn't going to be giving her the details of his journey anytime soon, so she pulled him with her into the kitchen. She thought he could most likely find his own chair, so she concentrated on bringing the fire back to life. That seen to, she poured him a hefty mugful of what had been so helpful to Mansourah, then set it down in front of him. He eyed the glass, then looked at her.

"Poisoned?"

"Mansourah drank copious amounts and is still breathing," she said, pulling out a chair for herself, "or so I assume. I tried it and I'm still alive, if that eases you any."

He took a deep breath, then threw back the entire glass without pause. He shook his head sharply, then rubbed his hands over his face. He looked at her and smiled faintly.

"Thank you," he said. "Forgive my lack of manners before."

"Long journey?"

"Shattering," he said. He tried to speak a time or two, then he rose and went to stand with his back to the fire. "He's evil."

"Your pony?" she asked. "I'd say he's just trying to impress you."

"He succeeded brilliantly," Acair said with feeling. He clasped his hands behind his back and looked at her. "I'm assuming that since we're both inside and not lying dead outside in a ditch that my mother extended her hospitality."

"She did," she agreed. "We might want to thank Mansourah for it. I believe your mother is inviting a pair of your cousins to come for a visit with him as the prize."

He pursed his lips. "I would have sympathy for him, but I'm fresh out of the same. I assume she locked him in a bedchamber so he won't flee during the night."

"He's enjoying the best guest chamber, or so I understand. We're enjoying the Lesser Parlor."

He opened his mouth, then shut it. "I was fully prepared to make a lecherous remark, but I'm too damned tired to try. You might have to carry me there, though."

"No food first?"

"I'd likely fall asleep in my porridge and smother myself. I will, however, tend the fire—"

"Nay," she said, rising and taking the fire iron away from him. "Go lean somewhere and I'll see to this. I don't have any means of restoring your face if you fall into the hearth."

"And what a terrible loss that would be," he said with a mighty yawn.

She had to agree, but she wasn't about to agree out loud. She banked the fire, then walked with him to the door.

"First one to the parlor takes the sofa," he said.

She wasn't entirely certain he wasn't serious about that, but he was beginning to slur his words so perhaps he was simply babbling with weariness. She did enter the parlor first, though, which left her less than a handful of minutes later stretched out on that perfectly comfortable divan, covered in a decently warm blanket. Acair took off his boots, then rolled himself up in a blanket a pace or two away. Silence descended save for the occasional snap and pop of the wood in the hearth.

She could have sworn she heard a hint of song in those flames.

She watched the fire for a bit, trying to decide if she were losing her wits or not, then gave up and looked over the edge of the cushion at her companion. Acair was watching the ceiling, no doubt looking for answers to mysteries she imagined she didn't want to know about. He had seen things, that lad there, things she absolutely knew she wouldn't want to encounter. It showed in his eyes in what were apparently very rare moments when he let his guard down. For all anyone else knew, for all he admitted to, he was simply a terrible worker of magic on an endless quest to do foul deeds.

She wondered how true that was.

She cleared her throat. "Was that your bedchamber Mansourah took?"

He looked at her then, then shook his head. "I slept in here in front of the fire, actually."

"To keep warm?"

"To keep a fire iron always hot and at the ready for the regular occurrence of one of my siblings attempting to do me in during the middle of the night."

She leaned up on her elbow and looked at him in surprise. "You can't be serious."

He smiled faintly. "Is it any wonder I turned out so well?"

"It is a miracle," she said honestly. "How many brothers did you say you have?"

"Six that belong to my mother. An indeterminate number who don't, plus those impossible elven troublemakers Sarait of Tòrr Dòrainn foisted off onto the world. My brothers didn't live here for very long, thankfully. Once they were old enough to toddle on off to the keep up the way, they did. I alone remained until I left to make my way in the world. I was, and likely still am, my mother's last, best hope for someone truly vile."

She smiled. "You must be such a disappointment to her then."

He looked at her seriously. "I believe I am."

She felt her smile fade. "Do you think so?"

"Tonight, I have no idea." He sighed deeply. "Her spells didn't slay me at the front door, which is unusual, but that may have been because she didn't want to frighten either you or that finicky prince of Neroche by having you see the mess."

"Do you never come visit her?"

"More often than the rest of the rabble," he said with a shrug, "but not as much as I likely should. So much mischief to make in the world, you know, and so little time. I have a very full calendar."

"I imagine you do," she said. She watched the fire for a bit longer, then found even that was too much trouble. "I should have tended your horse—"

"He's off hunting," Acair said with a yawn. "I've no doubt he'll find somewhere warm to curl up after he's filled his belly. He'll regale you with all his adventures in the morning, I'm sure."

She didn't doubt it. She rested her chin on her hands, then realized she looked as foolish as any young girl gaping at her first sight of a handsome nobleman.

"You'll have to sleep eventually," Acair said, opening his eyes and looking at her. "Difficult when you have me to look at, I know, but perhaps possible with enough effort."

"How is it possible you can look so tired but still be able to talk so much?"

He smiled. She closed her eyes in a last-ditch effort to save herself, but perhaps it was too late. She opened her eyes in surprise as she felt him take her hand and pull it toward him.

He kissed her palm, then put her hand on his chest and covered it with both his own.

"You were worried," he murmured.

"I wasn't," she countered. "Not for a moment."

"You're a terribly bad liar," he said, looking at her. He smiled wearily. "Do you truly think I would abandon you to the clutches of that prissy archer from Neroche?"

"I thought someone might catch you and kill you, rather," she said frankly.

"Me?" he scoffed. "Never. I always emerge alive and unscathed." He paused. "Relatively unscathed, if I'm to be entirely honest. But always alive." He reached up and brushed her hair back from her face. "Always."

She wasn't sure how he could possibly guarantee that when he had nothing but a quick smile and an impressive collection of curses to hand.

She was beginning to agree with his mother that magic was a very useful thing to have.

She would have asked Acair for his opinion on the matter, but he was asleep. She knew she would wake with her hand numb and her arm likely feeling as if it had been pulled from its socket, but she wasn't about to take her hand away.

She was tired, that was all. She was tired, she thought the fire might keep her awake all night with its song, and she wasn't entirely sure she wasn't dreaming the whole of her life. If she weren't dreaming, she wasn't sure she wanted to think about what her life looked like when she was awake—

She turned away from the thought because it was maudlin and ridiculous and because she had things to do, secrets to uncover, and one terribly beautiful but impossibly reckless man to keep safe so he could save the world and rescue her grandfather.

All without magic.

She rolled her eyes and promised herself a full morning of work in whatever stables Acair's mother might possess. It might be her only hope of regaining her good sense.

She closed her eyes and fell asleep to the song of the fire weaving its way into her dreams.

Eight

A cair woke to a kink in his neck and pain in his face. The latter he assumed came from the fact that he was sitting on the floor of his mother's library with his face pressed against books placed on shelves he'd built for her during his youth. He wasn't sure when he'd fallen asleep, but he had the feeling it had been somewhere between an extremely tedious treatise entitled *Meithian Archers of Note* and a collection of rather bawdy tales about women of a certain profession from Gairn. That the books were written by the same author had obviously been enough to send him to seek refuge in sweet slumber.

In his defense, he had arisen at an appalling hour and that after a journey that had been beyond unpleasant. Running for leagues had been nothing out of the ordinary. Having his horse find him, refrain from biting him long enough for him to heave himself up onto its back, then subsequently turn itself into a bitter, screaming wind that had left him on the verge of screaming himself had been another thing entirely.

Truly, things had to change in his life very soon.

That was precisely why he found himself where he was, trying to make a thorough search of books he had apparently preferred to use as a resting place for his visage. He was likely fortunate the lamp he'd lit earlier hadn't burned the entire place to the ground. He supposed he'd been asleep long enough to render a lamp useless, which would no doubt save his eyes a decent amount of strain, but he didn't imagine it would do anything to relieve the pains in his head. At least he'd managed to sleep in peace and security.

His choice of safe havens was, as he tended to tell anyone who would listen, rather limited. The odd armoire of one or two more notable wizardesses, a discreet guest chamber belonging to a rather feisty and morally questionable queen, and the wine cellar of a rather nearsighted king were the only places he could count on without fail. He had known his mother wouldn't be any happier to see him than anyone else—something that he supposed would have hurt his feelings if he'd had any feelings to hurt—but he certainly would have engaged in a hefty bout of groveling—or shoveling, which would likely be the case and brought him back full circle to those rather unpleasant days spent in Léirsinn's barn doing just that—to buy them all some peace. He suspected he might be engaging in that activity fairly soon, so there was no reason not to get it out of the way as soon as possible.

He sighed deeply, opened his eyes, then squeaked in spite of himself.

His mother, a woman who inspired that sort of squeaking in

most people she encountered, was sitting on a comfortable chair
not a handful of paces away from him, watching him thoughtfully.

He looked up above his head on the off chance a spell was
waiting there to fall upon him, checked both sides of the field, as
it were, then straightened carefully.

"Mother," he said politely. "Good morning."

"What do you want?" she asked without preamble.

He shifted in a vain attempt to ease the unpleasant stiffness
in his back, then heaved himself up and onto a stool that was
mostly used to reach the upper shelves. He wondered if honesty
or subterfuge would serve him better, then decided there was no
point in not continuing on with his greatest of failings.

"I'm here for a list of evil mages."

"List," she said with a snort. "A list of several books full of
that sort of thing, you mean."

"Well," he said, "aye, though I would settle for that volume of
mine that contains all father's enemies of note, as well as all the
lads I've bothered to consider."

She harrumphed, then reached over and pulled out a slim
leather book just to the right of the one he'd stopped at. He looked
at her.

"Mother," he chided. "You put that there whilst I was
napping."

"You deserve it," she said shortly. "You never write, never
come to visit—"

"I'm visiting now," he pointed out. "And I chopped wood for
you last year."

"*Rùnach* chopped wood for me last year," she said, "whilst I
was about the heavy labor of making certain his dreamspinning
lady didn't unravel me entire house."

"Well, I must agree that Aisling of Bruadair is terrifying," he said, suppressing the urge to shiver. He'd had more to do with Bruadairians over the past pair of years than he had ever wanted to. If he never saw another one, it would be too soon.

"Rùnach is up there on the same shelf with her, love."

"Which is the only reason I didn't slay him the last time I saw him. Not," he added quickly, "because I feared his puny powers, but because I didn't want to grieve his bride and upset the balance of the world."

"Good of you."

"I thought so."

She handed him the book. "I don't know what you think you'll find, but there it is."

He opened it just to make certain his dam hadn't decided to liberate the proper pages and replace them with detailed notes about the grooming habits—or lack thereof—of his brothers. Finding everything as it should have been, he closed the book and smiled at his mother.

"Delightful," he said. "Just what I needed."

She looked at him narrowly. "You could have made that list from memory, my lad. What are you looking for truly?"

He would have invented some lofty-sounding errand to throw her off the scent, but it was his mother and he'd inherited from her the whole of his ability to obtain details from even the most reluctant of victims. Distracting her from ferreting out the truth would be difficult, if not impossible.

He sighed deeply. Where to start? He was there for answers to several vexing questions, beginning with who was creating those pools of shadow he seemed to be finding in untoward places and ending with who had created the spell that continued to prevent him from delighting and astonishing everyone around him with his mighty magic.

It also might have been useful to know who was chasing him, particularly since he had the feeling it wasn't just the usual collection of workers of substandard magic he tended to offend.

If he happened to help himself to a few spells he'd jotted down and left folded up beneath tins of healthful herbs he was positive his mother would never disturb, so much the better. It could count as a bit of housework, which might earn him a kind word or two.

"I don't know, Mother," he admitted. "I am besieged by a handful of vexing mysteries. More shocking still, I find myself without a decent idea of where to turn."

"Take the path leading to that red-haired wench," she said wisely.

"Do you think so?"

She blinked. "Are you asking my advice?"

"Ye gads, nay." He paused, then considered. "I wouldn't completely discount it if you cared to give it."

She felt about in her hair for what he could only hope wasn't a dagger or a witchly wand of some sort. She pulled a pencil free, licked the tip of it, then drew forth a notebook from the pocket of her apron, all the while watching him as if she expected him to suddenly leap up and rush off.

"What are you doing?" he asked carefully.

"Making a note of this historic moment. I'll find out later whether or not the world cracked in two during the same."

He pursed his lips. "I am not above the occasional bit of humility."

She blinked, jotted down something, then looked at him

again. "I would guffaw—indeed, I imagine I will after you go—but I'm too stunned at the moment to indulge."

"Indulge away," he said wearily. "It won't be the worst thing I've endured so far this year."

"I understand you've been on an apology tour."

"From whom do you understand that?" he asked politely.

She shrugged lightly. "Can't say I'm able to bring to mind the exact teller of that tale. Word gets 'round, you know."

He imagined it did and whilst he wasn't sure he wanted to know who was spreading that word around, he thought he might be able to latch on to a name or two just the same if pressed.

"I'm assuming you'll give me the details," she continued, "considering I've given you refuge."

"Happily," he said. He couldn't say he cared for gossip—well, if he were to be completely honest, he didn't care for silly, useless gossip, but tales of riches and rumors of things that might be useful in the odd spot of blackmail, aye, he wasn't above bending an ear for that sort of thing. His mother cast a wider net for items of note, but her days of making as much mischief as he indulged in were perhaps discreetly behind her.

Perhaps. With Fionne of Fàs, one never knew.

"It is true," he conceded, "that I've spent the last several months spreading sunshine and happiness from one end of the Nine Kingdoms to the other. I imagine I can find things you'll want to make a note of, but you might want to wait until I'm better rested lest I forget important details."

"Hmmm," she said studying him. "I would certainly prefer that you be at your best for the grilling, so we'll leave it for the moment. As for the other question that you tried to so neatly sidestep, why are you here? Past the obvious need to show me that feisty little miss of yours, of course."

He suppressed a snort. If Léirsinn still wanted to speak to him after having encountered his mother, he would be fortunate indeed. The other thing, though, he wasn't above addressing.

"I don't know what you've heard," he said slowly, "and want even less to find out who's been yammering on about my activities, but the truth is, I am looking for a particular mage. I might need a rather lengthy look through your books to find him."

She waved her pencil at him. "You're starting in the middle, which you know annoys me. Begin at the beginning and concentrate on your troubles, something I'll thoroughly enjoy. I'll keep an ear cocked for details you might inadvertently reveal. Before you get yourself launched, however, I will tell you that I heard that that delicious prince from Cothromaiche had you for supper a month or two ago."

"He *invited* me for supper," Acair corrected. "He and that meddling half-brother of mine, Rùnach, lured me to a pub where they were very unkind to me, never mind scarce having the manners to pay for my ale."

"Rùnach chopped wood for me—I believe I mentioned that before—so I'm not inclined to disparage him. Besides, I understand he saved your life in Beul."

"Unfortunately," Acair said, rubbing his chest to ease the sudden tingling there. It was as if the damn spell Rùnach had healed him with had heard itself being noticed and was clamoring for more praise. "I took a blade meant for Rùnach's bride and he restored me with some elvish rubbish instead of mercifully letting me die. I'm still troubled by the aftereffects of it."

"Fadaire?"

He nodded grimly.

She licked her pencil again and waved him on. "Continue."

He supposed if anyone would understand the terrible affliction of his straits, it would be his mother, so he obliged her.

"As you've obviously heard," he said, settling in for a decent
recounting of his continuing nightmare, "I've spent the past
many months—I try to forget the exact count in deference to my
mental state—going about apologizing to various offended
crown-wearers in order to make reparations for a modest piece
of business, the particulars of which slip my mind at the moment."

She only pursed her lips and continued to scribble in her
book.

"I had thought my days of prostrating myself before kings,
ministers, and their puffed-up ilk were over, but, as you heard, I
found myself summoned to supper with both Rùnach and
Soilléir."

"I would have given much to have been eavesdropping on
that conversation."

"No need, for I'll give you the details freely. There was very
little chitchat and no inquiries about my health. I had scarce
begun to imbibe a rather undemanding pint of ale when I was
put off my drink by their telling me that my days of acting
against my nobler nature were not yet over and that there was
more for me to do to bring peace and justice to the world."

"Beginning in Sàraichte," she said slowly, looking up from
her notes. "Or did I mishear that rumor?"

"Nay, you have that aright."

"Auntie Cailleach told me she'd seen you in the market, trail-
ing after that lass of yours like a lovesick pup."

He didn't want to know where that conversation had taken
place or what else had been said. "'Tis true, that."

"Where did you meet your horse miss?"

"That is an interesting wrinkle in this otherwise very dull

piece of cloth," he said, watching her to see if she might want to make a note of how poetically he was stating things. She snorted, which he supposed was the best he was going to get, so he moved on. "I had encountered Léirsinn because as part of my continuing punishment for, again, I haven't a clue what, I was informed I would be spending a year in a barn, shoveling horse droppings and waiting for someone to steal my best pair of boots. That, by the way, happened before a single day had passed."

His mother glanced at his feet, then lifted her eyebrows briefly. "Poor you," she said unsympathetically. "So, you were in a barn, you met that red-haired beauty, then what?"

He made himself as comfortable as possible on his perch. "I've gotten ahead of myself, actually," he said. "To rid myself of those two profoundly irritating busybodies—you know which ones—I agreed to a year without magic to avoid having to forgo giving the stuff up for a century."

His mother gasped. "A century?"

"Appalling, isn't it?" he asked. "'Tis no doubt why Soilléir opened the negotiations with such a span of years. I bargained it down to the aforementioned and equally preposterous year, but you can imagine my thoughts about that. After I left that whoreson and Rùnach trying to come up with funds to pay for their drinks and mine at that truly dire little pub in the middle of nowhere, I trotted off into the gloom, fully intending to duck off the road and scamper away to lie low until they'd forgotten about me."

"Then to resume your usual business of making glorious mischief?"

"Exactly," he said, feeling a rush of affection for that terrifying woman there. "Unfortunately, I hadn't gone but half a league before I realized I was being followed by something vexatious."

His mother glanced at the spell that was currently curled up in the corner, feigning sleep. It was starting to alarm him a bit more than usual, that thing there. He'd always felt it possessed some sort of shape, but the longer it followed him, the more it began to resemble a shadow of a youth. There were times he suspected it was making rude gestures at him from behind his back, but he knew he shouldn't have been surprised. Whoever had created it had had a very rudimentary and juvenile sense of jest.

"What does it do?" she asked.

"I understand that its sole purpose is to do damage to my innocent self should I dare breathe out so much as a word of a spell."

"Shocking," she said, looking genuinely startled. "And if you, as they say, slip up?"

"That spell will slay me," he said.

"Why the hell did you agree to such a stupid thing?" she asked in astonishment.

"I didn't agree to it," Acair said shortly. "I *only* agreed to the bargain of no magic and that only because *your* beloved Soilléir threatened to turn me into a birdbath if I didn't."

She pursed her lips. He wasn't altogether sure she wasn't trying to keep from laughing, but there it was. His situation was ridiculous.

"Well, he definitely could," she allowed.

He looked at her suddenly, wondering why he'd never thought to ask her the question that had clouted him so suddenly on the side of his head. "Could you turn *him* into a birdbath?"

She clutched a pearl necklace she wore, something that he wasn't entirely sure wasn't made from calcified souls of those she'd frightened the very hell from, and manufactured what he imagined she supposed was a look of horror.

"Why would you ask?" she hedged.

"Because your dear aunt Cailleach said I possessed power that left Gair's looking like rubbish," he said. "Or words to that effect."

"She exaggerates."

He suspected his great-aunt didn't do anything of the sort, but it was obviously going to take more effort than simply asking to have an answer from his dam.

"I'm not going to let that go," he muttered.

She looked slightly pleased, if such a thing was possible for her, then tapped her pencil against her chin. "I have to ask— because I'm a bit pressed for anything interesting to do at the moment—why you find yourself somewhere besides Fuadain of Sàraichte's barn, if that's where you were meant to serve out your sentence."

He wasn't sure if she didn't know or if she were simply trying to dig a few details out of him, but he supposed in the end it didn't matter. Answers were the price for being allowed to hide under her very utilitarian but terrifying spells of protection, spells he would certainly be having a closer look at whilst she was napping.

"The tale is long," he warned.

"I have all day."

He started to thank her for having cleared the decks for him, as it were, when he was interrupted by trills of laughter coming from the front parlor. He was absolutely certain that wasn't Léirsinn making that noise, though not altogether certain Mansourah of Neroche wouldn't make that sort of noise if pressed, but he paused just the same and looked at his mother.

"Who is that?"

She smiled blandly. "I invited a pair of your cousins to come to take in the view. You'll hit upon which ones without having to peek around the corner, I imagine."

"Ah," he said, wishing he weren't so damned tired. "I remember Léirsinn having said something about that."

"I wasn't going to keep that handsome young prince all to myself."

"Generous of you."

"One of my greatest faults," she said seriously. "Besides, I owe Fiunne a favor. Actually, I might want a favor from those two rapacious gels at some point, so no sense in not doling out those sorts of chits whilst I'm able, don't you agree?"

"Heartily," he said, not having to look far for where he'd obviously come by many of his best strategies.

"Now, continue on with your tale," she said. "You were in Sàraichte, then what?"

He supposed there was no reason not to tell her about the entire sorry business. "This is where things become a bit dodgy," he admitted. "I hadn't been in the south but a day or two when I noticed that Léirsinn was seeing what I can only call spots of shadow. I thought perhaps they were patches of spells laid by the local wizard to lighten purses without the effort of leaving his fire, but I began to watch what happened to those who stepped in them and concluded that I was judging poorly."

His mother frowned thoughtfully at him. "What happened when you stepped inside one?"

He spared the briefest of moments to be gratified that his mother would have expected nothing less of him, then permitted himself a shudder at the memory.

"I felt as if a part of my soul had been torn from me," he said.

"I managed to wrench myself free, but it was absolutely excruci-ating." He shook his head. "I wouldn't repeat the experience for anything, though I think it's been different for others. I've heard there are those who seem to crave a tussle with the damned things."

She studied him. "I don't suppose you'll tell me who told you that."

"I vowed I wouldn't."

"And *I* vow I don't recognize you. You'd best get through this year quickly lest you lose yourself entirely." She tapped her pen-cil against her notebook thoughtfully. "So, lest you sully your vaunted code by a bit of dishing with your mum, let me state it for you: you're here to try to find out who might have created both the spots and that thing in the corner."

"That was my plan," he agreed.

"You also needed a place to hide for a bit."

"I'm not above accepting aid," he conceded.

She studied him for a lengthy moment. "I have wood that needs chopping."

"Done."

"And a roof that needs to be patched."

He took a deep breath. "I'll put a whip to Mansourah."

"That delightful prince of Neroche will be too busy for that sort of rough labor, so I'll find a hammer for you." She stuck her pencil back in her hair, slipped her notebook into her pocket, and pushed herself to her feet. "I'll give your tangle a bit of thought." She hesitated, then looked at him seriously. "I wouldn't step in any more of those spots, were I you."

"Excellent advice."

She continued to chew on her words before she finally shook her head as she headed for the door. "I'd keep my companions out of them as well, but that's just me. Giving, always giving, am I."

"Indeed, you are," he agreed.

He watched her go, then considered that last piece of advice. He hadn't asked the particulars, but he wondered what Léirsinn had experienced when she'd backed into one of the damned things in Miach of Neroche's kitchen garden. Well, he knew what he'd heard, which was the sound of her screams, as terror-filled as if she'd peered into the pit of hell itself. She hadn't volunteered details and he'd honestly been too weak-kneed to ask her.

That had to stop, truly. He was a damned fine black mage, ruthless in his schemes, and absolutely relentless in pursuing the delights provided by stirring up trouble. Too much more time spent looking out for others and he would completely lose himself in that vat of stickiness labeled *Do-Gooding*.

He opened the book his mother had handed him and had another, more leisurely look at it. He imagined she'd kept it under her pillow simply because she'd known he would come looking for it—it was something he would have done, which meant he'd likely learned it from her—but now that he had it in his hands, he honestly wasn't sure he wanted to see what it contained.

Then again, as he'd had to recently remind himself, he wasn't a coward. He was hungry, however, and he'd apparently spent most of the morning unconscious on his mother's library floor, so it was obviously past time he went to see if Léirsinn was safe and whole. Surely, though, he would be forgiven a quick visit to his mother's stewpot first.

He tucked his book under his arm and made his way back toward the Greater Parlor, a room that was hardly ever used for anyone less than those of royal blood. It was tempting to trot right on past so as not to be privy to the carnage, but unfortunately his curiosity was simply too strong to be resisted. He peered around the corner and assessed the situation.

Mansourah of Neroche was currently sitting on the fancy divan that his mother reserved for the use of those she truly wanted to impress. He was flanked by none other than Acair's own cousins, Mòday and Mùirne of Cael. Acair didn't like to speak ill of women, but those two there were trouble. They singly had a cache of spells that should have given that prissy prince pause, but together? Acair would have hesitated to meet them both in a deserted ballroom.

Mansourah shot him a look of pure pleading. Acair was momentarily moved by it, but alas, he had things on his plate that demanded his attention. He shrugged helplessly, held up his hands in a further gesture of helplessness lest the first have been lost on that dolt there trembling into his teacup, then made a hasty exit stage left before either tears or spells erupted.

He paused in the middle of his mother's main passageway, though perhaps terming it that was giving it a grander title than it deserved. The house was modest, cluttered, and simply saturated with spells. Then again, it was his mother and she tended to get a bit distracted whilst about her work of keeping a detailed and completely disinterested history of the world. He couldn't say he blamed her for setting spells of ward to keep herself safe. The spells of death she collected like others might collect figurines were, he knew, just for the amusement of watching powerful mages squawk and beg for mercy when they ran afoul of them.

He was beginning to suspect he had inherited quite a bit of her less savoury side.

He nipped into the kitchen for a quick bite and a drink of something he hoped wouldn't kill him. He then managed to elude what was at her front door only because he tossed a coat out first to test the waters, as it were. His mother's spell fell upon it, giving him the chance to duck out to the side. His own spellish companion exited with him, then paused to face off with his mother's spell. Surprising, that, but nothing he wanted to investigate further. He left them to it and darted around the side of the house.

He noted the enormous nature of the woodpile there in the distance, then promptly ignored it in favor of carrying on toward his mother's modest set of stalls. That she didn't own horses had never deterred her from always being prepared for them. He suspected Léirsinn was likely there, conspiring with his pony. He paused and considered the possibility that perhaps she was teaching the beast a few manners, something that definitely needed to be seen to. Perhaps leaving them to it for a bit wouldn't be unthinkable.

He leaned against a part of his mother's house that didn't look as if it had been plastered with faery sugar, then decided the shadows of her house were too much like the shadows he was trying to avoid. He found a spot in a goodly bit of sunshine, leaned against a fence post, then took his book and considered things he hadn't before it.

If he opened it and saw the name of someone he didn't want to encounter—

He rolled his eyes at himself. He had already set foot to a path that was going to lead him places he absolutely didn't want to go. He'd known that the moment he'd been tossed in Ehrne of Ainneamh's dungeon—nay, it had been sooner than that. It had been at some point during the shoveling out of Léirsinn's favorite horse's stall when the damned nag had tried to bite him. He'd known he was in trouble. The rest had simply been what followed along after trouble was first encountered.

He opened the book and started with the first name written there.

He thought it might turn out to be a very long day.

Nine

Léirsinn leaned against a stall door in a surprisingly luxurious little barn and watched Acair's horse work his way through his breakfast. She wasn't sure she had ever seen a horse eat grain that quickly, but the ponies she was accustomed to didn't . . . well, the truth was, she wasn't accustomed to the dietary habits of horses who could change their shapes, so what did she know? Sianach might actually be on the reserved side and she was judging him too harshly. At present, he was snorting opinions at her instead of fire, so perhaps that was the best she could hope for.

She shivered and wondered if she might be better served to ask him to spew out a flame or two. She was chilled to the bone, but if she were to be honest there as well, it had absolutely nothing to do with the bitterness of the winter morning surrounding her.

It had everything to do with the book she held in her hands.

She hadn't come to the barn to read, she'd come to take her mind off things she hadn't wanted to think about. Difficult, perhaps, to forget about magic and its makers when she found herself firmly ensconced in the home of a witch, but not impossible. A little shoveling of manure and soaking of grain had seemed like the best idea she'd had in days.

Instead, she'd found a book on a stool in the barn, sitting negligently next to tools of her trade. She'd picked it up, of course, because she was absolutely daft. There was no other excuse for it save blaming her damnable curiosity on too much time spent in the company of Acair of Ceangail, who was likely going to meet his end immediately after he poked his nose once too often where it wasn't meant to go.

Once she'd taken the small volume in hand, there hadn't been any reason to argue with it when it opened to a particular page she hadn't asked for but couldn't help but read.

Gair of Ceangail lived a thousand years before he wed Sarait of Tòrr Dòrainn, youngest of the five daughters of—

She'd shut the book and dropped it back on the stool. It had remained there as she'd tended Acair's horse, but those words had echoed in her mind like a song with a tune she didn't particularly care for but couldn't forget just the same.

She had wanted to know about Gair, hadn't she?

At the moment, she couldn't remember why, though she could name at least half a dozen reasons why she didn't. Unfortunately, all those reasons vanished like a bit of mist after sunrise and she found herself picking the book back up and opening it.

The spell of Diminishing, which could take from a mage every last drop
of his power and leave him a mere husk—

She wanted to shut the book, truly she did, but she couldn't
bring herself to. As the innkeeper in Eòlas had said, Gair had
been a terribly elegant man but ruthless in his pursuit of power,
spells, and elven princesses. He had apparently come to a bad
end trying to steal vast amounts of power from some well—

"He's still alive, you know."

Léirsinn almost fell over the stall door into what she was
absolutely certain was not a pile of clean straw. She picked up
the book she'd dropped, then looked at Acair's mother, who definitely hadn't been standing next to her a heartbeat before.

"You startled me," she managed.

"I startle everyone," Fionne of Fàs said with a shrug. "It's my
stock in trade." She nodded at the book. "You're reading about
Gair."

"How did you know?"

"Your expression is an equal mix of horror and fascination.
It's how everyone looks when they read about him."

"I found this book on that stool over there," Léirsinn said.
"Sitting all on its own."

The witchwoman of Fàs smiled. "Of course you did, lovey,
because I put it there for you. I thought you might be interested
in the sources from whence your would-be lover springs. Me, you
have to interview all you like. Gair is more difficult to reach."

"Would-be lover," Léirsinn repeated faintly. "Ah, we aren't—"

"Why the hell not? He's handsome enough, isn't he?"

Léirsinn wished the woman wasn't standing in the way of her
collapsing on that extremely sturdy stool. She tried leaning

against the stall door, but Sianach kept bumping her elbow with his nose. Acair's mother looked her over, then turned and walked over to another stool placed near enough the first that easy conversation could be had. She sat, patted the seat next to her, and looked at Léirsinn expectantly.

Léirsinn took a deep breath and went to sit. She looked at her hostess and decided perhaps there were things that could be gotten out of the way first.

"I'm still not sure what I should call you," she said. "I don't want to be impolite."

"I've been called many things, but I would hope those sorts of words aren't rattling around in your pretty head. You may call me Fionne, or Mother Fàs if you prefer. I'll call you Léirsinn, unless you prefer Red."

"Mistress Fionne, if that suits," Léirsinn said carefully. "Given your reputation, I suppose you can call me whatever you like."

Mistress Fionne looked pleased. "I'll call you by your name, but don't think I won't call you other things behind your back. Now, to answer the questions you aren't asking about my former lover, he is still alive. One of Sarait's sons shut him up in a garden and used an extremely dangerous spell to drop all his power down a well and seal it there." She shrugged. "I always thought Gair would come to a bad end, but that didn't stop me from having several sons with him."

"Acair obviously inherited his good manners from you."

Mistress Fionne laughed heartily. "And so he did, though his pretty face comes from his sire, it must be said. I'd pay good money to see you manage my youngest son the way I've just watched you manage the shapechanging beastie in that stall. My maternal instincts prevent me from smothering Acair in his sleep, so I fear the task of bettering him—or doing him in, actually—falls to you."

Léirsinn wasn't sure if she should laugh or weep. "Indeed," she managed.

"Indeed," the witchwoman of Fàs said. She slid Léirsinn a sly look. "Do I frighten you?"

"You terrify me."

Mistress Fionne looked terribly pleased. "I do my best, as always. Now that we've sorted Acair—the annoying little git—let's move on to you. You said yestereve that you had no magic."

Léirsinn wondered if perhaps blisteringly swift changes of subject were usual fare with the woman sitting next to her, but decided she would learn the truth of it without having to ask. "Thankfully, nay."

"Can't say I haven't shared your opinion from time to time, though it comes in handy."

"I've never had it to miss," Léirsinn said carefully, "and to be honest, I didn't believe it existed until quite a while after I met your son." She paused. "I'm not entirely sure I'm not still imagining things."

"Understandable, dearie, but foolish." She leveled a look at Léirsinn. "Who is your father?"

"Saoradh of Sàraichte," Léirsinn said, then she wondered if perhaps she shouldn't have been so forthcoming so quickly.

Mistress Fionne pulled a book from her pocket and drew a pencil forth from where she'd obviously stowed it behind her ear. She considered, then made a note in her book. "Your mother?"

"Muireall of An Caol," Léirsinn said. She'd already put her foot to the path, so perhaps there was no sense in not continuing on. "'Tis near An Cèin, or so I'm told."

Acair's mother nodding knowingly. "Horse lovers, that lot. A few clutches of elves in An Cèin, but they keep to themselves, so you likely wouldn't have encountered them." She considered, then jotted down a few things before she snapped her book shut and put it back in her pocket.

"Does that mean anything?" Léirsinn asked, because that seemed like a reasonable question to ask.

Mistress Fionne shrugged. "I'll have to investigate a bit before I can say anything. I don't know much about your father's family save that his brother, your uncle, is not a pleasant sort."

"I would have to agree."

"I'm sure you would, gel. I would suspect, apart from anything else, that your suspicions about your lack of magic are correct. The truth is, I wouldn't mourn it if I were you. Look what became of Gair. Black magery is a dodgy business. Acair had best watch what he steps in, wouldn't you agree?"

What Léirsinn thought she could agree about was that Fionne of Fàs was either too damned observant for anyone's peace of mind or she had magic Léirsinn didn't want to know about. She looked at Acair's mother and took note of the knowing look there.

"About stepping in things," she began slowly, "I have some experience with that."

"I'll just bet you do," Mistress Fionne said with a snort, "but we won't talk about barn delights. Tell me more about places you've put your foot that you didn't intend to."

Léirsinn wasn't sure what she should or shouldn't say, but she already started down that path of madness so perhaps there was no reason not to keep on with it.

"I was standing in the king's garden at Tor Neroche when I stepped backward into a particular sort of shadow." She took an unsteady breath. "Now I can see things."

Mistress Fionne studied her for a moment or two. "What sorts of things?"

Léirsinn suppressed the urge to shift. "I can see things about people," she admitted, wishing she had anything but that to discuss. "I'm beginning to think I'm losing my mind."

"Keeping company with my son will do that to a gel," she said without hesitation, "but I likely shouldn't tell you that. As for anything else, your sight might be merely a sharpening of ordinary horse sense, or it might not. What do you see about me?"

"I'm afraid to look."

Mistress Fionne laughed, a sound that was reminiscent of Mistress Cailleach's booming fishwife's voice. "Can't say I blame you, but not to worry. I won't turn you into a shrubbery if I don't like what I hear. Again, I'm sure I've heard worse."

Léirsinn wasn't going to lay odds on that because it was a bet she didn't want to lose, but it didn't look as if Acair's mother was going anywhere until she'd been properly looked at.

It was true that she hadn't seen anything unusual since that terrible moment in the garden at Tor Neroche, not even in Eòlas, which was a bit strange. She didn't fancy looking about presently for a pool of shadow to step in to rekindle her unwholesome ability, but she supposed if she were going to try something absolutely daft, there was no better place to try it.

"Well?" Fionne prompted.

"I'm not sure how to make the attempt," Léirsinn admitted.

"Just look," Fionne said with a shrug. "Unless you want me to make my own pool of shadow for you."

Léirsinn didn't want to think about where that might lead, so she shook her head before Acair's dam trotted off with that idea. She wasn't entirely sure she wasn't still imagining it all, but perhaps that could be debated later. She had, after all, watched the woman in front of her drop magic on Mansourah of Neroche's arm and restore it to its original perfection. Hard not to suspect other things were possible in her presence.

She closed her eyes, then opened them and *looked* at Acair's mother.

It was as if she'd had a heavy woolen blanket of sorts pulled from where it had lain over her eyes. The witchwoman of Fàs was still sitting there, only at the moment, Léirsinn could *see* who she was in truth.

Acair's mother was . . . well, the woman was a tree. Not a straight, majestic pine or a supple, rustling aspen. She was an ancient, twisting oak that bore leaves that Léirsinn was certain fell when commanded and only landed where permitted. There were nooks and crannies and sinewy branches that likely should have given any unwary traveler pause. It was a mighty tree that Léirsinn suspected didn't care what wind howled around it or how much snow fell atop it. If unusual birds, misshapen sprites, and assorted other creatures from myth and legend nested in those branches, neither the creatures nor the tree seemed inclined to complain.

She blinked, and the vision was gone. She took a deep, unsteady breath.

"I see."

Mistress Fionne tilted her head to one side. "Do you?"

"Do you care if I do?"

Mistress Fionne smiled faintly. "Not a bit, lass, but you don't expect anything else, do you? That isn't to say that I wouldn't pull you out of the way of a bolting horse if necessary, but you've strong opinions yourself and no need of my approval." She shrugged. "My life's work is to make records of happenings.

Hard to make good ones if you're too caught up in those happenings."

Léirsinn was absolutely thrilled to talk about something else. "Have you always kept records?"

Acair's mother sat up a bit straighter and patted her hair. "Of course not. I've had loves and losses and ruined more than my fair share of dinner parties. After a few centuries, though, stirring the proverbial cauldron becomes a bit commonplace. I now have a steady stream of visitors, which keeps my mind sharp, and I live to torture my sons, which warms my black heart. What else is there?"

"Horses?" Léirsinn managed.

The witchwoman of Fàs laughed a little. "I suppose there is that, but my riding days are over. I'm not opposed to a turn about the old place as an icy wind or a terrifying dream, but for the most part I'm happy to stay in my own shape and make mischief as I can. Miserable people put a spring in my step, so I like to help that sort of thing along whenever possible. As for the rest, the world continues to turn and I continue to watch." She shrugged. "Trees seem to enjoy that, don't you think?"

"What I think isn't worth trying to repeat," Léirsinn said, feeling a little faint. "How did you know what I saw?"

"You aren't the only one who sees," Mistress Fionne said archly, "and I do have a polished glass, gel."

"You frighten me."

"And we're back to where we started," Acair's mother said pleasantly. "What do you see in my son?"

"Good manners and a flawless face."

"You know from where he gets those, but that wasn't what I was talking about. Have you peered into his soul?"

"Unwillingly," Léirsinn admitted. She thought about how she'd seen Acair in the king of Neroche's garden, standing in the moonlight in all his terrible beauty, with his soul so perfectly balanced between light and dark she half feared the slightest breath would destroy him. She looked at his mother. "I saw him in the gardens of Tor Neroche as I stepped in one of those spots— or after, perhaps. I can't remember. I'm not sure I can adequately describe the vision."

"I'm not sure he would care to hear it," Mistress Fionne said frankly, "but you might tell him just the same to vex him." She took the book about Gair and rose. "You're new at all this business, so I wouldn't worry."

"I'm not sure this is anything I want to be involved in, even if I knew what *this* was," Léirsinn said seriously.

"A quest, lass," Mistress Fionne said, "or weren't you told?"

Léirsinn wasn't sure she could adequately respond to that, so she settled for simply gaping at Acair's mother.

Mistress Fionne rested her elbow atop a stall door and looked at her seriously. "Gel, I would hazard a guess that there's been a lad or two from the noble rabble who's marched off into the darkness whilst wondering why they were where they were."

"Do you think so?"

"I *know* so. Most of those Heroes you read about have their heads full of rocks. Pretty, but not all that bright, if you know what I'm getting at. As to your purpose, I'd say you're not here by chance, but I'm not much of a believer in coincidence." She paused. "Speaking of things to look at, I'd like a peek at the charm you wear."

Léirsinn put her hand over her heart before she thought better of it. "How do you know?"

"Because I can see it burning through your tunic, that's how."

Acair's mother paused. "That and I had a wee chat with my aunt Cailleach recently and she said she'd given it to you. Her gifts are very powerful."

Léirsinn decided abruptly that she didn't particularly want to know how and when those two women had met over tea. She pulled the charm out from under her shirt and started to ease the leather cord over her head, but Mistress Fionne stopped her.

"No need for me to get too close to that."

Léirsinn didn't want to admit that her hand was trembling, so she ignored it. "Why not?"

Acair's mother looked at her with eyes that were so clear and knowing, Léirsinn almost flinched.

"Because it would likely burn me to cinders." She peered at it, then pulled back. "Cailleach never gives anything away, as you know by now. That she gave you this is unusual."

"It was very kind."

Mistress Fionne snorted. "That isn't the word I would use, but I'm more cynical than most." She looked at the charm once more, then shook her head. "'Tis true that you have no magic, girl, but you will breathe fire."

"With respect, that doesn't make any sense at all."

"If I told you what I saw . . . well, in your case, you'd likely just march on ahead without taking my advice, so why should I offer it?"

Because she was a witch, apparently, and likely knew all sorts of things that might be useful to know. Léirsinn would have asked her to divulge a tidbit or two, but it was too late. The woman reached out and stroked Sianach's nose, complimenting him lavishly on his propensity to nibble on her son, then walked off humming something that was so terribly out of tune, Léirsinn almost flinched.

She followed more slowly, then paused by Acair's horse. She stroked his face as well, then found herself completely overtaken by the memory of another hand on a different horse's forelock. That hand had belonged to the king of the elves—one group of them, actually—who had healed her stallion Falaire of an arrow wound that she was certain had slain him.

Acair's mother had used a different sort of magic the night before on Mansourah's arm, but it seemed to have worked equally well.

It was odd, that healing magic.

She leaned against the stall door and allowed herself to consider other things she hadn't wanted to before. Her grandfather's illness, for instance. It had come upon him suddenly and left him nothing more than a shell of his former self. It had been so devastating to her as a girl that she'd accepted it without looking for a possible cause, but when she'd told the tale to Acair, he had been convinced a foul magic had been to blame.

She wondered if a less-foul magic might reverse that.

She suspected she might be in the right place to find that out. The witchwoman of Fàs couldn't be heard any longer, but she had no doubt stridden off to do something Léirsinn was certain she wouldn't want to know about. She stroked Sianach's cheek, reminded him to behave himself, then took herself off to see if there might be anyone else with answers for her.

What she found instead was the son of a witch leaning negligently against a sturdy fence post, his nose buried in a small book and a frown marring his perfect brow. She stopped in the middle of the yard partly because for the first time ever she was wearing boots that completely repelled the snow, but mostly because seeing Acair of Ceangail generally resulted in that sort of stopping.

Bad mage he might have been, the sunlight didn't seem to mind him. It fell from the sky, lightly touched his hair on the way down, then lovingly wrapped itself around him.

She wondered if stepping in that pool of shadow had not only ruined her sight but damaged any last vestiges of her good sense as well. She had to ruthlessly suppress the urge to snort, mostly because she could hear Sianach indulging in a bit of equine laughter behind her and she suspected that pony could read her thoughts.

Acair, however, seemed incapable of doing anything past reading his book. She could have beaned him with a tree branch and he likely wouldn't have noticed. Perhaps she was more valuable to him on their quest than she'd suspected.

A quest, she reminded herself, that she had found herself unwittingly and unwillingly pulled into, a quest that seemed to have an equal amount to do with righting wrongs and getting rid of that spell she knew without looking was lurking in the shadows of a tree not ten paces from the mage in question. She was still trying to come to terms with anyone being *able* to use magic, never mind anyone in particular being trailed by a spell that didn't want him to use any of that magic.

Magic, she reminded herself, that quite possibly could be used for good.

She jumped a little when she realized Acair was currently watching her instead of his book. He pushed away from his post and crossed the yard to her.

"I was coming to find you," he said, tucking his book under his arm, "but I became distracted."

"I was chatting with your mother in the barn."

"Did Sianach bite her?"

"I don't think he dared," she said.

"Did she bite you?"

She smiled slightly. "Thankfully, nay."

"I'm not sure why I don't inspire that same deference in either of them, but the day is still young." He smiled and offered her his arm. "A seat by the fire?"

"It would definitely be a step up from a seat in a dungeon," she said.

"We can only hope. With my mother, one never knows."

She took his arm and walked back toward the front door with him. She thought she might make it inside before she asked the question that burned in her heart, but realized she wasn't going to manage it. She stopped him.

"Do you think my grandfather is truly afflicted by a—" She tried, but she couldn't force herself to use the word.

"A spell?" he finished.

"Or something that looks like that but seems more reasonable."

He smiled briefly, then sighed. "I don't know what to think about your grandfather," he said slowly. "I find it curious that, as you say, he was fine in the evening, yet so different the next morning. I can't bring to mind a commonplace, unmagical malady that would have rendered him so thoroughly incapacitated. Something that dire would have simply killed him."

She nodded, then met his gaze. "Can you heal him?"

He hardly looked surprised, which left her wondering if he might have considered the same before.

"My bent lies more toward dismantling things," he said carefully, "but I could attempt something a bit more, ah, altruistic, if you like."

She tried to smile but found she couldn't. "Would you?"

He looked suddenly quite winded. "Of course, Léirsinn," he said very quietly.

"That would be very kind."

"Just this once, though," he said seriously, "then I'm back to my usual business of trying to overthrow kingdoms and rid the world of monarchs sporting curly toed slippers. I will also, of course, deny any involvement in your grandfather's rehabilitation."

"I'll only admit to watching you at your worst."

"I would appreciate that."

She turned toward him and rested her head against his shoulder for a moment or two, not because she didn't want him to watch her weep but because she was resting up for all the questing they still had in front of them. If he reached up and smoothed his hand over her hair, just once, well, she wasn't going to make a fuss over it.

She finally stepped back. "I suppose I'll need to carry on with you for a bit longer, just to hold you to your word."

"Or you could come along because you're safest with me," he said.

"That seems unlikely," she said before she thought better of it. "What with all those black mages who seem to be following you everywhere."

"I'll concede that, but nothing else." He looked at her gravely. "I would appreciate your company, actually. My heart is ashes, Léirsinn, and you breathe fire." He shrugged helplessly. "I have no more answer for you than that."

She stopped just short of gaping at him. "You say the damndest things."

"You said you wanted a lad—if you were in the market for

such a thing, which you insisted you weren't—who expressed
sentiments of some maudlin sort. Daily, if memory serves."

"That wasn't just maudlin."

"*Definitely* don't spread that about." He eyed the door behind
her. "There's a spell sitting on the roof there that I believe my
mother set specifically to vex me should I try to enter the house.
I'm not sure the back door is any safer." He looked at her. "Are
you willing to try a window?"

She supposed that might be the least of the things awaiting
her, so she nodded and followed him around the side of the house.
The thought of his perhaps being able to heal her grandfather,
though . . . that was almost more than she dared hope for.

Besides, that was so far in the future that even she with her
newfound clarity of sight couldn't begin to see how it might come
about. She was hundreds of leagues away from the only home
she remembered, keeping company with two lads of royal blood
who wanted to kill each other, and trying to avoid dying thanks
to any of the numerous souls who apparently wanted to kill
Acair but might miss and snuff out her life by mistake.

She put her hand over the dragon charm she wore and wondered if there might be anything to Mistress Fionne's unwilling-
ness to even touch it.

She just wasn't sure she was ready to know.

Ten

The witchwoman of Fàs wasn't humming any longer.

Acair reshelved a rather tattered copy of *Scenic Byways in Durial*, shuddering over the content as he did so, and realized that not only had his mother stopped humming, she had deserted him entirely. He looked about himself in her rather substantial library only to find himself quite alone.

He leaned his shoulder against bookshelves that would likely remain standing long after the world had ended—his mother had her priorities, to be sure—and wondered when she had abandoned him to his own devices.

He had started his search for the obscure and perilous directly after luncheon. He had been joined by his mother and Léirsinn whilst leaving Mansourah of Neroche the unenviable task of trying to entertain two women who would likely wind up brawling over him.

He was fairly sure that after a pair of hours, Léirsinn had pled the excuse of more barn work as a means of escape, something for which he absolutely couldn't blame her. His mother, however, had remained in the trenches with him. She had entertained him with an admittedly impressive repertoire of Durialian drinking songs for the better part of the afternoon, most of the time merely humming the tune, pausing now and again to burst forth into a verse or two before descending into wheezing laughter over the lyrics.

His mother was, he had to admit, a woman of extremely eclectic tastes.

He wasn't sure when she'd left him or, more to the point, where she'd gone, which meant he needed to find her before she said or did something untoward and sent Léirsinn fleeing off into the gloom. His horse-mad miss had refused to divulge what she and his dam had spoken of in the barn, but he was certain it couldn't have been good.

He made his way to the parlor, but it was full of prince and rapacious cousin multiplied by two, so he withdrew silently before he was noticed. The passageways were distressingly free of any red-haired vixens, so he settled for a hasty trip to the kitchen.

It was unfortunately lacking the woman he lo—er, was rather fond of, but his mother was definitely there, sitting in her rocker near the hearth. She was knitting heaven only knew what, but he didn't see shards of glass sparkling in her yarn by light of the fire so he supposed it might be something as innocuous as a scarf.

His spellish companion was slouched in a chair—actually, it was slouched in what Acair noted was the chair he'd always sat in as a lad. That thing there was looking more like a surly youth with every day that passed, which he supposed he should have found damned unnerving.

He needed to bump *find maker of that bloody thing* up on his list of things to attend to.

He leaned against a bit of wall that separated the kitchen from the rest of the house and allowed himself to entertain memories he hadn't in decades, maudlin fool that he was. He would have to share them with Léirsinn later, perhaps as his good deed for the day.

His mother had never lived at the keep, something he'd never thought to question as a child then never had the heart to question as an adult. His father had been a cold, particular man and perhaps the thought of bringing his lover into his home had simply not been to his taste. His mother's house was roomy enough, but he couldn't deny that he had rejoiced when each of his brothers in turn had packed up their things and moved on to the keep to live with their sire.

He supposed it could be said that he'd lingered at his mother's fire longer than he should have, but she hadn't complained—well, she'd complained endlessly about his cluttering up her salon and eating all her veg. Somehow, he'd still managed to spend an inordinate amount of time at that very table, poring over this grimoire or that collection of magelike scratches. It was a little startling, actually, to see how comfortable that damned spell seemed to be, sitting there as if it wasn't full of death and destruction.

If he'd been a more superstitious soul, he might have thought he was looking at himself.

He cleared his throat carefully to alert his dam that conversation was coming her way. It wouldn't have been the first time catching her by surprise had resulted in her flinging a knitting needle and leaving a mark.

"Mother?" he said politely. "Knitting anything interesting?"

"I don't know," she said absently. "I'm thinking and it keeps me hands busy." She shot him a look. "Come and sit. I've almost rounded out a few thoughts you might be interested in."

He imagined she had. He pushed away from the wall, then walked over to the table, yanked his chair out from under that spindly fingered piece of mischief, then sat down. If he stepped on its sorry self as he did so, so much the better.

The spell picked itself up, hissed something foul at him, then went to stand by the fire, silent and watchful. Acair did his best to ignore it, though it was a powerful reminder of just how impossible were his straits.

He waited for his mother to finish her row. She set her knitting aside, then reached for the teapot. She pushed a cup toward him, then paused before she poured. "Tea?"

"If you drink it first."

She poured him a generous amount, then helped herself to the same. "You still have wood to stack and a roof to tend. I'll kill you a different time when I don't need your labor."

"The gods weep with relief, no doubt," Acair said.

He waited for his mother to lift her cup before he lifted his, then he waited a bit more before she smiled very briefly and applied herself to her brew. It didn't fell her immediately, which he supposed was reassurance enough for him.

"What have you discovered?" he asked politely.

She set her cup down and looked at him seriously. "You need to go find pieces of your lost soul."

He felt his mouth fall open. He was fairly sure that wasn't

attractive, but damnation, the woman said the most appalling things without any warning at all.

"Do what?" he managed.

"You need to revisit the places of your worst deeds and look for the pieces of your soul you've left there. You'll never manage what you need to against what hunts you otherwise."

"What absolute rot," he managed. "Rubbish."

"You came here for answers—"

"Actually, I came here for a *list*—"

"Which wouldn't serve you anyway, which is why you're here for answers," she finished. "Now, shut up and listen to wisdom." She started to speak, then eyed him suspiciously. "Are you listening?"

What he was doing, with more commitment to the activity than he was comfortable with, was wondering if his mother had lost her wits. It was a thought that genuinely left him without a single useful thing to say. He could only stare at her helplessly, which he supposed was enough for her.

"Let's review," she said slowly, as if she thought he might have reverted to trotting about in short pants. "What happens when a mage uses black magic?"

"Glorious business that leaves every other mage in the surrounding environs wishing he had even half the skill or courage to attempt the same," he said promptly.

She blew a stray curl out of her eyes. "You wee daft bugger, give me an answer of less than five words."

Acair rolled his eyes then. "He loses a part of . . ."

He stopped speaking. He did that because he suddenly found that five words were not quite enough for a proper answer. Along with that came a realization that he supposed he should have been clever enough to have made long ago, which was how thoroughly he'd underestimated the woman sitting across the table from him.

He'd done the same thing with his great-aunt Cailleach, of course, and she'd cuffed him so hard for the same that he was fairly sure he would never hear again as well out of his left ear as he had before. But this was his mother, the woman who puttered in her house with her books and her pencils and her quills. This was a woman who spun and knitted and pulled out a cloth now and again to polish her reputation as one of the most terrifying spellweavers in the world.

This was also his dam who chortled over arrogant monarchs laid low and annoying mages brought to their knees with a proper bit of retribution.

He was beginning to think he was more like her than he'd feared.

She was a silent recorder of the madness that went on in the Nine Kingdoms, but he wondered what had made her so. Eulasaid of Camanaë had been a ferocious and constant champion of goodness and right. He wasn't sure what his mother had dabbled in and he didn't think he wanted to ask her.

But a fool she was definitely not.

He took a deep breath. "When a mage uses black magic," he said slowly, "he loses a part of his soul in the bargain."

She poured herself a bit more tea, then held up the pot with a questioning look. He shook his head and waved her on to her libation. She sipped, then sat back.

"What a fascinating observation," she said, looking at him as if she were sorely disappointed in his cleverness. She waited, then made a noise of impatience. "I can't believe you don't see the connection."

He couldn't either, but it had been a very long fall to which he suspected he would add an even longer winter. He was definitely not at his best.

"Connection?" he ventured.

She threw a tea towel at him. "Those damned spots, Acair! Have you forgotten so quickly what they do?"

"I hadn't, but that doesn't follow," he said, grasping desperately for anything useful to say. "Léirsinn didn't lose a part of her soul when she stepped in one."

"Well, the feisty little wench certainly lost her peace, didn't she?" She looked at him sharply. "Have you not talked to her about what happened that night?"

"I haven't had the courage," he said honestly. "Nor the time, actually. We've been too busy with fleeing from those who want me dead to have a proper chat about anything else."

"You might want to make time for it."

He stared at a biscuit hiding behind the teapot, not because he was hungry but because he was trying to give himself time to digest what she'd said. He finally gave up and looked at her.

"So," he began carefully, "what you're saying is that those spots are black magery?"

She lifted a shoulder slightly. "I'm not saying anything. I'm simply making an observation."

He tried a different tack. "You said I needed to go find parts of my soul that I've traded for the glorious pieces of business I've seen to over the years. Why?"

She shrugged and sipped.

He shifted to another spot on the metaphorical chessboard for a different direction from which to attack. "Are you telling me that I don't have enough soul to see to this quest?" he asked, trying to dredge up as much offended dignity as he could muster.

"I'm not *saying* anything," she said with a snort. "You have an annoying habit of putting words in others' mouths."

"I like to get right to the point."

She shook her head. "You are an insufferable little clot, but very skilled at reading between the lines."

"That's because my mother never *says* anything," he said pointedly.

"And where would be the sport in that?" she said with a smile that sent a shiver down his spine. "I would never see you at *all* if I didn't give you some reason to pop in and out every now and again to remind me just how clever you are."

He leaned his elbows on her table and looked at her seriously. "I am that insufferable, I'll admit it."

"Yet here you sit at my table, unpoisoned." She shrugged. "You might want to consider the condition of the field before you march into the fray."

"The field and my own stash of weapons?"

"As I said."

He rubbed his hands over his face, then looked at her. "Mother, I don't need to tell you that trying to even bring to mind all the places I've perpetrated mischief would be impossible."

"Perhaps just the most egregious pieces of it, then."

He was tempted to laugh, but it occurred to him that he could think of several places that would qualify for that. They happened to coincide quite nicely with places he didn't want to go, peopled by rulers and whatnot he absolutely preferred to avoid encountering without his magic to hand.

He shot that damned spell leaning negligently against the hearth a dark look, just on principle.

"It seems very protective of you."

Acair blinked. "What?"

"Your lanky companion there," she clarified. "It tutted at me this morning when I considered dropping a gilded volume of Nerochian heroic lays on your head whilst you slept."

"You could have killed me with that pompous trumpeting of their imaginary deeds."

"Indeed I could have." She picked her knitting back up and shot him a very brief smile. "But you've such a handsome face, I couldn't bring myself to mar it."

He grunted at her, because he hardly knew how to respond to that. He watched her knit for quite a while before he finally managed to chase down the thought that had scampered across his mind when she'd first brought up the business of the day. He had another sip of tea, then set his cup down before he dropped it.

"So," he said slowly, "since we agree that the purpose of those spots of shadow is to steal souls—at least for the most part—am I to assume you believe there is a particular mage behind the laying of those spots about?"

She leveled a look at him that had him smiling in spite of himself.

"I'm wearing another man's boots, Mother. I'm not at my best."

"That shouldn't affect your wits, Acair."

He hoped it would be only boots he would lose before the entire thing was set to rights. "Then let me rephrase. Who do you have in mind for the starring role in this drama?"

She paused in the middle of her row, looked about her as if to make certain she was alone, then leaned forward. "It is rumored that to say his name is bad luck—"

"That's Mochriadhemiach of Neroche," Acair said promptly. "I say his name all the time and look at me." He held open his arms. "Still breathing."

"And incapable of using your magic."

"That isn't little Miach's fault, but I digress. Go on."

She had to knit a bit longer before she apparently found the wherewithal to voice her opinion. "I could be very mistaken about this, of course. This man dropped out of tales hundreds of years ago, though I've heard . . . well—"

"Please don't hesitate on my account," he said when it looked as if she might not finish.

She considered, then shook her head. "I could be daft."

"Mother, of all the things anyone might call you, *daft* is not on the list." He tried to smile, but he feared it had come out as more of a grimace.

She sighed deeply. "Very well, if my memory hasn't completely failed me, the mage I'm thinking of went by the name of Sladaiche. He was born, if the tales are accurate, in a place that once rivaled Bruadair for beauty. The country, small as it was, doesn't exist any longer, but you could look for it in an archive perhaps." She paused, then shook her head. "I think it best to keep the true placename to myself."

He felt a shiver go down his spine. Even his spellish companion had sunk down on a stool there by the hearth, where it commenced gnawing on its fingernails in fright. Acair shot it a warning look, then turned back to his mother. He supposed it would take a decent amount of digging to find a name for that sort of place, though he wasn't afraid to look. At the very least, he could bring to mind a pair of locales that might have spewed forth such a lad.

"His name means *thief* in his language," she said absently, "though he has used different names through the centuries—"

"How do you know so much about him?" Acair asked in astonishment. "And who is he?"

She waved away his question. "I've given you his name, you'll find his place of birth on your own I'm certain, and his purpose was ever to steal souls."

Acair gave it a decent bit of effort, truly he did, but there were times his mother talked in such circles that he honestly couldn't make head nor tails of anything she said. He shook his head in frustration.

"I don't understand why he would bother," he said finally.

His mother rolled her eyes. "In truth, Acair? Name me a trio— nay, a single reason why you destroy men."

"I don't destroy them," Acair said. "I woo the women, vex the husbands and fathers, and pilfer kingly jewels and priceless art because it gives them all something to talk about. What else has a king to do these days besides stomp about and weep over losing his favorite landscape?"

"You have a point there," she agreed.

"The acquisition of power I can understand," Acair said, "but what in blazes would you do with a soul?"

She fingered her pearls which he still wasn't convinced weren't more than they seemed.

"Why did your sire spend so much of his life perfecting his spell of Diminishing?" she asked.

"Because he was—still is, in theory—a peerless mage and an arrogant whoreson," Acair said grimly. "What else was *he* to do with his days? There is never enough power to be had."

"That isn't the point of the question," she said impatiently. "Why did he *need* that spell?"

"To obtain more power," Acair said, "something we just discussed." He looked at her helplessly. "What decent mage doesn't want that?"

She blew a curl out of her eyes. "I despair, truly I do. Let's look at this from a different direction. What did Gair leave of those whose power he stole?"

"Lads grateful they merited his notice, no doubt," Acair said without hesitation, though he supposed he didn't particularly want to think about that overmuch because he had seen what his father's tender ministrations could do.

He had felt the shudder in the world when his sire had loosed the power of Ruamharaiche's well, intending to take it for his own. He had himself managed to arrive too late to stop the madness, but he'd certainly had an eyeful of the aftermath. Actually, he'd closed Sarait of Tòrr Dòrainn's eyes so even in death she wasn't forced to look at what her husband had done.

He wasn't sure he would ever forget that.

He had done what he could for his half-sister Mhorghain, at the very least, then watched from afar, wringing his hands like a fretful alewife until he was certain she would be safely hidden. If others had seen to the rest of Sarait's children, he hadn't argued. He'd been simply crushed with invitations to dinner and attempting to carve out the odd hour to make lists of foul deeds to be about as quickly as possible. He hadn't had time for any of his other step-siblings.

He looked at his mother. "Father left them as shells," he said flatly.

"Exactly."

Acair thought of Hearn of Angesand telling him about his son—Tùr, he suspected—who had stepped in a spot of shadow once too often and wound up empty and mad as a result. He thought of Master Odhran, who had been left sitting, a lifeless shell of himself, before a cold hearth.

Was the same mage responsible for both deeds?

Did that mage now possess the spell of distraction he himself had left in Odhran's back workroom?

He shoved aside the last thought as unimportant. Any mage worth being called such could have fashioned the same. More important was what was being done to those who had apparently simply been in the wrong place at the wrong time.

He looked at his mother. "I don't like the sound of this."

"I'm not sure *this* cares what you like."

"But surely this mage is dead by now," Acair said, wondering if it would make him look weak to reveal how greatly he wished that might be so.

"Most likely."

He didn't like the way she'd said that, as if she wanted to believe it but couldn't bring herself to.

"I recoil from the very idea of looking dense as a rock," he said, "but I still don't understand why any of this matters. Let's assume, if we must, that this man is still roaming through the world, hunting for souls. The question is, why would he bother?"

She looked thoroughly disappointed. "You *are* a rock. What have we been discussing?"

"Magic."

"*Black* magery," she said pointedly, "for which there is a terrible price."

"I haven't paid a terrible price," he pointed out.

"I'm not sure you've paused long enough in your wild swathcutting through the Nine Kingdoms to know what sort of price you have or have not paid," she said seriously. "Or it might be that whilst you trumpet your deeds as if they were fashioned of the depths of hell itself, you don't use all that much dark magic." She looked at him. "Or do I have that awrong?"

"I use what's expedient—"

"Which is generally not Olc," she said pointedly, "or Lugham, or a trio of other magics that I don't even like to mention. General naughtiness, Acair, is not black magery in a proper sense, something you should understand by now."

"I'm trying to turn over a new leaf," he muttered.

"One could hope so," she said with a gusty sigh, "which is why what I've told you is so important. Sift through all the knowledge I've put in that empty head of yours and tell me what you learned today."

"A black mage loses a piece of his soul every time he uses an evil spell," he said wearily. "So?"

She threw her napkin at him. *"So?"*

He set her napkin aside and suppressed the urge to swear. "What difference does it make? There is a price to be paid for using *any* magic. There is no possible way to avoid that. The only thing one could hope for was an endless supply . . ."

He stopped speaking. That happened, he supposed, when one actually listened to what was coming out of one's mouth.

His mother only shook her head, no doubt in despair.

"There is no final price paid when one has an endless supply of something that sustains him," he managed faintly.

"Such as what the country of Neroche gives its deliciously gallant young king," she said, nodding. "I'd think twice about going up against Mochriadhemiach of Neroche, me lad. He has the entire reserves of that enormous country as his underpinnings and if you think he doesn't know that perfectly well by now, you're mad. He could throw all manner of spells at you for decades before he was even forced to yawn."

"He does seem rather perky," Acair conceded.

"As would any black mage with a proper supply of . . . well, what shall we call it? Power? Enthusiasm?"

"Souls?" he said hoarsely.

She slapped her hand on the table, sending teacups rattling. "Of *course* souls, you idiot. Think on it! A mage who never pays a price for his black magic? Your father lusted after power, which would have allowed him many things, but in the end all the power in the world didn't serve him and it would have eventually destroyed him because of the magic he used. But a mage who can trade *others'* souls for magicmaking will never tire, never pay a price for his spells, never find himself in a position where he's at risk of being stopped."

"Ye gads," Acair said faintly.

"Well said."

He took a deep breath. "Then the purpose of those spots of shadows is made clear."

"And so it is." She paused, then shook her head. "I've said more than I should have."

"For once, I believe I agree with you," he said. He wondered if there might be enough daylight to apply himself to fixing her roof or if some vile spider would slay him if he tried to stack wood in the dark. At the moment, he thought that might be preferable to what he faced. He pushed his chair back. "Thank you for tea, Mother."

She eyed him over her spectacles. "Off to do foul deeds, my son?"

"Stack wood, rather."

She nodded and a substantial ball of werelight appeared over his head. "The sun will set eventually," she said. "Lots of wood waiting for you, of course."

He nodded his thanks, then whistled for his minder spell to come along with him. If it snarled at him like a rabid dog, so much the better. It was a pity he couldn't use it to hide behind, but it seemed to be more comfortable hovering behind him. At least he knew what to expect from it.

A mage stealing souls for unlimited power. He shook his head over the elegance of the thought. He wondered why his father hadn't attempted the same, but Gair was a man with an insatiable desire for praise. Stealing power was messy and loud. This was something else entirely. If Acair hadn't stepped in one of those spots himself, he never would have noticed them and he certainly wouldn't have known what their purpose was.

Quiet work indeed.

He paused at the door to the kitchen, then turned and looked at his mother. "I don't suppose you have any ideas where I might find a few more details about this mage we won't discuss."

She shook her head, looking more unsettled than he was comfortable with. "He was an afterthought, truth be told."

"What made you think of him?" he asked, because he was terribly curious and had no sense of decorum when it came to conversations in his mother's kitchen.

"I was thinking about your father, if you want to know," she said stiffly, "and what a right proper bastard he was, wanting all that power that wasn't his. I started to knit, then one thing led to another, and . . ." She shrugged helplessly. "My mind is ofttimes simply too much for even my knitting to contain."

"Mother, you are a wonder."

She blinked, then she colored a bit. "Get on with ye, ye wee fiend, before I toss a spell of death your way just for the sport of it."

He'd had experience with just that sort of thing from her, so he got on with himself, avoided the sitting room he wasn't entirely certain didn't contain the muffled sounds of a prince of Neroche being smothered by women with spells, then crawled out the spell-free window he generally used for that sort of thing. He made his way without hesitation to his mother's woodpile.

He had things to think on.

There had once been a mage who had created a spell to steal souls and his name meant *thief*.

He supposed it might be time to start another list.

Eleven

Léirsinn looked at the back door of Fionne of Fàs's house and wondered just how the hell she was going to get past the spell that was hanging down there, peering at her from where it was apparently lounging outside on the roof.

She scowled, but that accomplished nothing at all except to remind her that that was exactly the sort of thing she'd been trying to avoid since she'd encountered Acair's mother in the barn the day before. She would admit that she'd managed to keep herself firmly in that uncomfortable place between denying that she'd seen anything at all in the king of Neroche's garden and telling herself it was simply a waking nightmare. She had reminded herself that she was a stable hand with a fondness for horses and a decent amount of skill in training them. She was neither witch nor mage nor any other sort of daft creature who saw things where things absolutely should not have been.

It hadn't helped all that much, to be honest.

On the other hand, she'd been very successful at not looking at anything so far that day. *Looking*, if she dared call it that. She'd refrained from looking at Acair during luncheon lest she see anything about him that might be considered magical. She'd ignored with equal enthusiasm his flirtatious cousins, his mother, and Mansourah of Neroche. She had happily sought refuge in the library after inquiring where the unmagical books might be found.

That her peace should end thanks to wanting to take an innocent stroll in the healthful air outside likely shouldn't have surprised her.

She glared at the spell she could see perfectly well there, which seemed to impress it somehow. It studied her for a moment or two, then retreated until there was merely a handlike shape lingering there. It waved her through, which she supposed either meant she would survive or the damned thing wanted her to come closer so it might slay her more easily.

She took a deep breath, then bolted through the doorway.

She didn't stop, choosing instead to walk with an enthusiasm another might have called panic until she reached the edge of the forest surrounding Mistress Fionne's house. She leaned over with her hands on her thighs and simply gasped in bitterly cold air until she had breathed in too much. She coughed for a bit, which seemed a reassuringly normal thing to do, then straightened and turned back toward the house.

There seemed nothing terribly odd about the scene. There was snow lying in drifts, more particularly in the shadows. Acair was on the roof, hammering and swearing. His mother was wandering about with a basket on her arm, bending every now and again to pick something up. Léirsinn imagined she was gathering the last of the year's nuts or perhaps a hearty tuber that had survived the snow so far. Surely that was the extent of it.

Surely.

After a moment or two, the back door flew open and out flounced two richly dressed, highly energetic women who looked a great deal like most other noblemen's daughters Léirsinn had encountered in passing at her uncle's manor. They were obviously on the hunt and Léirsinn didn't need to ask for which prince that might be. Acair's mother spoke with them for several minutes before they walked back inside, their shoulders sagging. Acair's mother shouted something at her son, up there as he was on her roof, before she too went inside the house.

All perfectly normal. Not a spell in sight.

Léirsinn wondered if she were beginning to lose her wits in truth.

She put her hand out to steady herself on the tree next to her only to realize she'd put her hand on a person. She jumped in surprise, then realized it was only Mansourah of Neroche, hiding like the very sensible man he was.

He put his finger to his lips. "I've escaped."

"Not for long, I'll warrant."

He shuddered. "You've no idea."

"Actually, I've been listening to them for two days now, and I think you're caught."

He opened his mouth, then shut it and shook his head. "I am not interested in marriage at the moment and if I brought home one of those gels, assuming I wasn't slain and divided as spoils between the two of them first, my brothers would finish me."

She smiled. "Are they so awful, then?"

He put his hand on the tree and sighed. "Acair's cousins?

Nay, in truth, they aren't. I would just prefer to watch all my brothers march on doggedly toward wedded bliss before I make the journey myself. What of you? Any black mages roaming about who tempt you?"

"Oh, not at all," she said, hoping she sounded confident and a bit aloof. "I have horses to train, manure to shovel, grain to prepare. No time for anything else."

He looked at her skeptically. "So if I were to wish very sincerely for that bastard atop the house to fall off and dash his head against a rock, what would you do?"

"Rush over to catch him, of course."

"Just as I thought." He nodded knowingly. "Whether you want to admit it or not, you have a rather bad case of heartburn for that lad there."

"I don't," she protested. "I'm just here to keep him safe."

"And that, my gel, is probably exactly what he needs."

Léirsinn couldn't imagine why, but she wasn't going to argue the point. She watched Acair on his mother's roof and it struck her just how ordinary he looked. There was honestly nothing about him except things she had seen in his eye a time or two— and what she might or might not have seen in the king of Neroche's garden—that would have convinced her that he was anything more than he appeared: an exceptionally handsome, terribly elegant man.

She looked at Mansourah. "Am I losing my mind?"

He smiled sympathetically. "What makes you say that—or do I need to ask?"

She watched Acair for a bit longer, then turned to him. "Have you ever seen him, well, you know." She waved an invisible witch's wand. "That."

"Ah," Mansourah said slowly. "That. As a matter of fact, I have."

"I'm not sure I believe it." She said that, but she supposed she might have to continue to repeat those words before she believed them. She might never have seen Acair work so much as a single spell, but she'd had a peep at his soul and she was absolutely clear on what she'd seen there.

Mansourah leaned his shoulder against his tree and watched Acair for a bit before he looked back at her and smiled. "He's a very bad mage, you know."

"Bad at maging," she managed, "or just bad in general?"

"The latter, assuredly. He's very good at the former."

"Do *you* truly think he's as terrible as everyone seems to claim?"

"Not that my opinion matters," he said carefully, "but I'll give it to you since you've asked. I've crossed paths with him several times in the past and been quite happy to have a full dining table separating us. He has very pretty manners, but he is not a man I would want to meet on the field."

"Yet you faced him over swords in that inn's courtyard, in Eòlas."

Mansourah smiled. "I didn't say I was excessively clever, did I? That was also a battle with ordinary weapons, which leaves us on equal footing. I could choose a freckle on his nose and put an arrow into it from three hundred paces without any effort, which he knows very well. But I would do everything including tucking my tail between my legs and bolting not to face him over spells. Again," he added half under his breath.

She smiled. "Details."

He snorted. "You're unkind to force me to embarrass myself,

but I'll indulge you this once. Acair and I once had a rather warm disagreement that I don't remember with pleasure. I was younger then and very overcome by my growing affection for a woman he had escorted to supper. We sat down at the gaming table after supper where I subsequently accused him of cheating at cards."

"Was he?" she asked in surprise.

"I don't think he needs to," Mansourah said ruefully. "And to answer your question, nay, I don't think he was. It was several years ago, I was far stupider than I am today, and he is who he is. I thought it might do him good to learn a lesson about what true power looked like."

She felt her mouth fall open a little. "You didn't."

"I am a prince of the house of Neroche," he said haughtily, "and he is a bastard." He paused, then laughed a little. "There you have my thinking at the time, which I freely admit was outrageous. The folly of youth, I suppose, but I was determined to prove a point. We exited our host's private solar, took up places in his back garden, and there I was taught a lesson in humility. The only reason I escaped Acair's elegant and very lethal spells— including a very nasty spell of death—was because his supper companion tempted him with a very fine glass of port, distracting him long enough for me to bolt. He followed me all the way home, of course, and 'tis only thanks to the superior quality of my family's spells that I managed to get inside the front gates and slam them shut before he slew me."

"Would he have killed you, do you think?" she asked.

He shook his head. "I'm not worth the effort. Someone else, though?" He shrugged. "I wouldn't want to speculate. I will say this, though: whoever has sent lads after him has only done so because they know Acair has no magic. I can't think of anyone who would dare otherwise."

"Will they kill him if they find him unprotected, do you think?"

"Absolutely."

"Yet you've helped him so far."

"I've helped *you*," he corrected, "though I will admit I haven't actively hindered him." He glanced at Acair, then shook his head. "'Tis difficult to change when those around you don't want you to. Miach offered him a bed inside the walls and my sister-in-law the queen asked me to come after you both and keep watch, which says much about their opinions. I suppose the least I can do is afford him the same chance I would want in his place."

"And if he never changes his ways?" she asked with a faint smile.

"I'll wait for an opportunity to put an arrow through his eye," Mansourah said with a smile, then his smile faded abruptly. "Damnation, I'm caught."

Léirsinn looked at the back door as it opened and Acair's cousins spilled out. They had obviously steeled themselves for another round of hunting.

"I'll go keep those two busy if you'll do me the very great favor of hurrying your lad along with his labors," Mansourah said seriously. "I would very much like to escape this place at first light tomorrow, not that any future locales will be any less perilous than this one. At least in some foul lord's dungeon I won't find myself fighting off witches eyeing me as a potential husband."

She supposed that might be preferable, but she also thought she might like to avoid any other dungeons. She'd already passed several hours in an elven king's pit and she had no desire to re-peat the experience.

She watched Mansourah walk off to collect his admirers, then leaned against the tree and thought about what he'd told her. A part of her wished she hadn't heard any of it.

The less cowardly part of her decided that she couldn't carry on any longer denying the truth.

She had latched on to every reasonable explanation for her recently acquired ability to see otherworldly things, everything from losing her eyesight all the way to losing her wits. Unfortu-nately, she currently found herself with no choice but to accept the undeniable and quite uncomfortable conclusion that the world around her was not at all what it seemed to be and she had no means of managing that.

She was beginning to have a painfully thorough amount of sympathy for Acair.

She looked at the spell sitting on the witchwoman of Fàs's roof and contemplated the truly improbable nature of what she was seeing. Very well, so magic existed. It was also true that she could see the bloody stuff in broad daylight everywhere she looked, with the notable exception of not having seen anything in Eòlas. Either the city didn't have very many spells cluttering up its streets or Acair's childhood home was simply overrun with them.

She was beginning to think her parents might be responsible for some of her current troubles. With all those tales of magic and Heroes and improbable things that they had taken such pleasure in retelling, it was almost as if they'd had an especial fondness for magic—

She shook her head before she traveled any farther down that path toward madness. Her childhood had been ordinary, short, and thoroughly lacking in anything unusual. Her older brother had been protective, her younger sister ethereal, and she the plain, uninteresting middle child who had survived where they had not—

She took a deep breath and let it out slowly. She didn't like to think about her past, mostly because there was nothing she could do to change it. Her parents and siblings were gone, and she was in a witch's house—or, her yard, rather—thinking that she might want to look for a terrible black mage who had vowed he would try to help her.

She wondered if she might be forgiven for simply setting everything aside for a bit and passing a few minutes helping a man who apparently loved his mother enough to fix her roof for her. She walked back to the house just in time to meet him as he swung down off the roof. She picked up a small bucket of nails and held it for him as he attended to something loose on the side of the house.

"Your mother says you never do any work here," she remarked.

It was surely a coincidence that his aim went awry and he hit himself instead of the intended nail. He cursed, sucked on his thumb, then glared at her.

"She might have that aright."

She ignored his grumbles. He was, in the end, no worse than any other surly stallion she'd known.

"She also suggested to me earlier that you're doing it to impress me," she added.

"I'm doing it so she doesn't poison my tea." He drove another nail home, took the bucket from her, and set everything down on the ground. "Somehow, I think my terrible reputation is more than enough to impress you."

She smiled. "Your cousins say you are a rogue of the first water."

"Flattering, of course, but I'm unable to admit to anything."

He didn't need to. She'd been caught on the way to the stables that morning by his cousins, women who had seemingly felt compelled to fill her ears full of Acair's conquests. One of the twins, she wasn't sure which, had been very clear that he traveled in circles so far above their own social station that they couldn't say for certain but suspected he had toppled more than just thrones.

Léirsinn wouldn't have been at all surprised.

He dusted the snow off a stone bench pushed up against the house, then invited her to sit. He collapsed next to her and groaned.

"I've done all I can to this damned nest of hers," he said, shaking his head. "If she poisons me, it will be a mercy. And don't look at me that way. I will absolutely *not* admit to anything that might paint me in an unflattering light."

She smiled, because he was absolutely incorrigible. "Do you ever have to use threats," she asked, "or do you just charm your victims?"

He drew his hand over his eyes. "Ye gads, self-reflection," he said with a shiver. "The places you've forced me to go, woman."

She watched him watch her with eyes she suspected had seen far more things than he would ever admit to. They were beautiful eyes, though, she had to concede.

He looked at her, sighed, then shook his head. "I have lived a long, indulgent life full of things I might regret and many other things I don't regret in the slightest. My lack of contrition over any of it is what keeps me heart protected, oy, as my mother would say. But since we're sharing secrets—"

"Are we?"

He shot her a look that made her smile. "We are," he said distinctly. "And given that such is the case, perhaps 'tis time you told me what happened to you in young Miach's garden."

"I deserve this," she said grimly. She looked over his mother's snow-covered ground for a bit before she turned to him. "I saw . . . things."

"More than just pools of shadow and my superior swordplay?"

"Your swordplay was spectacular," she agreed, "and I thought you fared very well against Prince Rigaud, who definitely looked as if he would have liked to have slain you. He is very powerful."

He went very still. "Why do I suspect you're not talking about his abilities with a blade?"

"Because *I* suspect you have a very suspicious nature which is no doubt what keeps you alive," she said without hesitation. "And aye, I saw more than I bargained for. I stepped in that shadow that I hadn't seen—"

"It *was* the middle of the night," he said.

"Or close to it," she agreed. She took a deep breath. "I don't think I want to think too long about what it did to me." She paused. "I'm not sure what it *did* do to me, but I could see Prince Rigaud's magic."

"What did you see of me?"

She blinked in surprise. "You've finished hearing about him?"

"Rigaud of Neroche is an ass who careens from one fashion disaster to another, apparently unable to find a polished looking glass," Acair said without hesitation. "I'm far more interested in all the lovely things you'll say about me."

She would have thought he had begun to take himself just a bit too seriously, but he had taken her hand in both his own and was stroking the back of it in much the same way she would have soothed a frightened pony.

She strove to match his light tone. "Your ruthlessness was terrifying."

"And all is right with the world," he said in satisfaction. "What else?"

"I've forgotten," she lied.

He looked a bit startled. "Is my power failing? Am I rusting from the innards out?"

"Nay, you seemed to be in perfectly foul condition, but what do I know? Now, if you had thrush, I might be able to discuss that with you for hours on end."

He shot her a disgruntled look, which she appreciated. He obviously knew she wasn't telling him the entire tale, but he didn't press her and she didn't volunteer anything. She wasn't going to be responsible for sending him in a direction he might regret. If he didn't already realize what was hiding in his own soul, she would have been surprised.

"I think my feet are fine," he said slowly, "but I thank you for the consideration. As long as my power seemed to be not leaching out of me, I'm content."

She nodded, then looked at her hand in his for longer than perhaps she needed to. It was better that than remembering how he had looked in the garden at Tor Neroche, standing there in all his terrible, undeniable power.

She was no coward, however, and she couldn't put off any longer facing the things she needed to. If that meant acknowledging things that made her uncomfortable, so be it. "Do *you* see?" she asked him.

He looked at her reluctantly. "See?"

"You know." She waved her hand negligently, gesturing at she hadn't a clue what. "Things."

He sighed. "I can see those damnable spots of shadow, as well as spells and whatnot that others feel compelled to send my way. I'm not as skilled at seeing things about people, if that's what you're getting at." He looked at her. "Is that what you're getting at?"

She groped for a way to avoid answering that, but in the end all she could do was return his look. "I'm admitting to nothing."

"And why would you? Surely it is enough to be rendered speechless by the perfection of my form and visage and that is definitely all you should admit to lest you cause a stampede of angry misses and mavens, come to trample you for delights they are sadly denied."

"Acair, please stop."

"Ah, how I love to hear my name said in such dulcet tones." He squeezed her hand briefly. "I'll humor you in this and we'll carry on with less interesting things. As for what we're discussing but not discussing, the ability to See is something that comes as a bloodright." He nodded at her. "We discussed that sort of business in Ehrne of Ainneamh's dungeon, if you remember."

"I'm trying to forget," she said.

"I can't say I blame you," he agreed. He looked out over his mother's backyard, then shook his head. "To be honest, I'm not sure *bloodright* applies as neatly with this. Normally, magic that finds home in your blood allows you to use spells that are your reward for putting up with your vexatious relations—"

"But with enough power, you can use whatever suits you," she finished skeptically. "Or so I've been told."

"By a very wise man," he agreed. "With Seeing, though, you could have all the power in the world and you still wouldn't do so properly unless it came from your own blood. There are those who possess the ability to see, of course—elves, dwarves, the odd local sorceress with something unusual sitting perched in her family tree—but that's a quotidian sort of business. Those who actually See, well, that's something else."

"Is there that much difference?"

"Do you want to know?"

"Absolutely not."

"I understand that for those who have it as their bloodright," he continued mercilessly, "'tis heady stuff. Dreamspinners can see the fabric of the world, or so I hear. Those lads and lassies from Cothromaiche are the most cheeky of all, for they can see what a soul's made of."

"Can you do this Seeing?" she asked.

He shook his head. "Not in the purest sense of it. My father is the son of an elven prince and wizardess of terrible power, both of whom you've met. Toss my mother's heritage onto the pile and there you have what I'm capable of. Nothing to rival that busybody from Cothromaiche, I'm sorry to admit, but enough to get by."

"Meaning you can pick bugs out of your veg in the dark?"

He smiled. "Something like that." He looked at her. "I understand for some 'tis a bit like having a layer of wool removed from over one's eyes. You might have an opinion on that."

"I'm too refined to voice it." If she were too unnerved to swallow properly as well, that was her business.

"And so you are. For all I know, 'tis all rubbish and I know nothing of it." He looked at her thoughtfully. "Why do you ask?"

"I didn't see any spots of shadow in Eòlas."

He choked. Léirsinn would have enjoyed that, but she wasn't entirely sure he wouldn't choke himself to death. She pounded him on the back until he held up his hand in surrender.

"I am well," he wheezed. He took several tentative breaths, then looked at her in astonishment. "What?"

"You heard me."

"What *did* you see, then?"

"Nothing," she said.

He stared off into the distance for a moment or two, then turned back to her. "I don't suppose you would want to remain behind here."

"Are you mad?"

He looked, for the first time since she'd first seen him, rather rattled. "I wish you would."

She studied him. "Why? What have you discovered?"

"Worse than what we already knew?"

"I don't know," she said uneasily. "Is it?"

"Much." He heaved himself to his feet, then held down his hand for her. "I need to walk."

She would have suggested a quick run to somewhere safe, but she wasn't sure such a place existed. She walked with him through what served as a path around his mother's house until she at least no longer felt chilled to the bone. Acair finally stopped and looked at her. She had seen him look bored, angry, dismissive, and impossibly arrogant. She wasn't sure she had ever seen him look that unnerved.

"Too late to run?" she asked.

"For me? Aye. For you?" He looked at her seriously. "It is never too late, Léirsinn, for you to remain in a safe haven."

"I cannot," she said lightly. "I breathe fire, you know. Your mother said as much. For all you know, you might require that sort of thing at some point in the future."

"I might," he agreed quietly, "though I'm not sure I can describe the lengths I will go to before I ask you to put yourself in harm's way for me."

"Don't be ridiculous," she said, attempting to sound brisk and businesslike. "You're a ruthless, evil mage with a terrible reputation who I'm certain never worries about the state of his companions. That, and you hid behind me in Angesand *and* the library without a second thought which tells us both all we need to know about your true feelings."

He smiled wearily. "I can only hope to avoid that sort of thing in the future."

She would have happily continued to poke at him, but the expression on his face stopped her. "What did you find that was worse, Acair?" she asked, not at all interested in the answer but knowing she had no choice but to have it.

He paused, then sighed. "My mother thinks a truly vile little black mage who lived eons ago has slithered forth again and is making trouble. Stealing souls and that sort of rot."

She blinked. "What?"

He held up his hands in surrender. "I didn't suggest it to her, she suggested it to me. Utter rubbish, of course."

That wasn't the word she would have chosen. She wasn't sure what to call what she'd just heard, but she thought *terrifying* might be close to the mark.

"Does she think he's making those spots of shadow?"

"I believe so, but I also think she may have been overcome by her recent matchmaking success, resulting in her making assumptions she shouldn't. I'm sure she's mistaken."

She suspected he wasn't sure at all. She continued on with him for a bit longer, waiting for him to spew out what she was certain he hadn't yet told her.

"About those spots," he said slowly.

She stopped and looked at him. "What?"

"My mother believes that in order to fight their maker, I must go round to scenes of past triumphs and collect pieces of myself

I left there." He glanced at her. "So I'll have as much of my black soul as possible available for the final fight."

She retrieved her jaw from where it was hanging halfway to her chest. "That's completely daft."

"Thank you," he said with feeling. "I agree."

She supposed the time to point out to him that a pool of shadow had ripped off a piece of his soul—his words, not hers—back in Sàraichte was not the present moment. It was likely the last place he wanted to return to. She watched him watch the forest for a bit, then cleared her throat.

"So," she began, "what now?"

He sighed deeply and looked at her. "I believe we should visit the scene of my first triumph, namely the cottage of the mage whose spell I stole right off his mantel."

She found she had absolutely nothing to say to that. The thought of Acair potentially knowing who seemed to be setting snares designed to steal souls was terrible enough. Having to scurry around to places where he hadn't been on his best behavior was likely going to be dangerous, if not fatal.

Believing that souls could be lost, collected, or used against another in a battle of magic was almost more than she, even with her newfound acceptance of a reality that had never been hers, could begin to believe.

"If the house still exists," he said carefully, "I suppose it would be as good a place as any to start."

She nodded, but could only hope it wouldn't be the place that finished them.

Twelve

Acair stood near the fire in his mother's kitchen and contemplated the dregs of something in his cup that might have risen to the level of poison with a goodly nudge. He had been at the activity for longer than he should have, but he was having thoughts that he wasn't sure he cared for, he who had never backed away from any unpleasant thought before. He had been up before dawn—an alarming trend he would put a stop to just as soon as his life was again his to call his own—pacing and wringing his hands.

Chasing after bits of his lost soul? Looking for a mage who collected souls like he himself collected spells? Yet another indeterminate number of leagues spent with that pampered puss, Mansourah of Neroche?

Appalling.

He noted something out of the corner of his eye and was

relieved to find it was his mother, not some new spell of death bent on his destruction. She was watching him far too closely for his peace of mind, which should have been unsettling all on its own, but there you had it. His mother was terrifying.

He rather liked that about her, truth be told.

"Aye?" he asked warily.

"Just watching the wheels turn," she said with a shrug.

Well, if she was going to do that, there was no reason in not clearing up a few last-minute things with her. "There is something that still puzzles me," he admitted.

"Why that red-haired vixen tolerates you?" she asked. "Me too, but perhaps she took a blow to the head recently and lost all sense."

He pursed his lips. "I try not to discuss it with her."

"Wouldn't want to scare her off." She walked into her kitchen, took the cup from him, then refilled it before she sat it and herself down at the table. She pushed it into an empty spot and nodded. "Tell Mother about your confusion, lad, and we'll see if superior wit and wisdom can carry the day."

"And if not?"

"Well, I'll make a note of it and rejoice after you're gone, of course." She patted her hair. "I'm on my best behavior for the moment. Never know when that luscious piece of goodness from Neroche might stumble into me kitchen for coffee and a biscuit or two." She lifted her eyebrows briefly. "I have a reputation for hospitality to maintain, you know."

Her reputation included mostly tales of what—and who—she buried in her garden, but he supposed that wasn't a useful thing to bring up at the moment. He sat down, sipped, gasped, then leaned his elbows on the table to avoid falling off his chair. The woman's coffee rivaled the king of Durial's ale for its vileness. In fact, he wasn't entirely certain the two of them didn't have some sort of foul contest going to see who could brew the most un-drinkable swill possible. It took him a moment or two to regain his composure, but when he thought he could speak with any success, he looked at his dam.

"Let us concede the point that a mage loses a part of his soul when he works black magic."

"Not all dark spells, of course. Just the truly vile ones."

"Don't suppose you've made a list of those."

"Didn't suppose I needed to, especially where you're con-cerned," she said, "but we'll discuss that later. Go on. You're hav-ing thoughts and I don't want to interrupt such a monumental event."

He would have scowled at her, but he was too unsettled to— an unsettling turn of events in and of itself.

"Let's agree on more dire pieces of magic," he said. "We could argue spells of death, surely, but I say we concentrate on Dimin-ishing."

His mother leaned forward, obviously ready to dish. Bless the woman, she had always been willing to get her hands dirty discussing things that would have made another witch swoon into her cauldron.

"Shall we discuss what's left of the victim, or what the work-ing of that spell does to the mage?" she asked. "Well, to your sire, actually, given that he used it so often that the effects might be more readily examined."

"Exactly that," Acair agreed. "We can say without quibbling what was left of those he plied his trade upon, which wasn't much."

"Lumps of sorrow and misery," she agreed. "Just my sorts of lads, but you know me."

Indeed, he did. He looked at her thoughtfully. "So, what is your opinion on what the working of that spell did to him? Did he lose parts of his soul in the bargain?"

She shrugged again. "There was so little of his black soul left by the time I met him, I don't know if I could answer that properly. Did he have no soul to start with, or did Diminishing cost him what he had left?" She looked at him with eyes that saw far too clearly. "Makes you wonder, doesn't it, what Ruamharaiche's well took of him when he lost control of himself there, if he had so little soul left. I understand he certainly didn't lose any of his power, but there had to have been a cost of some kind."

"I'm not traipsing to Shettlestoune to ask him," Acair said grimly.

"Don't look at me for that answer," she said. "I'm not even sure knowing the particulars would aid you, not that he would admit what it had cost him. If you want my advice, think on that name I gave you."

"Sladaiche."

"I believe that's the one."

"From whence did he hail, did you say?"

"I didn't say." She pulled his cup away from him. "Best toddle on off and find out for yourself."

He rose, leaned over and kissed her cheek, then leapt back and dashed for the door before she cuffed him.

"Oh," she said, "one last thing."

He had to admit he didn't care for the tone of her voice or how just the sound of those words seemed to bring everything in the world to a grinding halt. He turned around and looked at her with a fair bit of reluctance. "Dare I ask?"

"I think you should go visit your grandmother."

He staggered. He staggered into the doorframe, true, which

he supposed was the only thing keeping him on his feet. "You cannot be serious."

"Think on what her library contains. I have limited myself to an unvarnished and factual record of the Nine Kingdoms, but she has collected an entirely different sort of thing. You should know, having nosed about in her library more often than you should have. Potions, oddities, rare and unusual books that might or might not have anything to do with the world as we see it." She nodded knowingly. "Faery tales aren't always what they seem to be."

"You want me to take my life in my hands and slip inside her house to look through her collection of *children's* books?" Acair asked incredulously.

"Dolt, where do you think those stories come from?" she asked in exasperation. "The man you may or may not be hunting faded out of all histories centuries ago. For all I know, he's older than that ageless prince from Cothromaiche. He was the stuff of legend when your sire started investigating him and that was centuries ago. If Gair could have found him, he would have. I suspect he's likely a miserable seller of porridge located on the same street as your tailor, hiding in plain sight."

"My late tailor, you mean," Acair said, "but the point is still well taken." He sighed and rubbed his hands over his face. "And you think Granny will tell me where he is?"

"I think your grandmother, my wee brat, will slay you the moment she claps eyes on you. She's bitterly disappointed in the way you turned out. You also nicked one too many of her little figurines. She paid a great deal for them from Roland of Gairn and his progeny, and you know how rare they are. A woman doesn't forgive that sort of thing."

"They made excellent hostess gifts."

"Which put her in the position of seeing her treasures in the glass cabinets of various noblewomen she loathes whilst she was unable to, for the sake of decorum, announce that the goods in question were actually hers."

Acair supposed it might be wise not to mention the other things he'd liberated from his maternal grandmother's cache of things he'd been certain she would never miss.

"I understand she has a tome called *The Book of Oddities and Disgusting Spells*," his mother said placidly. She picked up her knitting. "Right up the old alleyway where you're concerned, I imagine."

He considered. "Think she would let me have a look at it?"

"Of course not." His mother snorted. "As I told you before, if you show your pretty face at her gates, she'll slay you as soon as look at you."

He tsk-tsked her. "Are you suggesting, Mother mine, that I sneak over the walls and do a bit of burgling?"

"I'm not suggesting *anything*, but make certain you take note of any new spells she has guarding her walls. She's terribly stingy with what she invents, which I find surprising considering how popular my diaries are. You would think she might want to figure prominently in one or two, but there you have it. Relatives are a mystery."

He couldn't have agreed more. He made her a low bow, then steered himself in the direction of loud weeping. He paused at the doorway of the fancy parlor and shook his head over the scene of devastation that greeted him. Mansourah was standing in the middle of the chamber, drenched to the skin by two wailing workers of magics that should have had *him* weeping. Acair cleared his throat loudly.

"You do know, ladies, that Prince Mansourah's twin, Turah, is even more handsome than he is."

His cousins turned and looked at him as one.

"Is he?" they asked, also in unison.

He suppressed the urge to shiver and instead carried on with the business of getting his little company underway. "Indeed he is, so there's plenty of Nerochian royalty to go around. No need to fight over this one when there's more to be had at home—and definitely a better specimen. I'd rush off and see for myself if I were you two."

The breeze left by their passing came close to knocking him off his feet, but at least the deed was done. Mansourah walked unsteadily over to him.

"I should kill you for the insult, but instead I find myself wanting to kiss your boots."

"Hold that thought," Acair advised. "I would also suggest not going home for a bit. They'll lose interest after a while, but I have the feeling that might take longer than you'd care for. You might want to warn your brother."

Mansourah smiled briefly. "Or I might not."

Acair looked on him with a friendlier eye and would have complimented him on that lack of brotherly compassion, but he didn't want to offer praise too soon. A few more opportunities to do a foul turn instead of a good one, then they might have something to discuss.

"I understand Léirsinn is outside trying to convince your pony not to stomp you to death when he sees you," Mansourah offered. "The sooner we interrupt her, the better."

Acair shook his head in wonder at the way things were looking up. Nastiness from a prince of Neroche, a mystery from his mother, and a potential bit of excitement at his Gran's. He thought it best to bid his mother a final good-bye, collect Léirsinn and Mansourah, and march off into the pleasant morning light whilst the winds were so favorable.

He didn't imagine that would last.

Several hours later, he was making his way through the forest to the north of his sire's rotting, bastard-brother-infested keep and marveling at how quickly the worm, as the saying went, had turned. He felt exactly as if he were walking over his own grave.

It was absolutely ridiculous, of course, but that was his life of late. No magic, no mischief, and no ability to properly astonish the glorious woman walking next to him, never mind giving that cloying prince of Neroche a proper send-off. All he could do was crawl about like a pitiful mortal, wondering when the next mighty mage would find him in the way and squash him like a bug.

Things had to change, and quickly.

That was precisely why he was stooping to the madness his mother had suggested of traipsing hither and yon to collect the bits of himself he had apparently left behind whilst about his three favorite activities, a list he supposed he didn't need to make for himself. He could hardly bring himself to think on any of them without indulging in a heavy sigh. So much havoc going undone was such a terrible waste. Telling his companions about his escapades had lifted his spirits briefly, but now he was back to the dull business of keeping himself alive long enough to have his magic back.

It took less time to reach the site of his initial foray into true shady-doings than he'd anticipated, though he supposed he should have expected that. He had been a lad of tender years, after all, venturing forth from Ceangail on his own two feet in deference to stealth. The appropriate spot had seemed quite a distance to him at the time, but he now realized that it was closer than he should have been comfortable with. He held up his hand to stop his companions, hoping they would ignore how that hand trembled.

"We're here."

Mansourah, to his credit, only frowned at the house sitting there on the sunnier side of the slope. Acair had little idea what sorts of things that lad there had combined as a strapping youth, but he imagined it had included what for those Nerochian lads might be counted as the occasional bad deed. Cutting the blooms off their mother's rosebushes, pushing over the occasional snoozing bovine, filching the odd bottle of wine from their father's stash of that nasty stuff from Penrhyn, who knew? It seemed to be the extent of the imagination of those northern lads, so he couldn't mock them for it. One lived with one's failings as best one could.

"Have you never been back here?" Léirsinn murmured.

"Return to the scene of such a prattish crime?" he said with as much disdain as he could muster, which unfortunately wasn't much. "Nay. I only revisit scenes of past triumphs. This doesn't qualify."

He supposed he didn't need to add that he was finding those visits increasingly difficult to make during daylight hours, but what was there to be done? He was a black mage extraordinaire and some people just had no ability to enjoy the odd ribald jest or the nicking of an irreplaceable portrait. That was hardly his fault.

But returning to a place languishing in the middle of trees

that he was sure clung to life through sheer willpower alone? Preposterous. It looked nothing more than what it was: a modest country house set on a small landhold where the owner had likely died without heirs, no doubt a fortnight or two after he'd taken a tumble off an orchard ladder.

Acair steadfastly refused to think about the fact that he had knocked just such a man off just such a ladder. That crotchety old bastard had been a mage. He certainly should have been able to take care of himself.

"Well, what now?"

"An excellent question, young Mansourah," Acair said absently. "I think a brief turn about the old place might suit."

"If you say so," Mansourah said doubtfully.

Acair excused himself and went to do just that. A careful scouting of the border of the orchard and house convinced him only that he'd been a fool to even set foot near the place, deliciously tempting rumors aside. If he'd had the wit the gods had given a common garden slug—something his mother was convinced he didn't possess—he never would have bothered.

He rejoined his companions, checked briefly for any untoward familiarity with Léirsinn on Mansourah's part that would spell the end of the man's life, then frowned.

"I don't see anything, but perhaps I'm not seeing what's there." He looked at Mansourah. "Don't suppose you'd care to have a look about, old bean?"

Mansourah took his bow in his hand, shifted his quiver of arrows to quite possibly a more advantageous locale on his back, then melted into the shadows of the forest.

"How does he do that?" Léirsinn asked, sounding a bit more breathless than circumstances warranted.

"It's likely how he manages free ale," Acair said sourly. "He sneaks up and poaches it whilst the lad who paid for it is distracted. I'm sure his technique has been perfected in just such spots as that rather rough pub we frequented in Neroche."

She gave him a chiding look. "I believe he's a very skilled bowhunter."

"Yet still so unwed," Acair said, shaking his head. "One wonders why, doesn't one?"

"One does," she agreed. "One is also a little surprised there isn't a line of noblewomen forming somewhere for your eligible self."

"I'm surprised by that as well," he said honestly. "I think there might be, but the trouble is I've yet to encounter anyone from that very long line whose first instinct was to stab me with a pitchfork. I might have to look further afield."

She smiled and he had to remind himself quite sharply not to fall into those limpid leaf-green pools she called eyes.

"You might," she agreed.

He reached for her hand and tucked it under his elbow before he dropped to his knees right there on that carpet of fallen pine needles and spewed out a maudlin sentiment or two. Her fingers were freezing and that in spite of the winter clothing—completely black, of course—his mother had so thoughtfully provided for them. If he and Léirsinn looked a bit like a pair of ne'er-do-wells out for a bit of burgling, well, his mother was nothing if not practical.

Mansourah, of course, would need to travel a few more leagues out of Fionne of Fàs's sights before he dared discard the lovely ermine-trimmed cloak and boots he was sporting. At least the man had managed to escape without committing to wed either of the twins he'd left sobbing into their porridge.

Love was a complicated business.

But so was the rubbish he was currently embroiled in, so he set aside those flowery thoughts for examination at another time and tried not to wonder if his mother might have sent him on an errand that would prove to be fatal, just for the sport of it.

He honestly wouldn't have been surprised.

He jumped a bit when Mansourah materialized next to him, then he glared at their companion.

"Magic?" he demanded.

"Skill," Mansourah said distinctly. "I could teach you, if you like."

When hell freezes over, was half out of his mouth before he thought better of it. He didn't imagine Mansourah of Neroche had anything useful to teach him, but he was in reduced circumstances. At the moment, he was open to quite a few things he would have otherwise dismissed.

"Did you see anything?"

Mansourah shook his head. "No spells, no animals, no one inside. Are you sure about this?"

"My mother claims I should be."

"Your mother also thinks I should wed one of your cousins."

"You could do worse," Acair said with a shrug.

Mansourah shut his mouth around whatever he'd intended to say and apparently settled for a look of consternation. "Miach would kill me."

"I'd be more worried what Queen Mhorghain would do to you, but that's just me." Acair looked at Léirsinn. "I think you should remain—"

"Nay."

He sighed. He wasn't sure what else he could offer her in the way of protection, not that she would have accepted it. He had a dagger down the side of his boot and a very large collection of insults at the ready to hurl in her defense. Perhaps that was the best they could hope for at the moment.

He nodded, then looked at Mansourah. "I must admit that I don't know exactly what I'm looking for," he began.

"Sometimes that's the best way to find it," Mansourah said easily. "Let's see what's inside."

Acair didn't want to feel a twinge of anything that couldn't be comfortably placed in the *Reasons to Murder a Prince of Neroche* saddlebag he'd dedicated to that middle-ish child of the terrifying Queen Desdhemar of Neroche, but again, there it was. His life could hardly be called his own at the moment. All the more reason to see if there was anything to what his mother had advised him to do. He nodded to his companions, then led the way forward.

The house in front of them turned out to be nothing more than a rustic little place that had obviously not been lived in for years. Spells hung in tatters over doorways and alongside windows. He opened the door, somewhat surprised to find it unlocked, then pushed it fully open. He ignored the shiver that went through him—exhilaration, naturally, not fear—and was more grateful than he should have been that a spell of something foul didn't immediately fall upon him as he walked inside.

A thick layer of dust blanketed everything, something he thought best not to disturb overmuch. There was unfortunately nothing to be done about footprints on the floor.

"There's something on the tea table," Mansourah said quietly. "An open book."

Acair didn't dare speculate, so he simply walked over to the table set there before the hearth and looked down. He wasn't sure there was any point in trying to read the damned thing, but his curiosity, as it usually did, got the better of him. He brushed aside the dust that obscured the top page and found a date written there.

"Almost twenty years ago," Léirsinn said in surprise. "Has the place been empty for that long, do you think?"

"I haven't been here in far longer than that," Acair said slowly. "I wonder—"

Léirsinn's fingers digging into his arm made him wince. He looked at her in time to watch her nod toward a spot next to the hearth. He looked in the direction she was indicating, but saw nothing. He glanced about the great room, but all he saw was his ever-present companion, that damned spell of death, standing a pace or two away from them, watching the hearth as well. Acair didn't suppose that was any sort of endorsement of anything save of his own blindness, so he looked back at Léirsinn.

"What do you see?" he asked, his mouth as dry as some parched bit of cursed soil in Shettlestoune.

"You," she said hoarsely. "A very young you."

"Bollocks."

She put her hand on the back of his elbow. "Your spell is going over to . . . ah . . . well, that younger you."

He could see his minder spell, true, but past that, all he saw was Mansourah of Neroche's shadow almost reaching the dust-covered hearthrug. He would have commented on the untidy condition of the house, but words failed him. He supposed that might have been from shock, but he wasn't certain he should be the one to offer an opinion on the matter. He watched in astonishment as the spell that followed him stretched out a bony arm toward the hearth.

The damned thing took what he could now see was a shadow of a lad of tender years by the hand—

"Oh, but this is absolute rubbish," he blustered furiously.

He had to do that because what he was watching was no longer what he was seeing. It was as if he'd been simply plucked out of his currently delightful life and deposited without care into his rather miserable past.

He saw himself at the fire, reaching up to take a spell from off the mantel. That younger him unwrapped the spell, examined it, then tossed it in the fire in disgust. A noise startled that poor, foolish shadow of a lad and he bolted, only a piece of himself caught on the door.

It was as if a bit of his soul remained there, unable to move, trapped in a place that was absolutely not suitable for a boy of ten summers, no matter his parentage.

He watched in what he could only term horror as an old man, the mage he'd knocked off the ladder on his way by, walked into the house, pulled the remains of the spell out of the fire, and shook off the sparks.

Then he turned and looked at Acair.

Not the young him, but the current him that was standing at present in a dust-covered gathering chamber, flanked by a woman he thought he couldn't live without and a royal princeling he knew he could most definitely jettison without regret at his earliest opportunity.

Or at least he thought the mage was looking at the current incarnation of himself.

It didn't last very long before the man turned his sights on that poor lad caught at the door. Acair didn't stop to consider whether or not it was foolish, he simply stepped in front of that young, stupid version of himself and protected the lad. He wasn't sure what he expected, but the look of absolute loathing he received from that mage by the fire—

Acair came back to himself to find his cheek stinging as if

he'd been smartly slapped, which he realized he had been and by that damned Mansourah of Neroche.

"You'll regret that," he growled.

"You were shouting," Mansourah said, looking rather startled. "Don't do that again, though I won't deny that I enjoyed the terror in your voice. Still, don't do it again."

Acair wondered if they'd lingered too long, but he was too caught up in a dream that had felt a damned sight too much like reality to do anything but stand there and shake.

"Ye gads," he managed, "I need a drink."

"I'll go see if all your shrieking called any of your bastard brothers to come admire the spectacle," Mansourah said grimly. "Be prepared to flee."

Acair hardly needed the injunction as he had no desire to remain behind and watch anything else untoward. He ignored the stinging of his cheek—surely Mansourah could have delivered a more gentlemanlike tap—and stumbled out of the small gathering chamber. If Léirsinn had to half hold him up as they left the house, well, he would ignore it and thank her later.

He finally stopped under the eaves of the forest, uncomfortably aware that he'd paused there all those years ago. If there was one thing to be said about the accursed soil he stood on, it was that it hadn't changed all that much so the spot was easily recognized. He leaned against a tree, concentrating on not looking as if he were desperately dragging air into his lungs. It was difficult.

He tried to look at the house sitting there so unassumingly in the clearing, but all he could see was that poor sniveling child so full of bluster flinging himself into the shape of something with wings. He also couldn't rid himself of the sight of that piece of his soul being caught on that door.

The worst, though, was the sight of that mage looking at him. At *him*, as if he had been standing in that gathering room in his present form, facing off with a mage in *his* current incarnation.

What he did know was that he would never admit to having toppled into a pile of snow when Mansourah stepped up next to him. Worse still was that he wasn't sure the lad hadn't materialized in the usual magicless way. The prince reached out and hauled Acair to his feet.

"Nothing to be seen," he said quietly, "but I don't like the feeling here. Where to now?"

"You know where to," Acair said, trying not to gasp for breath. "We've already discussed this at length."

"I thought you were trying to torment me," Mansourah muttered. "Are you certain?"

The truth was, there was only one other place in the whole of the Nine Kingdoms he wanted to visit less than he wanted to skip off to his maternal grandmother's house, but things were what they were.

"Of course," Acair said. He reached for Léirsinn's hand. "I'm sure we'll be invited in for tea."

"That's what I'm afraid of," Mansourah said honestly. "Any more cousins I need to keep a watch out for?"

"And by telling you as much, rob any of those cousins of the opportunity to pursue your charming self?" Acair said. "I think discretion is the order of the day." He looked at Léirsinn. "Let's be off, shall we? More delightful adventures await."

She said nothing, but he could tell she was worried. He would have reassured her that he had everything under control, but the truth was, he didn't.

He started to march off with a cheery spring to his step, but it was difficult. As much as he didn't want to admit it, he felt absolutely shattered by what he'd seen. He wasn't sure what he'd expected to find inside that house, but it hadn't been what he'd seen. Damned unnerving, that.

He also didn't appreciate that rubbish his dam had foisted off on him about his needing to collect bits of his soul that he'd left behind. Surely an insignificant piece of naughtiness such as the one perpetrated in that house didn't count. If he'd left anything behind, it had been his dignity, courtesy of his hasty flight away from the bloody place.

But the worst thing of all was his inability to shake the sensation he had of being watched.

He glanced casually at Mansourah only to find the prince of Neroche studying him with a hint of a frown creasing his noble brow. He prided himself on his ability to carry on an unspoken conversation across a ballroom, so he saw no reason not to attempt the same at the moment.

Do you sense that we're being observed? was what he would have asked but imagined he didn't need to.

Dolt, what do you think?

Acair mouthed a vile insult and had a smirk in return. He turned away and shook his head. What was the world coming to when he could exchange friendly banter with an insufferably virtuous royal of that stripe and not have tummy upset afterward?

He wasn't sure he wanted to know.

What he did know, however, was that whoever was watching them was playing a terrible game of chess. Perhaps it wasn't even as lofty as that. He felt a bit like a mouse in a stall, darting frantically about whilst being watched by a fat, lazy cat who blocked the only exit. Time was being bided, and he had the feeling he was intended to know the same.

All the more reason not to be absolutely helpless in the face of that deadly game.

He would see what his granny's inner sanctum had to offer in the way of details he might need. He wasn't sure at the moment if it was more critical to identify who was stalking him or who had made the spell that was also stalking him. It was odd how both seemed to be about the same foul work. He didn't want to believe that both were linked to the same mage, but what did he know?

Nothing was what he knew, nothing past the need to keep Léirsinn safe and unravel the threads tightening around him.

He set his face forward and carried on.

Thirteen

There were strange things afoot in the Nine Kingdoms.

Léirsinn could scarce believe she was considering the like. She who had never given thought to anything past what the port town of Sàraichte might hold for her, now contemplating the state of the entire world? It was almost too ridiculous to be believed.

She wasn't sure that word didn't apply itself rather handily to the whole of her life at present. Her current circumstances were proof enough of that.

She had recently flown—flown, not ridden—for endless hours on the back of a black dragon who tended to nip if his master got too close but who liked to nudge her hand or warm her feet with his remarkably soft, fire-snorting nose. She was wearing clothing gifted her by a witch who seemed to believe she might be engaging in nefarious doings in her future and should be dressed appropriately.

That same witch had sent her son on a quest to search for lost parts of his soul, though what he was supposed to do with them if he found them was anyone's guess. She had listened to Acair and his mother discuss the particulars on the way out the door the morning before and only her own vast amounts of self-control earned over years of refraining from snorting had kept her from doing the same then.

Or at least it had until she'd gone to that dusty, deserted little house and had a good look inside. A *look*, if she could term that business properly.

She'd been a little surprised by the lack of spells, true, or anything that might have indicated it was a mage's house. What had left her speechless had been seeing that lad of ten summers, or, rather, the faintest shadow of a lad of about ten summers, trapped on a piece of wood that had seemingly splintered off the main door.

She'd suspected that she'd been looking at a part of Acair's soul.

The strangest thing of all had been watching Acair's minder spell reach for that piece of soul's hand and pull it along with them as they fled—

She pulled herself away from that memory before it unnerved her more than it had originally. She forced herself to concentrate on the business at hand, which seemed limited at the moment to standing a few paces away from two men who alternated between insulting each other and—an admittedly recent development—considering nefarious plans together. If she'd been a more frivolous woman, she might have decided that she had stared at their painfully handsome selves a bit too long and it was time to look for somewhere to sit before she swooned into a snowbank.

She wasn't one to feel fragile very often. It took a certain amount of spine to face off with four-footed stallions. She was accustomed to correcting ponies with a sharp tongue and keeping stable lads in check with nothing but a look. Those two there were definitely not stable hands, however, and she was so far out of her normal routine that all she felt capable of at the moment was staring at them stupidly and wondering how anyone managed to get anything done with them in view.

Mansourah had lost the very regal-looking clothing Fionne of Fàs had so kindly gifted him the morning before and was dressed in simple hunter's garb. If she had been a maid looking for a husband, she would have happily entertained his offer. No wonder Acair's cousins had been so dazzled by him.

Acair's gear was suited more to nefarious deeds than a visit to a prospective father-in-law, though she supposed she shouldn't have expected anything else. He wasn't in the market for a woman any more than she was in the market for a man, especially one who looked like he did.

Or so she continued to tell herself with an increasing lack of enthusiasm.

At the very least, they made a very dangerous pair, those two. They were also conversing instead of threatening to kill each other, which she thought might be an improvement over their usual interactions. She wondered what they'd been discussing while she'd been lost in thought, then decided perhaps it wouldn't be that difficult to guess. The endless chewing on the same topic had been what had left her daydreaming in the first place.

"We can*not*," Acair said, sounding faintly exasperated. "She'll sense anything you use."

"I'm not sure how we accomplish this without it," Mansourah said. "I have spells—"

"Your Highness, what you have are children's charms," Acair said seriously. "Do you honestly not know who she is? She'll see through anything you think you'll hide behind, then you'll gravely regret your cheek when you find yourself at her supper table, *if* you land at her table, which I can't guarantee. She might serve you supper, or she might *have* you for supper. Trying to sneak into her house will likely result in the latter, no matter your parentage."

"So, you're suggesting I hide in the woods like a common criminal whilst you trot off to do a bit of snooping."

"My stock in trade."

"Well, that at least is something I agree with," Mansourah said, with feeling. "As you will, then. Léirsinn and I—"

"Wait," Léirsinn said, putting her hand up, "I'm not staying behind."

Mansourah looked at her in surprise. "I think it would be terribly unwise for you to venture farther here. I wouldn't go near Cruihniche of Fàs without being prepared to use both arrows and many powerful spells, no matter what Acair says."

"But I can see things," she protested.

"So can he," Mansourah said briskly.

"Parts of his soul that he's lost?"

Mansourah shut his mouth apparently around whatever else he'd planned to say, then looked at Acair. "This is daft."

"But apparently quite a thing," Acair said. He pursed his lips. "I'm not enthusiastic about what thing this might be, but I fear Léirsinn has a point."

Mansourah sighed deeply. "I don't like this and I hope we don't regret what this stirs up. Well, you'll need werelight—"

"We'll manage," Acair assured him.

"Or spells of defense, at the very least," Mansourah finished pointedly. "You know I can't save you inside those walls."

Léirsinn fully expected Acair to toss off some cheeky remark about spells, sword skill, and Mansourah of Neroche's lack of both, but he only shook his head and clapped Mansourah on the shoulder.

"We'll manage," he repeated with a brief smile. "Don't worry yourself into a state whilst we're away or my sister will shout at me. Besides, I'm a terrible black mage with a foul reputation, remember? This is the kind of thing I do for sport."

"With a woman in tow?"

Léirsinn stepped between them before Acair could answer, mostly because she already knew what he would say and the subject had been discussed too much already. She was going to help him however she could and continue to tell herself it was simply because she needed his aid in the future.

She embraced Mansourah briefly, then turned and walked away before she could see his expression. Acair had said he needed a peek at one of his grandmother's books, so to his grandmother's solar they would go.

Though she could hardly believe he had been willing to come so far for only that.

Acair caught up to her immediately, then continued on with her into deeper shadows. She realized after a bit that whatever else he could do, the man could certainly walk without making a sound. She gave up counting the times he put his hand out to stop her, then nodded for her to follow him around some hazard or other. Obviously, he'd done that sort of thing before.

In time, the forest began to seem a bit more regimented, as if the trees had been instructed to grow in a certain pattern and they hadn't dared argue. She could make out a hint of a road in the distance, but Acair didn't lead them to it. He continued to walk a path that he seemed very familiar with for reasons she imagined she could divine without any help.

The lines of trees ended suddenly, and an enormous clearing appeared. She stumbled to a halt, then gaped at the sight of the large, stately home there in front of them. It made her uncle's manor house seem like a potting shed. She wasn't sure it looked like a very welcoming sort of place, but it was definitely grand.

Obviously, they had arrived.

She looked at Acair, but he was only studying his grand-mother's house thoughtfully. He reached for her hand, but said nothing. He was wearing gloves his mother had gifted him, sup-ple black leather ones that Léirsinn wasn't sure his mother hadn't laced with some sort of spell to aid him whilst he went about his nefarious deeds. The pair she was wearing was equally well made—and no doubt equally enspelled—but she hadn't looked at them past putting them on.

At the moment, all she knew was that Acair's hand was far steadier than hers, but perhaps she shouldn't have expected any-thing less. It wasn't as if he hadn't climbed over walls in the dead of night before.

"I'm not sure I asked you what you saw," he said absently. He looked at her then. "When was it?"

"Yesterday morning," she said faintly, "at that mage's house, and do you think this is the proper time to discuss it?"

He shrugged. "A bit of distraction before battle."

She'd heard of worse ideas, she supposed, but not many. "I can't remember," she lied. "What about you?"

He smiled grimly. "I saw the mage I stole that spell from."

"Did you?" she asked in surprise. "And?"

"Nothing more interesting than that," he said, "and fortunately for us all, I've decided it was simply my imagination fueled by my mother's profoundly undrinkable coffee."

"You must have a good imagination, then."

"Either that, or she's a terrible cook," he said solemnly. He paused, then shook his head. "The man I imagined I saw looked damned familiar, I'll admit, but I still can't place him." He paused. "'Tis possible but highly unlikely that I was too busy being startled to take a proper note of his features."

She wasn't sure if *startled* quite described his reaction, but she thought it might be better to move right past that. "I thought you were just putting on a show to throw Mansourah off."

He shot her a brief smile. "Of course. It wouldn't do to have him see my softer, less murderous side. One must keep up appearances, you know."

"Must one?"

He sighed deeply. "In my business, darling, I fear 'tis all too true. Black magery is a ruthless trade. A terrible reputation is sometimes all that lets me sleep peacefully at night."

She was beginning to wonder if he ever had a peaceful night's sleep, but she decided that it wasn't a useful thing to wonder aloud. She didn't protest when he pulled her close and wrapped his arms around her. If he trembled, he didn't say anything about it and she didn't point it out to him. She was too busy trying to smother her own unease.

That's all it was, of course. She was never afraid. She had faced feisty stallions and come away the victor. She had bested the demons that flanked her uncle—metaphorically, of course—and learned to ignore them. When she had realized that Fear was stalking her, she hadn't run away from him or demanded that he leave her be. She'd told him to take a leaning position against the nearest horse fence and keep his bloody mouth shut.

Unfortunately, she wasn't dealing with her fear at the moment. She was facing things utterly beyond her normal challenges with not a spell to hand nor any magic to use.

She refused to think about how far she'd fallen that she was even considering the like.

"Are you—" Her voice cracked and she had to clear her throat. "Are you ever afraid? In truth?"

"Never," Acair said seriously.

"Not even now?"

He snorted lightly. "This is akin to a bit of bother over having a fine dining establishment reserve the wrong table for me."

"You are a disgusting man."

He laughed a little, something she was fairly certain she'd never heard him do before. He sighed and rested his cheek against her hair.

"And so I am. Clever you for seeing it." He paused. "Would this be an inappropriate place to offer a maudlin sentiment about your own charming self?"

"Completely," she said. "Besides, you'll just make an ill-advised comment about the color of my hair, I'll be forced to blacken your eye for it, and then where will we be?"

"I'll claim I was in a brawl with a dragon. It will add to my rakish air, I assure you."

She imagined it would. She sighed deeply, then stood, warm and relatively safe wrapped in both his cloak and his embrace, until she grew too restless to simply stand about any longer. She pulled away and looked at him seriously.

"What will your grandmother do if she catches us?"

"She will embrace me like the long-lost grandson I am and shower me with accolades and kisses." He paused. "Or she might send minions."

"I don't like the sound of that."

"You wouldn't like the look of it either, which is why we shall nip in and out without any trace of our having been there." He reached for her hand. "We'll try the back entrance. No one ever uses it."

"Are you going to tell me why?"

He smiled briefly. "The minions are more terrifying there, of course. To me, that makes the success of slipping by their snoring selves all the sweeter."

"Of course."

She watched a squirrel scamper up a tree, then turn and chirp at them. It was as he spat out a bit of fire that she realized it was Acair's horse. Well, he seemed to be settling in for the duration, which she supposed was all she could ask. She looked at him pointedly before she walked away with Acair, hoping it wouldn't be the last time she saw the damned beast. It wasn't as if either of them had magic enough to fly off under their own power.

Magic. What a ridiculous business.

She was beginning to see, though, why someone might want a bit of it.

The forest was still and the air so cold she was almost certain she could hear her breath as it fell softly to the ground. What she did know with absolute certainty was that she was having no trouble seeing the spell that lay draped over the trees they walked under. She would have mentioned it to Acair, but she had the feeling he had enough to think about at present. The silence wasn't helping her keep her fear in check, though, so she cast about for a topic that didn't involve things she shouldn't have been able to see.

"Can you tell me about her?" she asked. She looked at him quickly. "Your grandmother, I mean."

"Of course," he said easily. "She is Cruihniche of Fàs, that being the name of the land we're crossing, and I don't think it much of an exaggeration to say she is one of the more terrifying souls I've encountered in my very long life."

"Is she worse than your mother and your aunt?" she asked.

He looked as if he couldn't decide if he should laugh or shiver. "My grandmother . . ." He shook his head. "She defies decent description, though I could start by telling you everything she is, then a bit of what she is not."

"I can scarce wait."

"You say that now," he agreed, "but tell me what you think after I make my list. What she *is* is a small, elegant woman, well-spoken, and old as the hills. She has a very long dining table that is endlessly filled by royalty, nobility, and hangers-on who wait months for the opportunity to take a seat. Her chef is beyond compare, her wine-steward without peer, and I've heard but never verified personally that she has wee faeries tending a greenhouse full of herbs and flowers used for beautifying delicate ices and cakes."

Léirsinn smiled. "That doesn't sound too bad."

"I've barely left the gates, if you know what I mean. What she is *not* is kind, merciful, welcoming, or lacking spells that send shivers of dismay down the spines of any number of rulers in the world."

"Does she use them?" Léirsinn asked, then shook her head. "Ignore that, mostly because I can't believe I've asked that."

He smiled briefly. "You've resigned yourself to the realities of several things with a marked lack of grumbling, something I'm sure my mother made note of. My grandmother isn't opposed to using spells, but she's as spare with their use as she is with the amount of tea she'll put in a pot to steep for family. Weak stuff indeed."

"Stingy or uninterested?"

"Choosey," he said. "She's as up to her elbows in foul deeds as the rest of us, but that tends to be overlooked in deference to the exclusivity of her salon. Or so it has been in the past." He frowned thoughtfully. "I'm beginning to think I've been too preoccupied with my own mischief to take the time to truly appreciate her accomplishments."

"Tell me again why we aren't going to the front door and knocking?"

He shot her an uncomfortable look. "I might have, as they say, nicked a knickknack or two."

She felt her mouth fall open. "You stole from your own *grandmother*?"

"It was retaliation for her having criticized one of my favorite cravats," he said promptly. "I took exception to her comments, perhaps a bit too loudly, which left her chasing me from her solar, then sending minions after me over her spike-topped wall. The hastiness of my exit resulted in a great and rather embarrassing rent in my favorite trousers. Revenge was imperative." He shrugged. "I will be forthcoming and say that one of her doilies was also the price for a particularly coveted seat at an extremely exclusive table."

She could only gape at him. "You great whacking snob."

"The supper was unparalleled."

"As was, I'm sure, the company."

"I fear I must agree."

She felt her eyes narrow before she could stop them. "There are times—more often than not—that I can hardly restrain myself from stabbing you."

He stopped, lifted her gloved hand, and kissed the back of it. Gallantly, it had to be said.

"That was before," he said.

"Before what?" she asked with a snort.

"Before I encountered a pitchfork-wielding, red-haired dragoness, and that is all the sentiment you'll have from me tonight. I fear to become too maudlin, lest you lose your resolve to vault over walls with me, something I think you shouldn't be doing."

"You know I'm not going to stay behind so don't waste your breath," she said shortly. "You told Mansourah you were here for your granny's book, but I suspect that isn't the only reason."

He tucked her hand under his elbow and nodded up the path. "It isn't, though I'm not particularly keen to discuss anything else lest listening ears I'm unable to see at the moment overhear my plans. You might want to keep an eye open for what we just saw recently, if you catch my drift."

She wasn't sure if he was referring to pieces of his soul or something else, but she supposed having a look at whatever caught her eye as he concentrated on other business couldn't go wrong. "Do you think you left something behind here?"

He blew his hair out of his eyes, then shook his head. "My dignity, more often than I care to admit, but none of that other rubbish. The worst I combined here was plotting thefts whilst enduring grandmotherly lectures about my failings as a mage and a gentleman."

"Then perhaps I'll just keep my eyes open for pieces of your pride."

He shot her a look. "You are *far* too free with those kinds of barbs at my expense."

"I am not afraid of you," she said, realizing as she said so that she believed it fully. "Besides, I have yet to see anything that leads me to believe you are anything more than your average showy stallion."

He squeezed her hand. "I only hope such will always be the case, poor soft-hearted sap that I have been reduced to." He nodded toward the house. "I think we might safely attempt a vault over the walls if you like, or we could simply try the gate."

"The gate sounds more reasonable," she said. "I might need a bit more practice before I start hurling myself over things."

He nodded, then paused once more. "One last thing that should be noted is that I am here under protest. If I had to make a list of places I didn't want to go, this would be the very last."

"Dead last?"

He seemed to consider. "Let's put it near the bottom—or the top, depending on your perspective. There are places I wouldn't set foot in again if my life depended on it, which is a different list entirely. Places where I *could* go but really don't *want* to go? My grandmother's house is somewhere on that list, very near the top. Her hall is dangerous, but not necessarily lethal." He paused, then looked at her. "Of course, that list was made with a pen dipped in a pot of magic, if you follow."

She had to admit to herself that she did, unfortunately. "Isn't she Mistress Cailleach's sister?"

"You would think that would benefit us here, but I fear not. They are sisters, but there's a reason my great-auntie is as far south as she can take herself without getting soggy. Well, that and my great-aunt is in Sàraichte because she thinks she might find someone with whom to have a—how shall we term it—ah, yes, a bit of a *romance*."

"Mistress Cailleach," Léirsinn managed.

"The very same."

"A romance," she repeated.

"The mind boggles, doesn't it?"

She smiled in spite of herself. "It does."

He didn't move. "Should something happen to me, I want you to get yourself to her solar. I may or may not have taken a spell and slipped it into a crack on the underside of her favorite chair."

"A spell?" she asked. "Written down?"

He shook his head. "One like what I couldn't find in Odhran's workroom. It will work, as that one would have, without any aid from me."

She nodded absently, because she wasn't sure she had the stomach to talk any longer about things she wanted to avoid, then it occurred to her just what he had said. She looked at him and had to make an effort to keep her mouth from falling open.

"You could use it, then," she said in surprise.

"In theory."

"And live."

"One could hope," he agreed.

"No wonder you wanted that other spell."

He nodded carefully. "Indeed."

She would have asked what the spell could do, but she wasn't sure she wanted to know. Either it dealt out death or turned whoever was in the vicinity—including her, she imagined—into mushrooms. With Acair, she just never knew.

He stared off down the path for a moment or two, then looked at her. "You're sure you won't remain here and wait for me?"

"How will you collect those flinty bits of yourself you left behind if I'm not there to look?" she asked. "Just so I know, is there some particular piece of mischief you combined here, or was it just general naughtiness and the pinching of doilies you should feel bad about?"

"Well, I didn't murder anyone," he muttered.

"What did you do, then?"

He dragged his hand through his hair. "If you must know, I stole one of her spells, then stepped aside when she blamed my older brother Garlach for it."

She frowned. "That doesn't sound like anything any other young lad wouldn't do."

"I was thirty-five at the time," he said. "A bit past being young."

She wasn't surprised. "Is that all?"

He shifted uncomfortably. "I can't be certain, but I fear she might have laid a spell on him that causes warts to spring up all over his face every time he sees a beautiful woman."

"How long did that last?"

"It is ongoing." He shrugged. "He's not a pleasant man and this, ah, affliction of his has caused him to lose what little chance he's ever had with even the most desperate of lassies. I should say that it serves him right given that he is completely lacking in any redeeming character traits, but . . ." He took a deep breath and blew it out. "I have suffered the odd pang of regret now and again for his plight, given that I was responsible for it. Or that might have been indigestion. I never can decide."

Léirsinn smiled in spite of herself. "Have you thought about just asking her to remove it?"

"And admit my part in it? She would likely take the damned thing off him and put it on *me*."

"Couldn't you take it from him?"

"The better question is, would I? The answer is, now that I think about it, nay."

"Did you do a good deed yesterday?"

He drew himself up. "I'm sure I did."

"I'm sure you didn't. This could count, you know."

He tugged her along with him down the path. "We'll need to move forward in silence now. Spells everywhere and all that sort of rot."

It took her a fair tromp along soft paths before she realized what bothered her the most. It was one thing to walk into his mother's house where she was fairly sure they wouldn't die. It was also something to be chased by black mages but trust that Acair would somehow get them to safety.

For some reason, she didn't care at all for their current errand or the feeling of the forest.

They were being watched and she had the feeling it wasn't by Mansourah.

"Acair?"

He smiled briefly. "Ah, my name. How it rolls from the tongue of a lovely woman, aye?"

"You're insufferable."

"But hard to look away from, I know. You needed something?"

"Does she know we're coming, do you think?" She paused. "Is she watching us?"

He shot her a look she had no trouble interpreting. She had the feeling he was just as aware of whatever was watching them as she was and that it most likely wasn't his grandmother.

For all she knew, it would be safer inside a witch's hall than outside in a forest where a mage prowled about.

She didn't want to think about why that might be so.

Fourteen

There was nothing like a bit of burgling to raise a man's spirits.

Acair supposed the whole exercise was made quite a bit easier by two unexpected boons. First was the fact that Léirsinn was proving to be very adept at pointing out spells he was too blind to see himself. Second, and perhaps even more critical to their survival at present, most of his grandmother's fouler minions were sound asleep at their posts. If he hadn't known better, he would have suspected there was something foul afoot.

But since that was usually him about his workaday activities, he brushed aside the unease and concentrated on the work before him.

The inability to use his magic wasn't even a bother at present. He never used it whilst about his current sort of business anyway. Where was the sport in that? With magic, he could have wafted in as an evening breeze, pinched what he wanted, then continued back out the same way, treasure in hand. But to enter a place guarded by spells and retrieve what he needed with naught but his wits and a decent bit of bluster? His life was full of delights, true, but a bit of plunder in the old-fashioned way was an especially delicious pleasure.

It was also safer that way, he had to admit. So many kings and landholders set spells of ward designed to shout out an alarm should anyone with magic creep over their walls uninvited. Suspicious bastards, but, alas, the world was not the paradise of his youth.

He considered the lay of the land, as it were, and the terrible little trolls he knew were guarding, even with just their snores alone, his grandmother's back door. He could bring to mind several rather unpleasant encounters with them, but perhaps he deserved nothing less. He had accepted invitations to his grandmother's house countless times, but he imagined she had kept a tally of the number of times he'd wandered uninvited into her private chambers to salivate over things behind glass and sturdy spells. If he'd found those to be the most interesting items in a grand house full of truly appalling things, who could blame him? His curiosity, as his mother would have said, was likely going to be the last thing he indulged.

But as he had no intention of skipping off into the eternal sunset anytime soon, he would simply take care, be quickly about his business, and get himself and the woman he lo—er, *liked* quite well back over the walls and away from the enormous manor house before his gran was the wiser. When he was at his leisure in a few months, he would take the trouble to make a proper investigation into things about that same grandmother that had puzzled him. There was ample history there for the studying.

For the moment, though, what he wanted was that book his mother had advised him to filch. With any luck, it might contain a list of crotchety old bastards who might have sent a tenacious, cranky spell of death after him to vex him. The sooner he solved *that* problem, the better off they would all be. Happening upon any stray bits of himself along the way would only be a boon. Indeed, he had the feeling he was going to need all the aid he could muster to finish the quest he'd so reluctantly started.

If he could also liberate that particular item he'd told Léirsinn about—something he'd never thought to need, actually— from under his grandmother's chair, he would consider the venture a complete success.

Léirsinn's hand was suddenly on his arm and he froze. He looked where she was pointing to find a fat, snoring lad half sprawled over the back stoop. He nodded, then very carefully walked with her to the back door. He picked the lock silently, then opened the back kitchen door. He stepped over the slumbering guardsman, made sure Léirsinn had followed him, then closed the door behind them. He silently turned the lock, then looked at her.

She only returned his look and shrugged.

He took a careful breath, then carried on.

He made note of the innards of his grandmother's home and realized that he tended to judge houses more on their ability to provide him with places to hide and less on their beauty. His granny fared well on both, though he couldn't say that her house extended any sort of friendly welcome. If she could have forced the very air he breathed into some sort of regimented order, he suspected she would have.

The hallways, as it happened, were replete with useful alcoves whilst everything else was placed at regular intervals, including furniture, plants, mirrors, and doorways. Even the carpets seemed terrified to buckle or lose track of any of their threads. He understood. He'd never made a visit during which he hadn't been excruciatingly aware of his appearance and manners.

It had made poaching a doily or two almost irresistible, he had to admit.

He spared a wish for even the faintest hint of werelight, but set the thought aside almost immediately. He could see well enough in the dark and that had the added benefit of not disturbing the slumber of any sleeping butlers, of which he found several on the journey down the main passageway.

He made the appropriate turns through the house, avoiding grand staircases where possible and keeping to the darkest of shadows everywhere else. He tiptoed with Léirsinn through a great room full of statuary that he wasn't entirely sure weren't his grandmother's enemies preserved for all time in marble—she shared some unsettling proclivities with his mother—and arrived finally at a particularly unassuming doorway.

He looked at Léirsinn but she was only watching him with wide eyes. He understood. The damned house was definitely built to intimidate.

He tried the knob and wasn't surprised to find it unlocked. For all he knew—and he thought he might have good reason for being cautious—his granny had had un-noticed minions following him from the moment he crossed the boundaries of her land. He hadn't sensed anything, but the uncomfortable truth was, his grandmother was a witch of the first water. He would have given much to have been allowed free rein in her private solar for even a single hour. He had attempted the same on more than one occasion, calling upon both his vast stores of charm and the ability to make a nuisance of himself, but he remained unen-lightened.

Hence the need for a bit of sticky-fingeredness.

He kept his hand on the doorknob for another moment or two, then decided there was nothing to do but press forward. Without magic, they wouldn't set off any alarms save ones nor-mally triggered by the average housemaid. He supposed he could don the persona of distracted manservant well enough in the dark. Escape would be difficult, but within reach. He had al-ready discussed the possibility with Léirsinn earlier, though he imagined she'd tried to put the warning out of her head as quickly as possible.

He let them in, looked about the chamber to make certain they were alone, then closed the door soundlessly behind them. He let go of a breath he hadn't realized he'd been clinging to so thoroughly, then looked at his companion.

"Well," he said, "we're here."

"Thrilling," she said, sounding as if it were anything but. "What now?"

"I need a book."

"I was afraid of that."

"They're useful."

"I wouldn't disagree with that," she whispered, "just with where you seem to think you need to look for them."

"I crave excitement like another might crave a bit of flight on the back of a spectacular horse."

She pursed her lips at him. "Let's discuss that later, after we've escaped."

He couldn't argue with that idea, so he turned his mind to a study of the chamber. He had never seen the book his mother had described for him, but knowing his grandmother as he did, he suspected she would have kept it either behind glass, behind spells, or behind her favorite decanter of port. There were bookshelves aplenty lining two walls, draperies covering windows on a third, then an enormous fireplace occupying the fourth. Chairs were set in a pleasing configuration in front of that hearth, chairs he was relieved to see were not only the usual ones set there, but ones that were comfortingly empty.

He identified a sideboard bearing a full complement of what he was certain would be delicate, exclusive liquors. It occupied a prime spot within that gaggle of bookshelves, which seemed to him the most likely spot to begin his search.

"Do you have a grandfather here as well?" Léirsinn whispered. "Just so I know if we should expect disapproval from more than one direction."

He smiled briefly. "Not to worry, we've only my grandmother to worry about. My grandfather ran off with a parlor maid before I was born, or so I've heard, but I've never taken the time to verify the truth of it. For all I know, my grandmother turned him into fire irons." He shot her a look. "It's been done before."

"By Prince Soilléir?" she asked uneasily.

"He certainly has the spells for it," Acair said, "but unfortunately he only uses his powers for good, or so he claims. I have absolutely no idea what he really does save endlessly put expensive creams on his visage to hide his age."

"Is he old?"

"Extremely, though you wouldn't know it to look at him." He shrugged. "Virtuous living, I suppose."

"I'm not sure I want to know more."

"I'm not sure I want to think about any more," he said honestly. "But remind me later if you're curious about either essence-changers or fire irons. At the moment, let's find what we need and escape whilst we still can." He nodded to a long sideboard. "We'll try there first."

He walked with her across a floor that didn't squeak—reassuring, he supposed—and stopped in front of a selection of bottles. He considered, carefully moved several to the right, then reached out and pushed on a square of wooden paneling behind them.

It opened soundlessly.

"Amazing," Léirsinn breathed.

He shot her a look. "I may have done this before."

"Less amazing, then," she said, "but not by much. What's inside?"

"Not purses made of my grandfather's innards, one could hope," he said grimly. He looked for spells adorning the opening, then hesitated and turned to Léirsinn. "Do you see anything dangerous that I'm missing?"

"Besides your minder spell next to you who's about to fall over into a pile of crystal decanters?" she said, reaching around him and making a shooing motion. "I can't see a damned thing. The fire isn't bright enough."

He couldn't see much either, but his ever-present companion wasn't hissing at him and he didn't sense anything else with his death uppermost on its list of things to see to, so he reached inside the cubby and felt about.

He ignored piles of gold, a trio of purses he wasn't sure *weren't* someone's innards, and a few crystal things he supposed were made of mages' tears. He found a trio of books and wasted no time in pulling them free. He checked the spines, then returned two, because he was feeling particularly virtuous at the moment. He took hold of his prize and looked at Léirsinn.

"Let's go."

"You aren't going to steal that," she said in surprise.

"Of course I'm going to steal it—"

"Didn't you learn anything from King Simeon's solar?"

"Aye, that I should pay more attention to those I make bargains with. Let's be away whilst we still can."

She gave him a look he wasn't entirely sure she hadn't learned from his mother.

"Didn't your mother say your granny might already be annoyed with you?" she asked.

"She's annoyed with everyone, so this won't worsen her opinion of me. Besides, 'tis obvious by the dust on this thing that she never uses it. She'll never miss it."

She pulled something out of the satchel slung over her chest and held it up. "Book, pencil. Your mother gave me both. Why don't you use them and leave everything here undisturbed? Then your grandmother won't know you've been here."

He had the feeling his gran would know anyway, but considered what Léirsinn held in her hands. There was something to be said for at least making the attempt to keep his visit a secret. He accepted the tools his mother had given Léirsinn, then had another look about the chamber as she lit a candle in the embers of the evening's fire. He waited for her to set the candle down in an advantageous locale, then took his grandmother's *Book of Oddities and Disgusting Spells* in his hands and tried not to give in to the temptation to chortle with delight. It even smelled exclusive.

He took a deep breath, then opened the worn leather cover.

The book didn't disappoint. It was such a treasure trove of appalling things, he could hardly decide where to begin. He flipped page after page simply brimming over with so much goodness about badness that he was finally reduced to feeling his way down onto a side chair so he could properly appreciate what he held in his hands.

"Well?" Léirsinn prompted.

He looked up at her. "There is too much here. I can't begin to decide where to start."

"Close the book, open it back up to a random page, then start copying."

"Oh, I couldn't possibly do that," he demurred. "What if I choose amiss? How do I favor one thing and slight another—"

"Acair, just pick something."

He was torn between genuine distress over having to make a choice and quite a bit of unreasonable delight over the way she said his name. He generally heard *my lord* and a rather alarming number of variations of *you bloody bastard* to suit even the most discriminating of ears. His name, though? Not many used that and never with the ease she did—

"Acair?"

He looked at her and blinked. "Aye?"

"You're half asleep and we don't have all night." She paused. "Do we?"

"I don't imagine we do," he said, dragging himself back to the matter at hand. He had to suppress the urge to simply wring his hands over an impossible decision. He looked at her. "I can't limit myself to a few notes. I could spend the rest of my life unraveling the mysteries and stalking the mages listed here—"

"If you don't choose five of each and do it now, you won't have any life in which to investigate them," she warned.

She had a point there. He forced himself to ignore how much more sense it made to simply pilfer the entire tome and hope for the best on his way over the walls. A choice it would have to be.

He sighed. "Very well, I'll try."

She held the candle up and leaned over his shoulder to look at the pages with him.

It took him several moments before he realized he wasn't seeing what was on the page. He was far too distracted by the woman resting her chin on his shoulder. He tilted his head to look at her.

"I can't concentrate."

"Shall I slap you smartly to help?"

"I think you might do more good if you stopped breathing in my ear."

"I'm not breathing, I'm wheezing in terror."

"I fear, darling, that it has the same effect."

She snorted at him and went to fetch a stool. She sat down and held up the candle. "Better?"

"Only a bit, but I am nothing if not disciplined." He gave her a quick smile, then attempted to concentrate on the task at hand.

He wished the damned thing had been divided properly into sections, one for lists of terrible spells and another for dreadful oddities that seemed to include names of mages scribbled in the margins. Unfortunately, it was simply a compendium of random spells, hastily scribbled notes about various mages he did and unfortunately sometimes did not recognize, and vignettes about happenings that he suspected it might take him years to study properly. He gave it his best effort, truly he did, but in the end, he had to concede the battle. He looked at Léirsinn.

"I can't choose."

"Are you sure?"

"Perfectly," he said. "We'll need to take it with us."

"I don't think your grandmother will be happy," she warned.

"I don't think my grandmother will have any idea it was me to nick it," he said. He handed her back her pencil and copybook, then paused. "Do you mind holding the prize as well? I have one more thing to look for."

She accepted his grandmother's book with the same enthusiasm she might have a live asp, but he couldn't fault her for it. He thanked her, then rose and strode over to the hearth. He didn't have to examine any of the chairs there to know which flowery, overstuffed bit of business belonged solely to his grandmother. He tossed the extra pillows onto another chair, virtuously ignoring the handwork adorning them lest he be tempted beyond what he could bear, and tipped the chair back.

He knew exactly what he was looking for and where it was to be found, and he wasn't disappointed. He reached out and came away with the other thing for which he'd come to his grandmother's lair.

A spell of un-noticing.

He held it up to the light, that sparkling thing that resembled a delicate piece of filigreed gold. It was as perfect as the day he'd fashioned it, which he knew shouldn't have surprised him. He had intended it to last for several centuries.

He could remember the afternoon of its creation with perfect clarity simply because he'd been at his own home that he rarely visited, sitting in his own private solar in front of the fire, and contemplating the vicissitudes of life. It had occurred to him that finding oneself in a tight spot now and again wasn't an experience limited to mages who were fools. He had never intended to be without magic, but he'd also been very cognizant that the world could be a dodgy place. His mother had muttered on more than one occasion something about *a pinch of prevention is worth more than a handful of faery wings* or rot of that sort. He'd never seen his mother caught unawares and he'd been fairly certain that even Ruamharaiche's well hadn't caught his father entirely flat-footed, so hiding the odd spell in places where he wouldn't find himself without absolutely dire need had seemed like a prudent idea at the time.

That he needed the like at the moment was absolutely appalling.

He came back to himself to realize Léirsinn had crossed the solar and come to a stop next to him. She was looking at the spell between his fingers with an expression on her face that he couldn't quite identify, but perhaps she was seeing things he couldn't. He'd seen that sort of look blossom into a bout of screaming—and indulged in the same himself, truth be told—so he quickly reached out and put his hand on her arm.

"'Tis only a spell," he whispered.

She shook her head as if she attempted to shake off the effects of drink that had been too strong. She looked at him in shock.

"It's beautiful," she managed.

"Well," he said, wondering if he should be offended or not, "I'm not completely without the odd redeeming attribute."

"Did *you* make that?" she asked in surprise.

He should definitely have been offended, he decided, but he just couldn't muster up the effort. He settled for a scowl. "Is that so unthinkable?"

She looked at him in a way that reminded him so much of Soilléir of Cothromaiche, he flinched.

"You made that," she said, as if she simply couldn't believe it of him.

"Shocking, isn't it?"

She shook her head, waving aside his words in frustration. "Nay, not that the spell isn't beautiful, because it is. I mean . . ." She looked at him as if she'd never seen him before. "You did that. Rather, you're *able* to do that."

"A trifle," he said dismissively, deciding abruptly it was less unsettling to be offended than it was to realize he was on the verge of coloring discreetly. "But feel free to heap more accolades upon my deserving head. I've had a rough go of things over the past few months."

"I don't think your arrogance needs anything added to it."

He was a bloody braggart, true. He looked at her knowingly. "I believe you might swoon."

"At the moment, I believe you might be right."

He tucked the spell into the purse at his belt, then looked at her. "We should go whilst we still are able to. I have everything I need."

She looked at him once more in consternation, then extinguished her candle and set it on the mantel. He took her hand, led her toward the door, then came to an abrupt and rather ungainly halt.

Damn, and so close to being gone.

He felt Léirsinn press herself close to his left side whilst that damned minder spell cowered behind him to his right. Léirsinn leaned up to whisper to him.

"I'm afraid to ask."

"Wise," he said, not because he was particularly spare with words, but because he knew what he was facing there.

His spell made no comment, but he hadn't expected anything else.

Every light in the damned solar suddenly blazed to life with a crispness that didn't surprise him in the slightest. He might have been tempted to do the same thing in their place, which he wasn't entirely sure he wouldn't be doing—and sooner rather than later.

"And here I thought we were going to escape death," Léirsinn murmured.

Acair had hoped so as well, but apparently not. Death was waiting there by the doorway, dressed in a perfectly pressed, starched-collared gown and boots that buttoned up the side. He knew about that preferred style of boot because he'd had ample opportunity to examine several pairs of them over the years as they'd kicked him in the arse on his way through the front gates.

At least he could say, with the exception of that one trip over the back garden wall where he'd made such a hash of his trousers, he'd managed to be ejected out the front gates.

He had the feeling the only place he was going to see this time around was the insides of his grandmother's dungeon.

He cleared his throat and prepared to make introductions.

Fifteen

❈

Léirsinn wasn't sure what she expected Acair's grandmother to look like, but the woman at the doorway wasn't it.

Cruihniche of Fàs was slight, elegant, and dressed so perfectly that Léirsinn felt as if she had weeks' worth of dung on her boots, not just a bit of dirt she'd done her best to leave behind just outside the back door. It had seemed a bit odd to her at first how the house itself had seemed on edge, as if it feared someone might walk through and find something out of place. At the moment, she understood completely.

She could hardly believe it, but if rumor had it aright, that delicate woman there was the sister of Cailleach of Cael and the mother of Fionne of Fàs. Léirsinn had no idea how the branches of their family tree twisted themselves around, but something definitely had taken a radical turn somewhere.

Acair stepped up and discreetly drew her behind him. "Grandmother," he said, making her a low bow.

"You odious little rodent," Cruihniche said crisply. "How dare you show your visage, no matter how handsome it might be, at my door!"

Acair cleared his throat. "If we're going to be entirely accurate, Grandmother, I'm not at your door—"

"You're in my private solar," she shouted, "which you well know. I refuse, Acair, to indulge your penchant for semantics." She motioned him sharply aside. "Let me see who you have hiding behind your sorry self."

"Ah, Grandmother," Acair began.

"*Now*, Acair."

He sighed, then looked over his shoulder. "Sorry," he mouthed.

Léirsinn shook her head in answer. Either both of them were going to escape their current locale, or neither of them would.

Acair sighed, then took a step to his right. "May I present my trusted companion, Léirsinn of Sàraichte. Léirsinn, my beloved and esteemed grandmother, Cruihniche of Fàs."

Léirsinn watched Cruihniche sweep her from head to toe with an assessing glance, then freeze. She looked as if she'd recently taken a hearty bite of a lemon, then her jaw suddenly went slack.

"Oh . . . I see."

Léirsinn wished the woman was merely reacting to an eyeful of Acair's minder spell, but it was obvious Acair's grandmother wasn't looking in that direction. She was looking at her.

She would have ducked back behind Acair, but two things stopped her. One, Acair seemed rather reluctant to allow her to use him as a shield, and two, she realized with a start that she might be the only thing that kept them both alive. She wasn't sure what was going through Mistress Cruihniche's mind, but it didn't seem to be thoughts of murder. She looked instead as if she'd just seen something that had knocked her firmly back on her heels.

Perhaps it was the dragon charm burning a hole in Léirsinn's tunic.

Léirsinn had to look down to make certain she wasn't on fire. The charm was rather warm to the touch even through the cloth, but she'd grown accustomed to it doing unusual things. If it saved them at present, she wasn't going to complain.

She wondered what she was supposed to do to humor Acair's grandmother, then decided there was no point in worrying about it. The woman was either going to slay them both on the spot, or—

Apparently, it was going to be *or*.

Cruihniche gave her another slightly alarmed look, then turned her sights back on her grandson.

"What is that other thing there?" she asked faintly.

"It is a spell," Acair said, "with nefarious intentions at the ready. Never fear, Grandmother, it has its sights only upon me, your humble and penitent scrap of progeny."

His grandmother considered that for a moment or two, then straightened her shoulders and pointed at Acair.

"Grandson, fetch the tea table," she said, seemingly laying hold on her strength. She shot Léirsinn another look, then shook her head and walked back over to the doorway. She bellowed down the hallway for refreshments to be provided, then slammed the door shut.

Léirsinn didn't want to know what those refreshments might entail, but as long as servants were delivering food and drink instead of chains and locks, she was happy to help Acair carry tea things over to a spot in front of the fire. She waited with him until his grandmother had arranged things to her liking, trying not to be too obvious about eyeing what foodstuffs were brought in and laid out. They didn't look lethal, but what did she know? She was in the inner solar of a witch, and she had no means of escape save her own two feet. She didn't think that boded well for her longevity.

"Sit," Cruihniche commanded. "We'll discuss your offenses after we've had a nibble and a sip."

Léirsinn sat where invited and tried to look as trustworthy as possible. She had the feeling she had quite a substantial amount of her companion's lack to make up for.

Cruihniche of Fàs—whatever title she preferred, though Léirsinn thought it best to just call her *Ma'am* and leave it at that—manned the teapot. Biscuits were provided, other delicate edibles placed just so, and whisky and rum were set well within reach.

Cruihniche shot Acair a steely glance. "Tea or strong drink?"

"Both, Grandmother, if you please."

Léirsinn sat up a bit straighter and wished for boots and a cloak that weren't so muddy when Acair's grandmother turned that same sharp glance on her.

"And you, my wee horse miss?"

Léirsinn started to ask the woman how in the world she would know anything at all about her past, then decided it was probably best not to know. It made her uneasy to think how often she'd made that same decision over the past fortnight, but perhaps with time it would grow easier.

"Whatever suits you, my lady," she managed.

"Harrumph," Cruihniche said, but poured just the same. She sipped at her own strengthening concoction for a moment or two, then set it aside and looked at Acair. "Surrender the book, grandson."

"But—"

"Now," she insisted. "Before I rip your arms off to have it back."

Léirsinn caught herself before she indulged in not only a look of astonishment but a hearty gasp. Acair's mother had been rather blunt, or so it had seemed to her. She had no idea what to call his grandmother.

Acair looked horribly torn. "Words cannot possibly express the marvelous and unique nature of this tome—"

"Which is why it was in my private and quite hidden cubby," Cruihniche said sharply, "not out in the open where any fool could pick it up and finger it. When, Acair, will you learn not to nose about in business that is not your own?"

He smiled a small, mischievous smile that should have felled every soul within a half-league radius. Léirsinn reminded herself that she continued to put up a decent defense against his charm with varying degrees of success, but that smile there was powerful stuff indeed. She had to tuck her hands under her thighs to keep from fanning herself, something she had never once in the whole of her life been tempted to do. Acair's grandmother, however, seemed utterly unmoved by the sight.

"Reprehensible attempt," Cruihniche said shortly.

"But, Grandmother," Acair said smoothly, "how am I to stop myself when the prize is so—how shall we term it?"

"Unattainable?"

"I *am* holding on to the book," Acair pointed out.

"Temporarily and only because I'm seeing how far out on the proverbial limb you'll go before you realize you've gone too far," she said.

"Curiosity is my worst failing," he admitted.

Léirsinn appreciated his attempt at honesty. She didn't think his grandmother was equally impressed, but it was, after all, Cruihniche's solar that Acair was invading.

His grandmother grunted at him. "Curiosity is your worst failing? When there are so many contenders for that spot, that is the trait you choose? I think I have a far different opinion." She looked at him pointedly. "Book."

He hesitated. "Might I simply look through it another time or two? Léirsinn has been supplied with pencil and paper for the express purpose of jotting down the odd thing we might find interesting."

Cruihniche frowned. "You don't want the entire thing?"

"Oh, I want it," he assured her. "I'm just trying to be polite by settling for less."

She had another sip of her tea. "If all you wanted was a look," she said, setting her cup down and shifting a platter bearing a cake closer to herself, "you could have just asked me."

"I didn't want to be a bother." He paused. "That, and the last time I came to tea—"

"You rifled through my fine linens," she finished. "Really, Acair, do you want to bring up the past at this particular moment?"

Léirsinn watched the exchange with fascination. Acair's grandmother was fingering that cake knife as if she intended to do damage with it, though why the woman didn't just reach for a spell was anyone's guess.

"Well, you did send minions after me, Grandmother—" Acair began carefully.

"Which was far less than you deserved, and you've now made up my mind for me." She set the knife down and held out her hand. "Book."

Acair gathered it to his chest and cradled it there reverently. "One more look."

Cruihniche leveled a look at him. "Do you truly want to brawl with me in front of my own hearth, child?"

"Nay, but I would endlessly sing your praises if you'd just let me make one more brief, casual study of this marvelous, one-of-a-kind foray into perfection on my way out the door."

"If I let you near the door, you'll just bolt."

He nodded. "I might, but at least then you would see me fleeing and know where to direct your thugs. Perhaps I don't need to point out that I could have simply turned myself into a discreet little breeze—"

"If you think, grandson, that I don't have the magic to keep you firmly trapped in your own current shape," she said mildly, "think again. If you further think I haven't the stomach to do worse, well, you're a disappointment and nothing but."

Acair blinked. "Could you? Or, more to the point, *would* you?"

Léirsinn found Acair's grandmother looking at her. "This is your doing, isn't it? This newfound politeness on his part?"

Léirsinn hardly knew where to begin denying anything to do with Acair's current condition. "Ah—"

"I sense a gentler edge to his general ruthlessness, which I find alarming. Did you do that?"

Léirsinn shook her head and pointed behind her at the spell that she didn't have to look for any longer. If it wasn't two paces behind Acair, it was lingering at her elbow.

Cruihniche looked at the spell, then lifted an eyebrow. "Interesting bit of business, that," she said slowly.

"Any suggestions on how to rid myself of it?" Acair asked quickly. "It is greatly hampering my ability to make mischief, and we both know how that grieves you."

His grandmother turned her attention back to him and her expression darkened. "I almost forgot about you in the excitement of encountering something that wants you dead. And to answer your surprisingly astute query, aye, I damned well could keep you in your own blasted shape and I don't need any spells of essence changing to do so."

"Your sister," he ventured, "Cailleach—"

"I only *have* one sister, dolt! You needn't remind me of my connection to her or her name."

Léirsinn would have smiled, but she didn't imagine that would improve matters any. She decided that perhaps it was best to just apply herself to her tea and stay out of the fray. She wasn't as adept at reading humans as she was horses, but she would have laid money on that woman there having a soft spot for her grandson. A very small one, true, but perhaps enough to get them back out the door while they were still breathing.

"Your sister who admires you to the very depths of her being said ours was the power I should be seeking," Acair said carefully, "not my father's."

"Bah, Gair is a spoilt little boy," Cruihniche said dismissively. "Why my daughter thought him to be such a prize I don't know, but who listens to their mothers in matters of the heart?"

"I wouldn't know," Acair ventured.

"I imagine you don't listen to her about *anything*, which is a mistake," Cruihniche said. She considered him then frowned again. "What do you want from that book?"

"I'm looking for a small list of mages who are up to no good."

"Small?" Cruihniche snorted. "Wishful thinking there, my lad. Perhaps you would do better to narrow things down. What do these mages do besides wreak your sort of havoc?"

Acair took a deep breath. "They steal souls."

Léirsinn looked at his grandmother and was surprised to

watch her go suddenly quite still. If the woman was breathing, she would have been surprised.

"Léirsinn, hand me your writing things."

Léirsinn didn't argue. She pulled out the notebook and pencil Fionne of Fàs had given her, then navigated the teapot and a set of stacked trays containing sweets she hadn't dared taste to hand Mistress Cruihniche both. The woman studied Acair for a moment or two, then jotted down a few things. She kept at it long enough that Léirsinn felt safe looking at Acair. He was rather green, something she could see quite well thanks to all the light from candles, lamps, and a roaring fire.

A fire that seemed to have a voice.

She shifted and looked at the flames, listening until she felt as if she were no longer at Cruihniche of Fàs's tea table. She was lost in a fire that sang something that tugged at her soul in a way she couldn't identify properly. Longing, or perhaps a need for something she couldn't name.

She felt as if she were being pulled into a dream.

The sensation alarmed her profoundly. It was one thing to watch otherworldly things happening to Acair and their horse; it was another thing entirely to have those sorts of things happen to her. She clutched the edges of the table and dragged herself back from a place she wasn't sure she wanted to go.

It was then that she realized that matters at the table had not improved any. Acair and his grandmother were glaring at each other, apparently engaging in last-minute negotiations about things Léirsinn wasn't sure she wanted to know about.

Cruihniche suddenly handed Léirsinn back her pencil, then threw the small book at her grandson.

"Be grateful."

Acair opened the book, then he froze. He lifted his head and looked at his grandmother in surprise. Léirsinn had rarely seen him not have at least something to say, but at the moment he seemed speechless.

Cruihniche laughed in a manner that was so reminiscent of Mistress Cailleach that Léirsinn could finally accept the familial connection. The woman nodded.

"That ought to keep you out of my private things for a few days at least. I've given you a few spells that might or might not turn on you and destroy you, along with a wee map that might lead you places you'll definitely regret having gone." She shrugged. "All the same to me." She looked at Léirsinn. "What can I do for you?"

"Ah," Léirsinn said, scrambling for something useful to say, "let us go free?"

Cruihniche laughed in a voice that was definitely reminiscent of Mistress Cailleach. "I will, if only to watch things chase your would-be lover there over the walls." She studied Léirsinn for a moment or two. "I believe, little one, that you might want to consider trying to acquire a few things that make you uncomfortable. Don't let Fear dissuade you, no matter how loudly he bellows. I tend to favor a different companion—let's call her Revenge—but that's just me."

Léirsinn could only gape at her.

Cruihniche laughed again. "Two souls rendered mute in one evening. It isn't a record for me, of course, but satisfying nonetheless." She pointed a long, bony, ring-encrusted finger toward the door. "Out, before I change my mind and slay you both."

Léirsinn supposed it would be rude as well as a bit dangerous to bolt without Acair, so she waited as he made certain everyone was politely helped up from the tea table. If he then wasted no time heading for the doorway and she followed hard on his heels, she didn't imagine anyone would fault them for it.

They weren't quick enough. His grandmother caught them both before Acair could open the solar door.

"Something slipped my mind," she said.

"Grandmother," Acair said carefully, turning and making her a very low bow, "I'm not sure how to thank you—"

"Aren't you?" Cruihniche asked smoothly. "I think you know exactly what will appease me."

Léirsinn had absolutely no desire to find out what that might be, but Acair apparently wasn't one to shy away from the difficult. He sighed deeply.

"I'll find a way," he said.

"You'd best succeed."

He hesitated. "If I might make an observation, they are, as you know, simply little tatted bits of—"

"They're *my* damned doilies!"

"I didn't realize you'd done the handwork yourself," he ventured.

She leveled a look at him that Léirsinn was rather happy wasn't aimed at her.

"I stole them from your grandfather's mistress, you idiot," she said shortly. She tugged on her collar, then smoothed down the front of her dress. "They have great sentimental value to me."

"As in, the thought of their being missed is something to chortle over during tea?" he asked.

"Perhaps," she said archly, "or perhaps not. I'm too well-mannered to admit to anything. You just concern yourself with fetching my damned doilies, you little rotter."

"Of course, Grandmother."

She reached out and poked him in the chest. "I want the one in Uachdaran of Léige's throne room."

"I didn't," Acair began, then he sighed. "Very well, I did."

"He keeps his bloody mugs of that undrinkable sludge he gulps down atop it, and don't think I haven't watched him do it."

"Scrying his private audiences?" Acair asked sourly.

"One amuses oneself from time to time with the doings of lesser souls," she said with a shrug. She looked at Léirsinn. "Remember what I said."

"I don't think I could forget it if I wanted to," Léirsinn said honestly.

Cruihniche reached out and opened the door. "I'm counting to one hundred before I set things upon you. Best trot on off into the Deepening Gloom quickly, don't you think?" She held out her hand toward Acair. "Kiss."

He did. Léirsinn supposed she shouldn't, so she patted Cruihniche's hand, then didn't protest when Acair grabbed for hers and pulled her out of the solar.

"How fast can you run?" he asked.

"Faster than you can, I'll warrant."

He smiled briefly. "No doubt. Stuff this into your satchel, will you?"

She took the notebook his grandmother had scribbled in and shoved it back into her bag. She looked at him. "Now what?"

"Pray she counts slowly."

Léirsinn supposed there was nothing else to hope for. She was happy that Acair knew where he was going because she was hopelessly lost.

She was also without a single sighting of any stray pieces of Acair's soul, but perhaps he'd left none of it behind, in spite of all the rather questionable things he'd done in his grandmother's house.

He paused at the entrance to some enormous hallway or other, swore enthusiastically, then reached again for her hand.

"Front door," he said with another curse.

"Why—oh, never mind," she said, because she could see what he saw. There were bright-eyed, sword-bearing creatures blocking every path except the one that led straight ahead. She didn't bother asking if Acair thought that would end badly for them because she suspected she already knew the answer.

"She must want that ale-saturated piece of lace very much," he groused.

"And this is her parting shot of good cheer?"

He pursed his lips. "I think you two might get on quite well if I weren't involved. Aye, I imagine this is just what that is." He took a deep breath, then looked at her. "Ready?"

She didn't suppose there was any alternative, so she nodded and darted across the polished marble with him.

What she assumed was the front entrance certainly was worthy of the name. She had never in her life seen doors so large or fine and she honestly couldn't remember the last time doors opened for her without anyone manning them. That she only shuddered as she hopped across the threshold instead of remaining rooted to the spot was perhaps less surprising than it should have been. The last place she wanted to linger was the grand house at Fàs.

She bolted with Acair down the path through a palatial front garden, along a tree-lined path that would have hosted at least half a dozen horses riding abreast, then through an enormous metal gate that started to close as they approached.

It was either good fortune or an ability to sprint perfected

thanks to many years of eluding ne'er-do-wells on her way back
from town, but she avoided being caught on the gates as they
closed. Acair had to leave his cloak behind, but she imagined he
thought it a light price to pay, all things considered. She continued to run with him until they reached at least the minimal protection of the trees that were a bit farther away than they'd
looked at first glance.

Acair skidded to a halt and she ran full into his back before
she realized what he was doing. She supposed the only reason
she didn't flatten him was because Mansourah caught them
both. She heaved herself upright, then felt something unpleasant
run through her at the look on the prince's face.

"We need to run," he said quickly.

"Why?" Acair wheezed, then he shook his head. "Don't answer. Pick a direction."

"Take your horse," Mansourah said urgently. "I'll hide us as
we fly. I say west, but that's only because I think we're being
driven in that direction."

Léirsinn flung herself onto Sianach's back as if she'd been
doing the same for years, didn't complain as Acair almost
knocked her off as he scrambled up behind her, then thought she
just might have to give that horse-turned-dragon an extra measure of grain the next time they were in a barn for having so
thoughtfully provided her with reins.

"I don't know that we'll manage this one," Mansourah said,
standing on the ground next to them. "There are things coming
after us that we won't like."

"My grandmother's minions," Acair said dismissively. "Easily
eluded."

Mansourah looked at him seriously. "I don't think so," he said
frankly. "Not this time."

Then he disappeared.

Léirsinn had become unfortunately familiar with the sort of spell Mansourah used to hide not only his tracks but theirs. She could still see herself, so she wasn't entirely sure what good it would do them. At the moment, perhaps any help was good help.

She forced herself to breathe normally instead of wheezing with what she didn't want to call fear. Acair's grandmother had advised her to send that sort of feeling to the back of the barn, which sounded a bit better when one was sitting in relative comfort in front of a fire instead of climbing fiercely up into the night sky on the back of an invisible dragon.

At least they hadn't encountered any pools of shadow—

She frowned and considered that, probably more grateful than she should have been for something to think on besides how far off the ground she was. Just as she *hadn't* in Eòlas, she hadn't seen a single spot of shadow in Acair's grandmother's house. She hadn't seen any pieces of Acair's stray soul lying about there either, but it was possible she'd been more distracted than she'd realized.

Either way, it was odd.

She also hadn't seen anything untoward at Acair's mother's house—save the witchwoman of Fàs herself, of course—but perhaps nothing was able to grow in the shadow of that mighty tree.

She considered that for a bit, then shook her head. The women in Acair's family were powerful witches who likely didn't allow anything unusual to take root on their land and in Eòlas, but she'd been too distracted by circumstances to have a proper look at anything.

Surely.

"Léirsinn."

She pulled herself away from her thoughts only to realize

how far they'd come without her having noticed it. The sky was beginning to grow light in the east. She twisted a bit to look at Acair.

"What?"

He looked grimmer than she'd ever seen him before.

"We're going to have to go faster."

Damn that fear she hadn't been able to entirely dismiss. "Why?" she managed, her mouth utterly dry.

He pointed over his shoulder, but perhaps that hadn't been necessary. It wasn't a cloud of mage following them, nor was it a darkness made by things she imagined Fionne of Fàs could send scampering with her wand.

It was something entirely different.

"Hold on," was the last thing he said before Sianach turned himself into something just a bit more substantial than a terrifyingly fierce bit of wind.

She hoped she could.

Sixteen

Acair had never thought all those years spent honing the ability to bolt past his brothers in absolute silence no matter the terrain would ever be so critical to his survival.

Of course, he'd been silent as a cat whilst about many of his own nefarious activities over the course of his lifetime, but that had been almost always simply for sport. There was nothing quite like the deliciousness of poaching something valuable from under the very nose of some snoozing royal or other and escaping without being marked.

The inescapable fact, however, was that his life had never hung in the balance during any of those pilferings because there had never been a moment, from the first time he'd set one of his brothers' knickers on fire, that he hadn't had magic to use for escape.

That he was currently running for his very life without any

ability to magically rescue himself was, in a word—and one he rarely used unless he was applying it to how he was certain he appeared to others—terrifying.

What he wanted perhaps more than anything was to wrap his hands around a certain Cothromaichian prince's neck, but he knew that wasn't going to help him at the moment. For all his faults, Soilléir of Cothromaiche was not a liar, damn him anyway. If he claimed he hadn't fashioned the spell following Acair like a lovestruck princess committed to a spectacular piece of rebellion, he'd been telling the truth.

Not that any of that aided him at present, of course. He was fleeing like a common criminal from an enemy he could sense like a bitter wind but couldn't for the life of him see, and he couldn't do a damned thing about it.

He had initially hoped his pursuer might simply be one of his gran's henchmen taking matters into his own hands, but those lads tended to stay close to home where they could corner their prey without overly exerting themselves.

He had also considered the possibility that the storm behind him was just the usual cloud of black mage out for a bit of exercise on a winter day, but dismissed that with equal certainty. Even after Sianach had plummeted to the ground and their little company had continued to flee on foot, the storm of mage hadn't gained on them.

Very odd that something that reputedly wanted him dead wasn't trying to catch up to him and kill him.

And then, very much out of the blue—nay, that wasn't accurate. With time, after having settled into a swift and steady run, it had occurred to him that what was following him wasn't a random mage out for a bit of sport or a clutch of lesser lads taking advantage of an unexpected opportunity for retribution.

They were being followed by the mage who had slain his tailor and stolen his spell in Eòlas.

He couldn't say how he knew that. Perhaps with a bit of time and a decent mug of ale, he could have nailed down why his thoughts led him in that direction, but at present, he didn't have the luxury for it. He could only continue to run and be grateful for the stamina of his companions.

He forced himself to try to work out in his head exactly where they were, though he didn't have as much success at it as he would have liked. They had flown for the whole of the previous night and the better part of the current day before he'd decided that attempting to blend into the forest below them might be a way to throw their hunter off the scent.

They had run for what felt like hours, though he was certain it had only been a pair of them. The sun had already begun to sink into the west behind them, which merely left him, for the first time in his life, not relishing the thought of a run in the dark. He had an excellent sense of direction, but the woods they were in were too close to the border of Durial for his taste. It was not a country he wanted to get lost in, for reasons he didn't particularly want to examine.

He cursed enthusiastically under his breath at the irony of his situation. He was where he found himself in a grander sense precisely because he'd refused to travel to see Uachdaran of Léige, king of Durial, and apologize for a minor piece of mischief that had likely not inconvenienced the king in the slightest. Many monarchs had rivers of power running under their kingdoms. Indeed, he couldn't think of a one who didn't have some sort of magic flowing through his land in some fashion.

He considered other likely suspects bearing up under that same sort of strain. Dreamweavers, mage kings, and wizards, to begin the list. Then there were witches, faeries, and other less welcoming creatures with magic at their fingertips in lands where he didn't care to go, to be sure. Indeed, what of those poor elves? They were victims of not only magic in their water, but magic that thoroughly drenched every damned bit of their country. Did they complain? Nay, they did not. They boasted of it to anyone who had the ability to sit for long periods of time and listen without pitching forward, asleep, into their suppers.

Acair suspected that the king of the dwarves had other things on his mind that he felt merited an apology, things Acair absolutely refused to apologize for. It wasn't his fault if the king's middle daughter—who he should have known was trouble from the start—had used him as a means to escape her father's iron rule. Indeed, considering what Acair had endured at her hands, the king should have been apologizing to *him*.

But given that he suspected hell would freeze over first, he thought it might be best to take stock of where they were and reconsider where a safe haven might be found. For all he knew, the creature pursuing him was Uachdaran himself, out for a bit of kingly vengeance. A detour south to even a marginally friendly elven haven might be just the thing to throw the old bastard off the scent.

He skidded to a halt in a clearing that simply opened up in front of him without warning. He almost went sprawling thanks to Mansourah and Léirsinn running into his back, but caught himself heavily on one leg. He straightened, then looked at the locale into where he'd run not only himself but his companions.

He felt that damned silence descend, as was its wont. He made a vow then and there that in all his other endeavors to come, he would herald realizations of his own stupidity and impending doom with loud and raucous cries.

A man stood there with a faint winter's sunlight streaming down on him.

"Run," Mansourah gasped. "I'll see to this."

Acair grabbed the prince by the arm. He looked at the man who had accompanied them in spite of his potential misgivings and no-doubt definite dislike of Acair himself, then shook his head.

"We can't run any longer."

"Aye, you can." Mansourah jerked his head toward Léirsinn. "Protect her, at least."

"Wait—" Acair began, but it was too late.

His hand clutched nothing simply because Mansourah had turned himself into something angry and dark that charged the man in the glade. It didn't last but a heartbeat or two. Acair watched Mansourah be caught, wrenched back into his own shape, and slammed into the ground at the feet of that mage.

The sight brought him up short. What sort of power was that? He had done the same thing to others, of course, but he was who he was. He'd never seen someone do it to anyone else, and he'd certainly never had the like perpetrated on his own sweet self. It was profoundly unsettling, but he gave that feeling the boot right off. He was nothing if not equal to any fight, no matter who his opponent might be.

He looked at Léirsinn. "Take Sianach and go," he said urgently. "Fly back to my grandmother's. She'll give you a safe haven."

She was absolutely white with what he imagined was fear, but she wasn't moving.

"Léirsinn," he said, putting his hands on her shoulders and coming very close to shaking her to see if she were enspelled or not. "You must *go*."

"I cannot leave you," she said hoarsely.

Well, the sentiment was appreciated, though he thought it extremely ill-advised. He took less than a trio of heartbeats to decide there was nothing to be done save hope she would have the good sense to flee if he fell. For all he knew, she thought he wouldn't.

He looked at her one last time, nodded sharply, then strode past her out into the glade before he thought better of it.

Actually, what was there to think on? That mage there was obviously accustomed to the theatrics of black magery and possessing a few decent spells, but surely nothing more. He had certainly dealt with much worse in the past. He'd been in full possession of his magic, of course, but just because he couldn't use that magic at the moment didn't mean he didn't have it still.

If nothing else, he would bluster his way through. He'd done it before.

He stopped some two-dozen paces away from the man and looked at him with as much disdain as he could muster.

"Face me if you dare," he said coldly.

The mage only shifted and looked at him from inside a heavy hood. He said nothing.

Well, that was annoying, but perhaps a sterner hand was called for. "Nothing comes without a price," he warned. "You will pay a heavy one for your cheek, I assure you."

The mage laughed, a harsh, cutting sound. "There is no price to be paid when I'm the one with all the spells."

"And why would you think you're the one with all the spells?" Acair asked softly.

"Because I know more about you than you think."

Shards of steel suddenly erupted from the man's mouth as he

spoke, a dozen impossibly sharp spikes that remained there, fixed, as his words slid past them.

Acair caught his breath. The sight was without a doubt the worst thing he had ever seen in his very long life of tiptoeing in and out of places he never should have gone. The spells the mage wove were simple, foolishly so, but they took on something entirely different as they came out of his mouth. They were horrifying.

Considering how many of those sorts of things he'd used in the past, he thought he might be something of an authority on the same.

He looked behind him to see if Léirsinn had actually listened to him and fled. He wasn't surprised to find that she had ignored him, though he genuinely wished she hadn't. She was staring at the man out in the clearing, looking as surprised as he freely admitted he felt. She looked at him.

"Who is that?" she mouthed.

He gave her his best *no idea but we'd best run very fast* look, which he was certain she'd interpreted properly. A pity that course wasn't open to him.

The other thing was, Mansourah of Neroche had suddenly risen to his feet and was throwing spells at that foul mage that left Acair almost blinking in surprise. Mansourah's command of slurs and insults was lacking, of course, but Acair expected nothing less. Obviously a few suggestions needed to be made.

The prince's collection of truly terrible spells, however, was genuinely surprising. That, he decided, was something that might make for a decent conversation over a decanter of very expensive port.

It occurred to him rather abruptly that whilst he was standing there, babbling nonsense in his own head, that pampered prince from that rustic hovel in the north was doing what had to be done. It was ridiculous and embarrassing and had to stop immediately.

He tried to think clearly, but for the first time in his life, he found he couldn't sort through everything before him. He began to feel a bit of sympathy for those mages he'd destroyed in his past, lads he had stalked, terrified, then sent off to their just rewards only after having left them groveling at his feet.

Damnation, but he was starting to see why there were places in the world where he just wasn't welcome.

"Acair," Léirsinn called, "look. Mansourah says . . . well, look!"

Acair forced himself to focus on the matter before him and knew as clearly as if Mansourah had shouted the same that the prince wanted him to flee. The spells were coming at that great-hearted archer like a rain of arrows shot from scores of bows. Endless, painfully sharp, impossible to elude—

Acair took a step backward in surprise.

He supposed that might have been the worst thing he'd ever found himself doing. He couldn't even credit it to an unfortunate stumble. It was cowardice, nothing less.

It was intolerable.

He gave himself a metaphorical slap across the face, stilled his mind, and forced himself to think clearly. He had the spell of un-noticing he'd retrieved from under his grandmother's chair, of course, but that would only buy him a moment or two more. It wasn't going to be enough.

When it came right down to it, the solution was simple.

What he needed was a spell of death.

He glanced casually behind him and found that his minder

spell was standing some ten paces away, watching not him but the mage standing in the middle of the clearing. He took an equally careful look out in the glade and found that their enemy was so wrapped up in his own spells that he wasn't paying heed to anything but the drivel coming out of his own mouth. He was currently creating a wave of darkness that dropped to the ground and spread out from his feet, slithering as it crawled onward.

Acair wasn't terribly fond of snakes, as it happened, so he reached for the first thing that came to mind. It was a spell of return, something he had used so often as a child with his brothers that it took no longer than a heartbeat to create it and send it flinging toward the mage there.

His minder spell whirled on him with an angry hiss, but he ignored it. He slipped the spell of un-noticing into his hand from where he'd stashed it earlier—just in case—up his sleeve, looked at Mansourah one more time, then flung that spell up into the air. It fell over him, Léirsinn, and that damned shadow of his like a gossamer layer of sparkling snow. That seen to, he began his most potent spell of death—

Only that same spell didn't rush away from him, it came at him. He watched his own spell of death be carried aloft toward him by that damned minder spell that certainly should have been more appreciative of how he'd tried to save its sorry arse—

He heard Léirsinn cry out, but he couldn't seem to turn toward her.

Mansourah fell, and he could do nothing to stop that either.

The only thing that gave him any pleasure at all was watching that mage leap back, fighting off his own creations that had turned on him.

Acair understood that, though he wished he didn't. He looked at his own minder spell, a spell not created by him but designed for him, and wished he'd had the time to reason with it. He hadn't done any foul magic, just a simple spell that he wasn't entirely sure he hadn't used a time or two on his mother's hens in the springtime when they'd strayed out of the coop. What harm could possibly be assigned to something so innocuous?

That spell of death was perhaps another matter, but he'd talked himself out of tighter spots, to be sure.

He took a deep breath. The game was being played to its very end and he wished he'd had the energy to cry foul and insist on a review of the rules.

Unfortunately, as it was, he could only watch death approach, loom up over him, and prepare to fall on him.

Damn it anyway.

Seventeen

The forest was gone.

Léirsinn supposed it wasn't, really, but it was as if a wall had slammed itself down in front of them, blocking out nothing but everything at the same time. The cloaked mage in the clearing was still frantically fighting off whatever it was he'd created that had turned around and was rushing back toward him. She had watched Mansourah fall, which likely meant he was dead, and she wasn't entirely certain Acair wasn't going to follow him to the grave.

She was sure, however, that she would never forget the sight of Acair facing off with that terrible worker of magic in the glade. Worse still had been actually seeing shards of steel coming out of that man's mouth, steel that became words that were spells of death and despair and things that made absolutely no sense to her, though she couldn't deny their reality. Those terrible

spells had soon been accompanied by things that crawled without ceasing toward them.

She had watched Acair weave his own spell and wanted to
stop him, truly she had, but she hadn't had voice enough to even
try. She had also failed to warn him about the spell that endlessly shadowed him, though she supposed there had been no
need. He had known what using magic would mean, yet he had
done it anyway.

His minder spell had slammed into him, stealing his breath.
He had fallen.

That damned spell of death now stood over him, studying
him as he lay there motionless. It leaned over him as if it wanted
to take what faint breath was left—

Léirsinn didn't stop to consider her plan, she simply threw
herself over Acair's chest and waited for his minder spell to fall
on them both and slay them. Acair was still breathing, barely,
but it was such labored breathing that she was absolutely sure he
would soon draw his last. She felt something very cold on her
back and braced herself to lead the way into that place in the east
where she'd been told there was no more sorrow or toil. At the
moment, she couldn't have cared less what was to be found there
if she could just get there without being in agony.

Yet still she breathed and still that terrible chill rested its
bloody hand on her back.

She turned her head far enough to look up only to find Acair's
minder spell looming over her. If she'd had it in her, she would
have screamed herself hoarse. She supposed she'd been wise
never to look it in the eye, but now that was all she seemed to be
able to do.

The horrors mirrored in those soulless eyes were absolutely
beyond anything she'd ever imagined.

She knew with a certainty she'd never felt before that she was going to die. She would go first, then Acair, then perhaps the entire world. It wasn't death so much as the thought that she had absolutely no means of stopping what was about to slay her—

Magic . . .

She looked up at the spell in surprise. She wasn't entirely sure it hadn't spoken to her, but at the moment she was sure she didn't care.

Magic? What a ridiculous thought. Her people knew horses, not spells. She was no different from them—

Send for him.

She looked at the spell, startled. "Stop that." Then she frowned. "Send for who?"

Soilléir . . .

"Why the hell would I want . . . to . . ."

She stopped speaking, because suddenly, everything she remembered hearing about the man came back to her in a rush.

He had spells of essence changing.

She blinked, then had to force herself not to shrink back from the thought that suddenly presented itself to her. If he could change things, change them permanently, could he not change her into a mage, or a witch, or some species of maid who could at least wave a wand and induce something besides laughter and eye-rolling in those so gestured at?

She pushed herself off Acair and heaved herself to her feet. She wrapped her arms around herself and wished more desperately than she ever had before that she was the sort who faced terrible things and managed them by bursting into tears.

Instead, all she could apparently do was shake.

She dropped to her knees and groped at Acair's belt for his purse before she thought better of it. If he'd been alive, he would

have made some lecherous comment, of that she was sure. That
he said nothing, but continued to lie there, seemingly not even
drawing in breath any longer, was the most alarming thing she'd
seen in a string of absolutely devastating sights.

She found the leather purse, then found she couldn't get it
open. A long, spindly finger that wasn't shadow and wasn't bone
came and touched the knot.

The knot vanished and the purse opened.

She thanked the creature that put its hand again on her back,
chilling her to the marrow, then yanked out everything Acair no
doubt considered precious. She dropped it all on his chest, ignoring the pattern all that power made over him, then pulled up the
single, golden rune that seemed to be fashioned of sunlight.

It wasn't the piece of business he'd pulled from under his
grandmother's chair. This was something entirely different. She
took the rune and held it up. Acair's minder seemed torn between hissing in anger and murmuring in pleasure. It reached
out that same bony, shadowy finger toward the sparkling rune—

"Nay," Léirsinn said, covering it in her hand. She pushed herself to her feet, stood over Acair, then looked at the spell. "You
may not have him."

The spell pulled back a pace or two, folded its arms over its
chest, and sent her a look of challenge.

You have no magic.

She was going to change that sooner rather than later.

She took a deep breath, then cast the rune up into the air.

The world seemed to hold its breath for an endless moment,
then it shuddered. Léirsinn watched Acair's minder spell back
away from her until it finally curled itself up into a little shape
that crouched at Acair's feet. It hissed a final time, then fell silent.

Léirsinn felt the world part behind her. She spun around,

steadied herself, then gaped at a place where a doorway had opened where no doorway should have been.

A blond man walked out of nothing and stood there, ten paces away from her.

She looked—very well, she *looked* at him and thought her eyes might catch on fire. Not in the way Acair tended to inspire—unrepentant flirt that he was—but simply because she felt as if she were staring straight into the sun that had fallen to the earth. She drew her sleeve across her eyes and the brightness was gone, but the impression of staggering power remained. She could see it stretching up toward the sky and down into the ground, as if the man in front of her had been some sort of tree fashioned of crystal and sunlight and spring rains that were endless and glorious—

She decided abruptly that she needed to make her home in a place with trees. Perhaps if she had them to hand where she could lean against them and have them send showers of needles and leaves atop her head, she might stop seeing them in places where only mortals should have been standing.

Or perhaps she simply needed to stop associating with mages and their ilk.

The blond man looked at Acair, then back at her. "Léirsinn of Sàraichte," he said mildly. "You called for me."

"Are you—" Her voice cracked, but she supposed that wasn't unexpected. She had been yelling at Acair's spell quite vigorously for longer than she likely should have. "Are you Soilléir?"

He smiled. She frowned because he was altogether too handsome and too young to command what imaginary power he was credited with, but she couldn't deny what she'd seen and how he'd simply walked out of nothing.

"I am," he said. "How may I aid you?"

She felt her mouth fall open, then she managed to retrieve her

jaw and glare at him. She gestured furiously at Acair. "Well, look
at him! How do you think you can aid me?"

Soilléir peered at Acair from a distance, something that
seemed thoroughly unhelpful. "He looks senseless, but his spell
is still over there keeping watch so I assume he isn't dead. What
will you have me do for him?"

She threw up her hands because that seemed preferable to
taking them and strangling the man in front of her. She'd heard
Acair express that desire more than once under his breath and
she was starting to understand what he meant by it.

"I don't know," she exclaimed. "Do whatever it is you do."

Soilléir studied her for a long moment. "That isn't why you
called me, is it?"

She didn't want to tell him what she'd been thinking, mostly
because it was beyond ridiculous. Men were men, stable lasses
were full of good sense, and the whole of her life recently felt a
great deal like a waking dream.

She looked around herself for a distraction but only wound
up looking at the place where the rune had somehow carved a
spot in the world. It should have seemed like nothing past a bit
of fresh air after the dust and fear that evil mage had stirred up
and sent crawling after her, but somehow it was something altogether different. She could see the fabric of the world, see the
threads of time and dreams and something that looked a great
deal like gold—

She stepped backward and sat down, hard, right on Acair's
belly. That he didn't move was alarming. What she was seeing in
front of her was worse.

She forced herself to look at the man standing in front of her.
Whoever, whatever he was, Soilléir—she couldn't bring to mind
at the moment where he called home—was full of magic so ter-

rible and beautiful, she could hardly look at him. He was the one, she reminded herself, who changed things and changed them for good. And if he could change things—events, crowns, destinies—perhaps he could change even her.

It was, after all, why she'd called him to where she was. She had thrown that damned golden rune into the air because she had deliberately set aside the part of her that disbelieved that he could do what she needed him to do.

She was going to trust.

She scrambled to her feet and took a pace or two toward him. "Change me."

He frowned. "I beg your par—"

"Change me," she said impatiently. "Change me into a mage. Then I can help Acair and save my grandfather. *Change me.*"

He didn't look at all startled, which led her to believe that he hadn't expected anything else.

"Give you magic, you mean?" he asked quietly.

She could hardly speak for the terror that had lodged in her throat. She knew she had come to the place where she was for exactly the step she was preparing to take, but that didn't make that step any easier. If she continued on the way she intended, she would never be able to turn off that path. Her life would be altered in a way that could never be undone.

She knew it was a choice she had to make, one she needed to make, one she would make freely and call the consequences her own.

"Aye," she managed. She pulled out the charm that Mistress Cailleach had given her. "Acair's great-aunt told me I could breathe fire, so I shall. You can help me."

Soilléir smiled faintly. "I don't think you want me to turn you into a dragon."

"Nay, but you could give me magic, then I could turn myself into a dragon."

"I don't think you understand—"

"What I *understand*," she said shortly, "is *that*." She stepped aside and gestured toward Acair. "I understand that. I understand that Acair used magic to try to save us and this is the price he paid. Mansourah of Neroche is likely dead and there's a damned mage over there where I can no longer see him who would likely slay us before he took the trouble to find out our names." She glared at him. "Look you what's become of us all. I can't save Mansourah, but I can save Acair."

He looked at her gravely. "There is a price and that price is dear."

"I *know* that," she said, through gritted teeth. "A piece of my soul or some other such rot. I don't care. We're in a bit of a rush here, if you haven't noticed. I think Acair is still breathing, but I'm afraid that won't last unless I do something fairly soon."

Soilléir considered. "There are many types of gifts, Léirsinn."

"I'm speaking of magic."

He nodded. "I know. And if you want the truth, there is none in your blood. No magic in the sense you're talking about. Sight, perhaps, but that is all."

"Then change that!"

He clasped his hands behind his back. "I could instead give you a handful of spells—"

"And if we encounter something that those spells won't see to, what then? Acair used that sort of thing and look where it got him."

"I imagine he didn't limit himself to a spell that worked on its own," Soilléir said with a faint smile.

"Does it matter?" she asked, hearing her voice break but finding herself unable to care. "This might count as his good deed for the day. I cannot stand by and see him repaid with death."

He sighed deeply. "I do this so rarely—"

"Make this one of those times."

He smiled very faintly. "You are persuasive."

"Terrified, rather," she said frankly. "And desperate to save those I love."

"I daresay," he said gently. He took a deep breath. "You should know that changing one's essence can produce results that I cannot foresee." He paused, then shook his head. "Let me rephrase that. I can change your essence and I might be able to see how it will affect you, but there are also things that might happen that I cannot control. You may find yourself facing parts of yourself that you don't necessarily care for."

"I'm traveling with Acair of Ceangail," she said pointedly. "Can I be worse than he is?"

He lifted his eyebrows briefly. "Time will tell, I suppose. I believe you are fond of him."

"Quite possibly, which is why I would prefer to have him alive. Since I don't think you're interested in coming with us on this journey, I need to be able to help him myself."

She realized she was talking more than she wanted to, but the truth was, she was almost out of her head with fear. Any hope of telling it to go off and linger in the verge was long gone. Fear was right next to her, with its arm around her shoulders, occasionally blowing down her neck with a cold, hard, unrelenting breath of ice.

She looked at Soilléir. "A favor first."

He tilted his head and looked at her in surprise. "What?"

She gestured toward Acair. "Heal him—but slowly. He'll try to stop me if he awakens too quickly."

Soilléir closed his eyes briefly, as if the thought pained him, then he opened his eyes and nodded. He walked over, knelt, then put a hand on Acair and wove his spell. Léirsinn supposed that if she'd been serious about becoming a mage she would have memorized what he was saying, but she couldn't. All she could do was listen to the words he spoke, words that caused bones to knit together and blood to run in its proper course, and the very essence of Acair of Ceangail to find its home in the usual way inside his admittedly superior form.

Then Soilléir rose, put his hand on her arm to draw her aside a bit more, then looked at her with pity in his eyes.

"Are you—"

"Aye."

Aye, she was certain, because there was only one path laid out before her, one way to escape a barn full of locked stalls and blocked passageways. The only way out was forward and she was the only one who could walk that path.

She looked at him and nodded, once, sharply. It was the best she could do.

He lifted his eyebrows briefly, then he began to speak. She supposed he did that for her benefit, mostly because she suspected he didn't need to give voice to the words he was saying. He might have spoken but a handful of words, or scores. She had no idea and felt no passage of time. All she knew was that she felt as if her soul had been turned inside out.

It was excruciating.

At one point, she found herself reaching out for something to hold on to. Acair's minder spell was there in its usual spot at her elbow. It nodded politely to Soilléir, then offered her its arm. She didn't think to find it strange that it had an arm or that she could use it to lean on. Or that might have been Soilléir's. She honestly couldn't tell.

"I need to breathe fire," she whispered.

She knew she had said those words, but she could hardly hear them for the song in her head. It felt familiar, as if she'd heard it before, but she couldn't place it.

"Let's start with simply calling fire. Here is a spell for that."

Soilléir's voice sounded very far away and small, but she memorized the words anyway. She wasn't particularly good at memorizing things, but she supposed that would need to change. She repeated the words faithfully, then heard a loud snap.

"Léirsinn!"

She looked up to find the entire forest alight with flame. She realized someone was calling her name. She was fairly confident it wasn't Soilléir because he was still standing there, simply watching her. She supposed it might have been Acair, but she was so tired, she couldn't keep her eyes open long enough to tell.

She felt arms go around her, which was very handy because they would likely save her from a nasty fall.

She fell just the same.

Eighteen

"What the bloody hell did you just do?" Acair snarled.

Nay, he didn't snarl. That didn't begin to describe the place of agony he'd spoken from. If he'd had any soul left to shred, he would have been crying out from a place in the midst of the tatters. He held a senseless Léirsinn of Sàraichte in his arms and wasn't entirely sure she would survive what she'd just done.

She was still breathing, which he supposed was something, but she was as pale as death. Acair looked at her, then at the trees on fire around them, then glared at Soilléir of Cothromaiche, that empty-headed wielder of ridiculous magic.

"Put out the fire," he snapped.

The trees returned to their unscorched state without even a single word being spoken, something that galled Acair to his very depths.

He was also exceedingly annoyed by the fire that appeared

from nothing fifty paces in front of him in a clearing that also hadn't been there before. He growled at his spell to follow him, shot Soilléir a look that should have had him scampering back to hide behind his grandfather's ermine-trimmed skirts, then carefully carried Léirsinn over to warmth and what he could only hope was a bit of safety. He looked over his shoulder, but the glade in the distance was empty from what he could tell.

Empty of that mage, empty also of Mansourah of Neroche.

Worst of all, though, was the seemingly lifeless woman he held on to. He sat down on a stump, cradled her in his arms, and tried not to weep.

"She asked me to give her magic," Soilléir said quietly.

Acair looked at the man who had sat down across the flames from him and wished he had the means to slay him, but then that would definitely end any hope of restoring Léirsinn to her proper state. He would slay him later, when he'd forced the damned worker of essence changes to put things to rights.

"You should have ignored her," Acair said bitterly.

Soilléir looked at him. "As you've managed to do?"

Acair felt his mouth working, but could find nothing in his extensive collection of slurs dire, disgusting, or damning enough to use in cursing the man sitting across the fire from him.

That Soilléir didn't mock him for it was even more alarming.

"I hate you," Acair managed finally.

"I know."

He supposed the bastard also knew that Acair never wept, ever. He couldn't bring to mind a single moment in the whole of his ninety-and-eight years of moving from one piece of mischief to the next where he had so much as troubled himself with a sniffle of emotion.

That tears were streaming down his cheeks at the moment was quite possibly the most—

Nay. Nay, that wasn't the truth. The most devastating moment of his life had been regaining his senses in time to watch the whoreson sitting across from him weaving one of his absolutely vile spells of essence changing over a red-haired gel who couldn't possibly have understood what she was asking for.

That she had done it for him was the single worst thing he'd ever heard in a lifetime of hearing terrible things.

He gathered what was left of his wits and looked at Soilléir.

"I will slay you," he said flatly.

"Do what you must."

Acair suspected that if he spluttered any more, his tongue would simply fling itself out of his mouth to spare itself any more frustration.

"When I have my magic back to hand," he said, "I will steep my worst spells in a mixture of loathing and bitterness until perfection is reached, then I will unleash the whole on you at a time and location when and where you cannot defend yourself. You will die a lingering, horrific death and I will stand over you the entire time and watch until the light fades from your eyes and you breathe your last."

"I look forward to it—"

"Shut up!" Acair shouted. "Have you no idea of what you've *done* to her?"

"I'm well aware of it," Soilléir said quietly. "And I'm sorry for it."

"Then why did you—never mind," Acair finished bitterly.

"Because she asked you to."

"Because she loves you."

"Ye gads, what absolute rot," Acair spluttered. He gathered Léirsinn a bit closer to him because he was afraid he would drop her, not because he was unsettled.

If he clutched her to him with a desperation that frightened him, well, who was to know? He wasn't altogether certain she didn't squeak, but that could have been that damned spell he couldn't seem to shake, leaning over his shoulder and peering down into her face. He flicked it away, looked at the woman in his arms that he lo—er, was fond of, rather—and watched her eyelids flutter.

That could have been from his tears dripping onto her face, but he wasn't going to investigate that any further.

She opened her eyes and looked at him. "You're shouting," she said hoarsely.

"'Tis better than weeping," he muttered. He glared at Soilléir just so the man wouldn't forget where his doom was sitting, then looked at Léirsinn. "I'm angry."

"Why?"

Where to start? He looked at her seriously. "Let's discuss it when I'm less angry and the focus of my ire has flapped away to seek safety behind the walls of the schools of wizardry." Not that he couldn't have tracked Soilléir down there and slain him on his way to the buttery, but that was perhaps not a useful thing to say at the moment.

Léirsinn sat up with more of his help than he supposed would be polite to mention. He situated her next to him on his perch, but kept his arm around her just in case. If she looked at Soilléir with a mixture of awe and horror, she was justified.

All he knew was that he wasn't at all ready to have the conversation with her he would need to about magic and magery of any stripe, so he continued to keep her close and turned back to his own business of wondering how best to put that damned prince across the fire from him to death.

"How has your journey been so far?" Soilléir asked politely.

Acair swore at him. It was the very least of all the things he wanted to do, so limiting himself to calling the crown prince of Cothromaiche's son names seemed like it could possibly qualify for his good deed for the day.

"Perhaps it would be more interesting to discuss instead *where* you've been so far," Soilléir suggested.

"Haven't you been watching?" Acair asked shortly.

"I try to leave people their privacy."

Acair gaped at him. "How do you say those kinds of things without your tongue catching on fire?"

Soilléir smiled. "Centuries of practice, my friend."

Acair realized Léirsinn was shivering. He would have given her his cloak, but he remembered having left it behind in his grandmother's gates. He jumped a little as a lovely thing came flying his way, but it had been that sort of day so far. It was a gentleman's garment, but it would certainly serve Léirsinn well enough. He grunted a thanks in the direction of its maker, then wrapped the damned thing around his lady.

He sighed. There was no point in trying to call her anything else any longer.

He put his arm back around her, settled her as comfortably as he could, then looked at his primary tormentor. He supposed there would come a time when he would have to examine what the bastard had used to heal him, but for the moment, he would leave the prancing Cothromaichian stuff dancing a set with the Fadaire already trapped inside his poor chest alone. There would be time enough later to see if both could be rooted out of him.

He looked at Soilléir. "After I saw you in Neroche where I

promised you a lingering death—something that keeps coming up, it seems—we decamped south for the library in Eòlas, where I thought I would see what sort of trouble looking for a book stirred up."

"It seems you managed that well enough," Soilléir said.

Acair sent the man his most murderous look simply because he was fairly certain there wasn't a damned thing in the whole of the Nine Kingdoms that Soilléir of Cothromaiche hadn't fore-seen to some extent. Why he didn't lend a hand more often was a mystery.

"I'm beginning to wonder if I just met what's hunting me," Acair said pointedly. "I don't suppose you would have an opinion on that."

Silence fell. As always, Acair didn't care for that sort of thing because he knew what it generally indicated, which was some-thing coming his way he absolutely wasn't going to like. Léirsinn was still breathing raggedly, but she had put her hand on his knee in perhaps a good-hearted attempt to keep him from kick-ing the life from the man across from them.

Soilléir, that preening do-gooder, was only apparently sifting through an enormous pile of words in an effort to choose the ones that would inflict the most pain.

"I might be able to offer that, at least," he said finally.

Léirsinn snorted. Acair was surprised enough by the sound that he looked at her. She smiled apologetically, but he shook his head. What a sterling gel she was and obviously possessing a superior ability to judge character. He patted her shoulder, then looked at the man he would happily crush like a bug under his boot the first chance he had.

"Do tell," he drawled, feeling slightly more like his old self than he had but a moment ago.

"I will tell you, but I need your help."

Acair blinked. "You what?"

"I need you to steal a spell."

Acair spluttered. He spared a moment to wonder if he would manage to take the dull dagger down his boot and bury it in Soilléir's gut before the man turned him into a slug.

"You want me to steal a spell," he repeated in disbelief.

Soilléir looked at his hands for a moment or two, no doubt deciding whether or not he should wring them, then looked at Acair and nodded. "Yes."

"Without my magic."

"Considering where you'll need to go to begin the hunt for it, I don't think magic would serve you."

Acair felt his eyes narrow. "And where, if I might be so bold, does this spell find itself—or do I even need to waste the breath it would take me to ask?"

Soilléir lifted his pale eyebrows briefly, but said nothing.

Acair realized he was on his feet pacing only because he ran into a rock so abruptly that it felt as if he weren't wearing boots. He cursed at the pain that shot up his leg, then cursed a bit more because the moment seemed to call for that sort of thing.

He finally gained control enough of himself that he thought he could look at his fiendish foe without wanting to throttle him. He clasped his hands behind his back where they wouldn't get him into any trouble by way of uncontrollable, rude gestures, then looked at the hapless grandson of the king of Cothromaiche.

"Where is this spell?" he asked.

"A better question might be, *where did this spell once find itself?* And the answer is my grandfather's library."

Acair thought it might serve him to refrain from shaking his head any more that day. He feared his wits were beginning to rattle around inside his skull in a manner that was unhealthy.

"And you can't go looking for this spell yourself?"

"From my grandfather's own solar?" Soilléir asked, looking horrified.

"Library," Acair said shortly. He dismissed Soilléir's look as badly done theatrics. The man would pinch his grandfather's nightcap off his head if it served his vaunted purposes.

Soilléir smiled. "Aye, library."

"You haven't hit upon the idea of simply walking in and asking for it?"

Soilléir shifted. "Well, that's the thing, isn't it?"

"Don't tell me your grandfather doesn't know it's missing."

"My grandfather doesn't know it's missing," Soilléir agreed.

Acair felt his way down onto a different log from the one where Léirsinn sat so unsteadily. Unfortunately for him, his arse's aim was terrible and he missed the whole damned thing. He lay on his back for a moment, looking up at the sky and wishing he were admiring it from several hundred feet off the ground instead of from a pile of rotting pine needles, then heaved himself back up and perched on that traitorous piece of wood.

"And what, again if I might be allowed to ask, does this piece of magic your grandfather doesn't know is missing actually do?"

"That's an interesting question," Soilléir said slowly, "but more interesting are the circumstances that seem to surround the theft."

"I can scarce wait to hear the details," Acair said, though he could think of several things he would rather be discussing. He paused, considered that, then shook his head. That wasn't true. If what Soilléir wanted from him included a trip inside Seannair of Cothromaiche's private nest, perhaps he was more interested than he wanted to admit.

"The spell is gone, but the rest of the book is intact. It was as if someone simply went into the solar—"

"Library," Acair exclaimed.

Soilléir smiled. "Just making sure you hadn't forgotten. It's as if someone merely walked in and cut a page from a particular book." He paused. "Not that you would have any experience with that."

Acair ignored the barb and concentrated on the matter at hand. "And you can't remember what the spell says?"

"It was the original," Soilléir said, "and not anything I was particularly interested in at the time, truth be told."

"Don't you people ever make copies of anything?" Acair said incredulously.

"The library is unbreachable," Soilléir said.

"Apparently not," Acair returned with a snort. "What did this spell do?"

"It's a spell of theft."

Acair rolled his eyes. "Pedestrian."

"It steals souls."

Acair was honestly rather grateful he hadn't been sipping anything because he would have likely put the fire out with his spewing. He grasped frantically for his last shreds of good sense. He was never afraid. He had walked in places that would have turned that prissy essence changer perched on that sturdy log over there white with terror, yet he himself had hardly raised an eyebrow.

He wasn't sure if that ice-cold hand that had taken hold of his innards was fear or the coldest of angers.

He settled for the latter, because the former was just too terrible to contemplate.

"Get out of my sight," he said with a haughtiness that he

feared wasn't nearly chilly enough for present circumstances. "Sending me off to do your dirty work? Disgusting."

"I think you've seen the spell before," Soilléir said quietly.

"Bah, what absolute rot," Acair said dismissively.

"I believe you threw it into a fire quite a few years ago."

Léirsinn squeaked. Acair understood and he wasn't entirely sure he hadn't made the same sort of noise right along with her. He rose unsteadily and paced, because that seemed like the most intelligent thing he'd done all day. He finally stopped behind Léirsinn and put his hands on her shoulders. To steady *her*, of course, not himself.

"How do you know *that*?" Acair wheezed. "Ye gads, man, do you have any idea what you're saying?"

Soilléir only looked at him steadily. "Aye, I do, and the answer to the first is that I did some investigating."

"Have you been spying on me my entire life?" Acair asked, thoroughly appalled by the notion.

"You were such trouble from the start that I likely should have," Soilléir said with a faint smile, "but nay, I haven't. If you must know, there was something surrounding that moment all those many years ago that drew my attention in a way few things have. You know I don't like to interfere—"

"Bollocks!" Acair shouted. He took a deep breath. "I honestly don't know how you live inside yourself."

"Centuries of practice," Soilléir said with a shrug.

Acair swore, because it seemed preferable to shouting. "Who stole that spell from your grandfather?"

"We're not certain."

Acair supposed he might hazard a decent guess. He considered the mage sitting across from him and decided there was no use in not asking a few questions whilst he had the chance.

"Have you ever heard the name Sladaiche?"

Soilléir looked as if he'd just been clouted in the nose. He pulled back, then looked at Acair with something that on another's face might have been called surprise.

"I haven't heard that name in years," he said carefully.

"But you've heard it before," Acair pressed.

Soilléir considered. "It cannot be the same man. That one was . . . nay, it can't be the same mage."

Acair crawled over the fallen tree and sat next to Léirsinn. "Perhaps you should let me decide that."

Soilléir shook his head. "I'm not sure I can bring to mind— well, actually you know I can but I don't wish to—from whence he hailed, but the country bordered Bruadair. Take that for what it's worth."

Acair wasn't unhappy to have Léirsinn put her arm around his shoulders, even if it was likely to keep herself upright. It was damned chilly and that in spite of the fire in front of them.

"He was exiled from his country hundreds of years ago for misuse of power," Soilléir said slowly. "Rumor has it he died a beggar."

"I'm suspecting that is wishful thinking," Acair said sourly.

Soilléir studied him for far longer than Acair was comfortable with. "If Sladaiche and this theft are linked in any way, I would be extremely careful—"

"I have no magic!"

The words hung in the air, there over the fire, where they crackled and popped as if they'd been a terribly dry branch full of sap. He looked at them until they faded, studiously avoided looking at Léirsinn, then fixed his glance on Soilléir.

"I have no magic," he repeated quietly.

"But you do have a quest," Soilléir said.

"I already *had* a quest!"

"This is an extending of that goodly work," Soilléir said mercilessly. "Your task is to find out where that spell has gone. I would suggest you pinch the original book for the companion spells, but that's only a thought." He paused. "I have the feeling that when you find that spell, you'll also solve several other mysteries that are keeping you awake at night."

"You should have told me that months ago!"

Soilléir only looked at him steadily.

"If you tell me you've been waiting for me to be ready for this new, unusual, and very unwelcome addition to something I was already doing under extreme protest," Acair said coldly, "I will stab you."

"You won't manage it."

"Oh, I will," Acair promised. "When you least expect it, you will find me standing over you, spell in hand, and you'll be powerless to stop me from sending you off to hell."

"Well, if anyone has the courage to try, it would certainly be you."

Acair wasn't sure if that was a compliment or an insult, then decided he might not want to think about it too much. "Why don't *you* steal the damned book yourself?"

"It wouldn't do—"

Acair was sure he hadn't howled, because a gentleman never howled except discreetly when the port he was sipping wasn't quite the thing, but whatever noise he'd made had come damned close to something that felt as if it had come straight from his soul.

What was left of that soul, apparently.

"You know," Soilléir said carefully, "it's an interesting spell that's missing."

"It's a terrible spell that's missing," Acair shouted. "How

could you possibly let something like that slip out of your own damned library?"

Soilléir looked a bit more helpless than Acair was comfortable with.

"My grandfather can be somewhat absentminded."

Acair found that there were simply no words left in what was left of his mind to use in describing his disbelief over what he was hearing.

He was also desperately regretting his lack of magic at the moment given what he thought might be a fortuitous breach in the bulwark around those Cothromaichian treasures, but he used a firm hand and all the terrible things all those months of do-gooding had caused to fester inside him to push himself away from that profoundly tempting thought.

It was a thought he would, of course, revisit at his earliest opportunity.

"Odd what those spots of shadow do, isn't it?"

A sharp verbal riposte was halfway out of his mouth before he realized it hadn't been Soilléir to speak, it had been Léirsinn. He looked at her in astonishment.

"What did you say?"

"Those spots of shadow," she said slowly. "They steal souls, just as that spell supposedly does."

Acair was happy to be sitting down. He felt Léirsinn's arm tighten around him, which he had to admit he appreciated for more than just the gesture of affection.

If those two things were connected, if he could find the mage using that spell to create shadows to steal souls . . . well, then the mystery would be solved. Repairing the damage already done would likely be a dodgy business, but perhaps he was more prepared for that than he suspected. His mother had advised him to collect bits of his own lost soul, so perhaps helping others to do the same wouldn't be all that hard.

Do-gooding. It was becoming a bad habit.

He rested his head against Léirsinn's, choosing to ignore her trembling, and considered the state of affairs in his life.

Spots of shadow, mages speaking in shards of metal, a prince of Neroche who might possibly be slain, and a spell dogging his steps that left him unable to defend himself were one thing. A woman he loved—there was no point in denying it any longer—now having magic she would no doubt come to regret having asked for, and no magic himself whilst his path led to a place where, he had to admit, he likely wasn't going to be able to restrain himself from dipping into the family coffers?

Impossible.

He looked at Soilléir. "Did you bring anything to eat?"

"I might have, but I'm not sure you'll have much time for a leisurely supper. You've distracted your friend over there in the clearing and I've given him a bit more to think about, but I sense that he's shaking off our spells."

"What of Mansourah?" Léirsinn asked.

Acair felt a pang in the vicinity of his heart. He looked at Soilléir.

"I cannot aid him," he said, finding it very difficult to get the words past his gritted teeth. "He deserves better."

Soilléir hesitated, closed his eyes briefly, then looked at them both. He pulled a pack out of nothing and held it out.

"Eat on the fly," he said, "though I would keep to your feet until you're deeper in the forest. I will do what I can for you here to purchase you a bit of time to flee. I will also do what I can for the prince."

Acair supposed that was the best they were going to get. He

also rose and took the pack because he was above all a pragmatist. He didn't waste time asking Soilléir if he couldn't just see to the whole damned thing himself because the very last thing he thought he could stomach at the moment was a lengthy lecture on allowing the world to turn as it wanted to without interference.

Damn it, there were evil things afoot. Why those didn't merit a bit of attention from that lad there . . .

It was obvious he would have to see to it himself, as usual.

"Thank you for the supper," Acair said. "Miach will appreciate your rescuing his brother, I'm certain. I'll be off to see to your dirty work for you."

Soilléir only lifted his eyebrows briefly and smiled.

Acair took Léirsinn by the hand and pulled her to her feet. He didn't stop her from embracing Soilléir briefly, though he would have preferred she use the proximity as an excuse to slip a dagger between the man's ribs. He shot his taskmaster a glare on principle, whistled softly for his horse, then started off into the darkness with his lady.

He had the distinct feeling he was putting his foot to a path that wouldn't lead to places he wanted to go, but that was nothing out of the ordinary.

He was starting to wish it were.

Nineteen

Léirsinn stumbled along behind Acair as he walked swiftly along a path she couldn't see, trusting that he wouldn't run her into anything. She had her hand on his back, which perhaps wasn't the most comfortable way to walk, but it helped her stay on her feet.

The chill on her face was bitter, but that helped her stay on her feet as well. The cloak the witchwoman of Fàs had given her kept her warm, but that also might have come from the fact that she was ablaze with a fever that she was fairly certain hadn't come from being close to anyone who had sneezed.

She tried to ignore the truth for a bit, but the truth was, she was beyond weary. What she wanted most of all was somewhere safe to sleep. It didn't matter to her if that safe place was a witch's hearth, a king's guest chamber, or a patch of ground under a starlit sky with a dragon keeping her feet warm and a prince of Neroche's spells keeping her from dying—

A prince of Neroche who might be dead.

She turned her mind abruptly away from that thought but all that did was leave her facing other thoughts she cared for even less. The last few words Acair had exchanged with Soilléir when he'd thought she wasn't listening were burned into her memory.

She cannot fight him and you're daft if you think I'll allow her to try.

But she might purchase you the time to escape—

Wasn't that why she'd wanted magic in the first place?

Acair stopped so suddenly that she ran into him before she realized what he was doing. He caught her, then put his arm around her and drew her more deeply into the forest. He leaned against a tree and pulled her into his arms, wrapping his new cloak around her.

"Danger?" she whispered.

"A handy excuse to indulge in a friendly embrace, rather."

She smiled in spite of herself. She supposed he wouldn't notice if her teeth were chattering so badly she thought they might be heard all the way back to his mother's house.

"You have a fever," he murmured.

"I don't feel very well."

"You feel very well to—"

"Will you stop?" she demanded in exasperation.

He tightened his arms around her briefly, then sighed deeply. "I'm trying to distract us both, I fear."

She was willing to admit that the thought was a good one. She rested her head against his shoulder and closed her eyes. It was probably as close as she was going to come to safety for the foreseeable future, so she thought she might want to take advantage of the moment.

"I've been thinking," she said finally.

"Kind thoughts about me?"

She lifted her head and looked at him. The dark wasn't quite absolute so she could see the hint of a smile on his face. "Those, too," she agreed, "but others as well."

He studied her. "Thoughts about magic?"

"I'm putting that off for a bit still," she said honestly. She chewed on her words before she managed to put them in an order that made sense to her. "If the spell that was stolen does what Soilléir says it does—and trust me, I'm finding it hard to take any of this seriously—"

"Even now?" he interrupted.

"I've only set half a forest on fire," she said solemnly. "That could have been someone else trying to undermine my confidence."

He rested his forehead gently against hers. "I'm fighting the urge to spew out a maudlin sentiment."

"Are you certain it isn't indigestion?"

"We have yet to ingest what that whoreson from Cothromaiche sent along," Acair said, "so, aye, I'm fairly certain my tum is still safe. But that wasn't what we were discussing." He straightened and tucked a stray lock of hair behind her ear, then pulled her hood closer around her face. "Go on."

She took a deep breath. "If that mage had taken that spell," she began, "and it does what it's supposed to do . . ." She looked at him. "Well?"

He blinked a time or two, then his mouth fell open. "If he had the spell, then he would have used it long before now."

"Exactly," she said. "Why buy a horse if you're not going to ride it?"

He took her face in his hands and kissed her.

She would have commented on that but he had released her and had begun to pace. She put her fingers over her mouth and watched him, not sure if she should laugh or weep. The man was exactly as she'd seen him in the garden at Tor Neroche.

Light and dark, good and evil, all perfectly balanced.

He stopped and looked at her, then froze. "What?"

"You are . . ." She blew out her breath. "I don't know what you are."

"Besotted," he said cheerfully, taking a step toward her.

She held up her hand and stopped him before he came any closer. "You're distracting, that much I can say with certainty. What do you think?"

"Many things, but I'll share those later," he said. "About our present business? I think you're brilliant. If the mage we're after had that spell—"

"He would be doing more than making spots of shadow," she finished. "Is that what you're thinking?"

He nodded, looking extremely relieved. "If he had the spell in truth, there would be nothing stopping him from using it. Either he is waiting for the perfect moment to spring his evil on the entirety of the Nine Kingdoms, or he doesn't have the spell."

"But he stole it."

"People steal many things."

"And you would know."

"I, darling, would absolutely know." He smiled. "We have just purchased ourselves a bit more time to save the world."

She shook her head and smiled in spite of herself. "Look at you, rushing off to engage in such a mighty piece of do-gooding."

He looked a little startled. "When you put it that way, I think I'm a bit unsettled by the thought."

"I'm sure you'll make up for it eventually."

He reached for her hand. "*That* is a piece of truth I can willingly embrace. Let's walk a bit more and I'll comfort myself with the same."

She nodded and picked her way through the forest with him for a bit longer until they found the path again. It was quiet, she would admit that, and she didn't feel the presence of a mage with Acair's demise first on his list of things to do. Then again, what did she know? She was a horse gel who had just had magic shoved into her veins.

Unless she'd imagined it all.

"Perhaps those pools of shadow are the best the man can do at the moment," Acair said suddenly.

"You mean, that's all he can remember of the spell?"

"Aye." He looked at her. "I think if he had that spell, we would all be soulless husks. Given that we aren't, I suggest that he is missing what he would very much like to have."

"Do you think he lost it?"

"Involuntarily?" he mused. "It would certainly be a tempting prize."

"If it was stolen from him, I wonder who did it?"

He shook his head. "No idea, but that might be a question we want to answer sooner rather than later." He took a deep breath, then looked at her. "I think a journey to Cothromaiche might be in order, but I think I'm in need of a quite utilitarian spell of death I tucked discreetly under a particular kingly throne. I'm not sure I want to use anything else at this point."

"Well, we know what happens if you do," she said, hoping that someday she would be able to forget the sight of him overcome by that minder spell's magic.

"We do," he agreed. He paused, then shot her an uncomfortable look. "I should warn you that the king of the dwarves is not one of my admirers."

"And yet you want to visit him?"

"Uachdaran of Léige won't have a clue I've been there," he said without hesitation, "because he would slay me as easily as to look at me if he did. It's over the walls for me whilst you hide safely behind a useful spell of un-noticing we're enjoying thanks to that busybody from Cothromaiche. I can, as it happens, show you how to create the same thing when we're at our leisure."

"Will you?"

He stopped and looked at her. "Unwillingly," he admitted slowly. He paused again, then shook his head. "Magic is a bit like fire. 'Tis easy for it to grow out of control."

"I won't let it," she said confidently. "For all we know, I don't really have it and Soilléir was just having me on."

He only sent her a look she couldn't quite identify, but it seemed a bit like pity.

"What is it?" she asked.

He simply shook his head and drew her into his embrace. "Nothing," he said hoarsely. "Nothing at all." He pulled away. "We'd best continue on our way. Soilléir likely distracted that mage only to the count of a hundred before he lost interest and wandered off to the nearest pub."

She imagined that wasn't the case, but she didn't want to linger in the area to find out. "A safe haven would be useful," she offered. "So you could show me what I need to know, if it weren't so utterly ridiculous to think I might be able to, well, you know."

He smiled, pained. "I do know, darling. We'll find somewhere, right after I nip in and out of Léige."

"Didn't you just say that was the last place you wanted to go?"

"It still is, which is why we won't be making a lengthy visit. In and out with as little notice as possible. We'll find a safe haven down the road."

She couldn't argue with that. She listened to him call for his horse, then prepared herself for another journey much farther off the ground than she wanted to be.

There was something, she had to admit after a night spent flying on the back of a marginally well-behaved dragon, about conceding that the world was full of things she hadn't known existed before.

Barn work was a sturdy, reliable bit of business that had shaped her days and given meaning to her life. She had relished the chance to ride glorious horses and, for the most part, avoid the doings of men much loftier than she was herself. Her life had been simple, predictable, and ordinary.

Then she'd watched Acair of Ceangail fumble with a pitchfork and known instinctively that her life would never be the same.

She had seen elves and kings and runes that sparkled with a light of their own. She'd survived a night or two in a witch's Lesser Parlor and slept uneasily on the back of a horse who had turned himself into something just slightly more substantial than a gust of wind. She had seen things that shouldn't have been there, but had been in spite of anything she thought.

She had set trees on fire with magic that had been dropped into her veins like a plague.

She still wasn't entirely certain how she felt about the latter, or if she even believed it. She had set trees on fire thanks to repeating words given to her, but that could have just as easily been something Soilléir had done to make sport of her.

With all she'd seen, she had to admit that she was as she'd been before.

Skeptical.

She turned her head and rested her cheek against Acair's back, primarily to block out the wind, but partly because it was comforting. She looked at the spell she could see hanging over them like a fine mist. It was something Soilléir had done, that much she knew. Un-noticing, she thought he had called it.

"I think we should land," Acair said, shouting over the wind. "I might fall out of the saddle, else."

She had no reason to disagree, so she patted his shoulder in answer, then held on as Sianach did a respectable job getting them out of the sky and onto a decent-looking road. She clambered off his back and had to stand there for a bit before she thought her legs would work as they should.

"Where are we, do you think?"

"Hopefully outside the king's border," he said wearily. "I think Soilléir's spell will provide enough anonymity that we might cross through the land without worry. The place is bloody cold, but we're dressed well enough for it. Let's walk for a bit, then we'll take wing again, pop in and out of the palace, then be off on our errand before another day passes."

She nodded and walked with him along the road. The air was chilly, but the sky was cloudless. She discovered that if she looked carefully enough, she could see the spell that surrounded them. She reached out and touched it, then jumped a little as she realized she could feel it. It was an odd thing, as if threads of silk were draped down in a curtain around them, floating along with them as they walked. It was beautiful, though, and she found herself becoming slightly disoriented as she looked at it.

It made her wonder if that was its intent.

She wasn't at all certain how long she walked in the morning sunlight, but it was long enough that she managed to take one of the threads and wrap it around her finger. The magic didn't seem to mind and given that she felt as though she were walking in a dream anyway, she supposed *she* didn't mind.

Walking into Acair's outstretched arm, though, brought her back to herself with a start.

She looked in front of them and found that they were sharing a road with people she hadn't noticed before. She supposed they were dwarves, though she wasn't entirely sure how to tell. Some of the men were of a shorter stature, others rather tall. They were sharp-eyed, those lads there, and carried weapons that mostly seemed to include battle-axes and the occasional highly polished sword.

A man stood in front of them all. He was shorter than the rest, but that was more than made up for by the height of the crown he was wearing. He was looking at them, yet not seeing them apparently.

"Uachdaran of Léige," Acair murmured.

She jumped in spite of herself. It was that moment, she supposed, when things truly began to go south for them.

It should have occurred to her that she was holding on to a thread of Soilléir of Cothromaiche's spell and that any sort of violent movement on her part would result in something untoward happening to that spell. Of all the things she expected, though, having the whole damned thing fall down in a heap around them was definitely not it.

The king's eyes widened and he pointed a finger sternly at Acair.

"You!"

"Ah," Acair began, "Your Majesty. A pleasure as always. Allow me to introduce my companion, Léirsinn of Sàraichte—"

"Seize him," the king commanded, then he paused and looked at Acair closely. "I heard you are forbidden to use your magic. Is that so?"

"Well," Acair said smoothly, "that is a bit of a—"

"Seize him!" the king shouted.

And that, Léirsinn supposed, was that. She looked at Acair as the king's men swarmed around him.

"Sorry," she mouthed.

He lifted his eyebrows briefly, but that was the last she saw of him as he disappeared under a cloud of dwarf and spell.

She reached for her own magic, but it was as if someone had handed her the reins to a mythical beast with six feet and fangs. She fumbled a bit with things she had absolutely no idea how to use, then finally looked at the king of the dwarves. He was watching her narrowly.

"Haven't figured out how to use it yet, eh, missy?"

She shook her head. "Not yet."

He grunted at her. "Come along, then. If you're keeping company with that little wretch from Ceangail, I'm not sure what I'll do with you, but you'll be safer inside my walls than out."

Léirsinn supposed he had a point, but she wasn't sure she was looking forward to discovering where he thought to house her.

Life was, as she had reminded herself more than once over the past pair of weeks, so much simpler in a barn.

Twenty

Acair sat in Uachdaran of Léige's dungeon and thought he might want to consider a new and goodly work of perhaps going about the Nine Kingdoms, extolling the virtues of forgiveness.

He wished he'd had the chance to discuss the same with the king of their current locale before the man had sized him up for any magical tools, then left his lads to wrap him in a spell of fettering and carry him off to a place where there were no doors. Not that there needed to be any doors on his current cell. The spells were, as it happened, impenetrable.

Was that a light?

His heart leapt at the hint of something besides unrelenting darkness, though he wondered why. The king was likely having him hauled upstairs so he could be summarily put to death.

He was rather surprised when, after his eyes had stopped

burning, he looked out of his cell to find Léirsinn standing there. She sank down to her knees and set the candle aside.

"Are you hurt?"

"Me?" he croaked. "Never been more fit and full of good humors. You?"

"He offered me a guest chamber," she said uneasily. "I pointed out to him that his favorite mount had thrush."

"You're handy."

"You've no idea." She paused. "I might also have come close to setting his audience chamber on fire. I believe it unnerved him."

Acair smiled in spite of himself. "Do tell."

She shifted. "I lost my temper. I think one of the tapestries nearest his hearth might still bear a singe mark or two as a result."

He would have laughed, but he wasn't sure he had the energy for it. "And then?"

She looked at him. "He's going to put you to death."

"Is he?" Acair asked lightly. "Such a pity."

"He doesn't like you."

"The feeling, as it happens, is quite mutual."

She looked at him with a frown. "I thought all was forgiven, forgotten, and left in the past. What did you do to him?"

Acair shifted. "The tale is long and tedious."

"I'm completely free of engagements for the afternoon, so say on."

He leaned his head back against the wall. It was freezing, which was a boon for the state of his pounding head. It was also damned cold, which was less pleasant for his backside, but he didn't imagine he was in a position to complain.

"The truth is," he admitted, "I may or may not have spirited away one of his daughters for a fortnight of pub crawling."

She rolled her eyes. "He has daughters?"

"Several. A son or two as well, I think. Terrifying souls, all."

"And?" she prodded.

"Are you curious about the results of too much quaffing of ale or how Papa Uachdaran reacted?"

She smiled. "I suspect there is much more to the story than a few mugs of ale."

"I refuse to admit to it."

He refused in part because he'd failed but mostly because he didn't want any eavesdropping guardsmen to remind the king about his true offenses.

He looked at her, looked at her hand that was so close to his but so completely out of reach, then leaned his head closer to her.

"I believe I need to teach you some spells," he whispered.

"What if I destroy the underpinnings of the palace?"

"It wouldn't be the first time someone had tried," he muttered, but he supposed clarifying that wasn't the best thing to do at the moment either.

He also imagined he could refrain from pointing out that Uachdaran of Léige wasn't as much of a purist as he might have wanted the rest of the world to know. That one knew spells . . . well, Acair wasn't one to recoil at much of anything save a poorly cooked plate of roast potatoes, but the dwarf king's spells—

Well, they were almost as vile as the ale he brewed, and that was saying something.

He looked at her seriously. "I had hoped we wouldn't find ourselves in such straits."

"I'll muck out a few stalls in the morning," she said. "Perhaps that will be enough."

He didn't hold out any hope for that. The truth was, he could only see one path in front of him and it wasn't one he particularly wanted to walk. He was going to die, Léirsinn was full of magic she couldn't control, and the fate of several no doubt critically important social events was in a total shambles.

Never mind the world and the chance to watch it continued to turn.

He was faintly surprised by how desperately he wanted to be a part of that. Unfortunately, he couldn't see how that was going to be possible unless something miraculous occurred.

He looked down at Léirsinn's hand on the other side of that invisible spell that locked him in the dungeon, then realized if he put his hand just so, it almost looked as if their hands were touching.

"It's very dark here," she said quietly.

"I'll give you a spell for werelight," he said with a sigh. "If you are determined to beat it out of me, I might tell you how to add a few things to it that scatter shadows of rodents about, just for the sheer sport of it." He met her eyes. "If you like."

"You are a very bad mage."

"I am a very *good* mage at bad magic," he said, wishing he'd been better at it. "But I'll only teach you virtuous and lovely spells, if that would ease your mind."

"I think I might like the one laced with rodent shadows."

He smiled in spite of himself. Murder, mayhem, mischief. He knew Léirsinn would never embrace any of them fully, more particularly the murder part unless she entertained thoughts of the same with regard to Soilléir of Cothromaiche, but she might be willing to get her hands a bit dirty for the good of the cause.

"Are the king's spells here strong?" she asked.

Ah, and there was the sticking point. He sighed deeply, then leaned his head back against the absolutely icy stone. "Unfortunately."

"Then we're going to die."

"Possibly."

"Are you honestly giving up this easily?"

He considered, then felt a bit of his old vim return. Léige was a terrible place to find oneself trapped underground, but he had extricated himself from worse places before. He might not have his magic available at the moment, but he had his wits, his fearlessness, and a horse miss who might likely burn the whole place to the ground before she found the means to apologize for starting the fire.

He looked at Léirsinn. "This might be a bit messy."

"A bit?"

"Very," he corrected. "But I'm going to teach you a few spells."

She looked like she might have preferred to be learning the location of the nearest cesspit so she could begin shoveling, but the woman was nothing if not courageous. He'd seen that for himself before.

He thought he just might love her for it.

Well, that, and a few other reasons.

"Acair, are you daydreaming?"

He looked at her seriously. "Actually, I was wondering where to go after we're free of this place. I believe it should be somewhere so drenched with romance that you'll be in the proper frame of mind to listen to me offer up a few maudlin sentiments."

Her mouth had fallen open, but she shut it with an audible snap. "You're daft."

"Besotted, as I said before."

"Mad," she corrected. "Absolutely barking. I don't want any maudlin sentiments, I want spells."

"And later?"

"I'll think about other things later."

He couldn't argue with that. He preferred not to think about what might come later, though he had the feeling it wouldn't be pleasant.

Léirsinn was full of magic she couldn't control and would likely pay a very steep price for, he was minus his very handy spell of un-noticing and definitely worse for the wear of his recent attempt to use even the most innocent piece of his own power, and they were both sitting in a dungeon completely impervious to any sort of digging. He knew that because he'd made a visit or two there in times past to taunt and annoy inmates who had run afoul of the king's sensibilities and found that the only exit was up the stairs.

It was, in a word, hopeless.

But hopeless was his fourth favorite thing, mostly because when he managed what was slathered in that sort of business, it made the rest of his accomplishments all the more glorious.

He looked at Léirsinn and smiled.

"Let's begin."